D0065904

BREAK
OUT

PAUL HERRON

BREAK OUT

A Thriller

GRAND CENTRAL
PUBLISHING

NEW YORK BOSTON

Copyright © 2021 by Paul Crilley
Jacket design by Rob Grom. Jacket photo of barbed wire by Paul Bucknall/ Arcangel. Jacket image of stormy sky/lightning by Shutterstock. Author photo © Paul Crilley. Cover copyright © 2021 by Hachette Book Group, Inc.

Grand Central Publishing
Hachette Book Group
1290 Avenue of the Americas, New York, NY 10104
grandcentralpublishing.com
twitter.com/grandcentralpub

First published in 2021 by Headline Publishing Group
First Grand Central Publishing edition: April 2021

Grand Central Publishing is a division of Hachette Book Group, Inc. The Grand Central Publishing name and logo is a trademark of Hachette Book Group, Inc.

The Hachette Speakers Bureau provides a wide range of authors for speaking events. To find out more, go to www.hachettespeakersbureau.com or call (866) 376-6591.

Library of Congress Control Number: 2021931426

ISBNs: 978-1-5387-3703-3 (hardcover), 978-1-5387-3705-7 (ebook)

Printed in the United States of America

LSC-C

Printing 1, 2021

For Jo

We survived, and there's no doubt we're stronger after everything we've been through. But still, after the couple of years we've had, I do find comfort in the words of one of the great philosophers of the twentieth century: "Things can only get better."

And for Bella, Caeleb, and the new member of our family, Callum. You guys are literally giving me gray hairs, but I love you all anyway.

When two hurricanes come into close proximity to one another, the vortices can pull together, merging to form a much larger superstorm.

The phenomenon is called the Fujiwhara effect.

Prologue

Three years ago

Three names. Three bullets.

I made them myself. Cast the slugs from lead mixed with Amy's melted-down wedding ring.

There's a fourth bullet too. A special one just for me. It sits on the coffee table, glinting in the afternoon sun. First gold, then red, tiny dents and imperfections picked out in the casing as the light slowly fades.

I stare at it all afternoon, like a recovering alcoholic contemplating the bottles in a hotel mini fridge. I eventually decide to leave it where it is. Imagining Amy's reaction is what tips the scales. She'd have kicked me in the balls for even considering it.

So I leave the last bullet behind in the house we once shared, the house we planned on raising our daughter in.

The house where Amy was murdered.

Something wakes you up. Something . . . other. Something that doesn't belong.

You lie in bed, listening intently. It's probably nothing. A car outside. A raccoon in the trash bins.

You check the clock by the bed: 3:46. Christ, you're never going to get back to sleep now.

You reach out for Amy . . .

She isn't there.

You touch the rumpled sheets. Still warm, slightly damp with her perspiration. The noise must have been her going to the bathroom.

You roll over. From this position you have a direct view of the bathroom. The door is wide open. The bathroom is empty.

There are rules for planning an ambush. I learned that in Afghanistan. In fact, there's a shit-ton of rules, collectively known as mission analysis (METT-TC—mission, enemy, terrain, troops available, and time and civilian considerations), and course of action development (COA DEV). I don't have the time, the backup, *or* the manpower for that kind of prep, but all the lists, all the rules, can be boiled down to four basic principles.

Planning, infiltration, actions on, and exfiltration.

Planning is the most important. You have to think the ambush through. Plot every last detail. Make sure there are no holes.

No mistakes.

You sit up in bed. Moonlight shines through the window, veiled by the net curtain wafting in the muggy midsummer breeze.

"Amy?"

No response. You get out of bed, head to the door, move out into the hallway. You lean over the banister. There's a light on downstairs. The kitchen.

"Amy?"

Nothing.

You hesitate, an uneasy feeling waking in the pit of your stomach. You can't explain it, but you suddenly feel that something is wrong. That something bad has happened.

The first job is to find a suitable kill zone. The place where the actual ambush will take place. A spot where the target needs to slow down is ideal, something like sharp bends in the road or a steep hill.

Whatever spot you pick, it's important to make sure the location has good cover for yourself. You don't want to be seen. Not until you're ready for the kill shot.

★

You slip back into your room and grab your police-issue Beretta. You ratchet the slide, flick the safety off, and move down the stairs. A small passage to your left leads to the bathroom, a spare bedroom, and the kitchen. The living room is to your right.

You pause, wondering which direction to go. Then you hear a noise. A groan? You're not sure, but it comes from the living room.

Generally, high ground is the best location for an ambush. Some natural obstacles to keep the enemy in the kill zone are a bonus. That allows the ambush force to control all phases of contact. I always preferred urban environments for that exact reason, but that's not an option here. Firing an M249 in downtown Miami is going to draw too much attention.

But it's Miami, I hear you say. Who the fuck's going to notice gunfire? Sure, I get it. But I don't want to take the risk. I might not get to finish the job.

You also need to figure out what kind of ambush you're planning. Hasty or deliberate. Hasty ambushes aren't prearranged. They're reactive, like when you're on patrol and stumble across enemy troops. If I was going to do that, I could just follow the bastards home and shoot them as they get out of their cars. No. I want them to suffer. I want to look them in the eye.

I'm going for a deliberate ambush.

One that I can plan. One that I can control.

I've already gathered the intel I needed to plan the mission. Their movements, their habits, their preferred bars, the name of their drug dealer...

You creep forward, gun held ready. The moonlight shines through the front window. The dresser's been ransacked, drawers pulled out, the contents dumped on the carpet.

Your gaze drops to the mess. Playing cards, coins, old USB sticks, bits and pieces lying every—

You freeze. There's a larger shape on the floor.

Your eyes skip over it. Something inside forces you to look away, some protective instinct. Instead, you stare at a photograph of you and Amy that's lying on the carpet. It's the one you took when she first told you she was pregnant. She's laughing. You're holding her from behind, the cell phone in your hand as you snap the picture in the bedroom mirror.

Finally, you drag your eyes back to the shapeless mass. Your heart pounds loudly in your ears.

So—the things I have control over: location of ambush. My own location in relation to the ambush. And of course the mission statement: torture and kill, slowly and painfully, with *extreme* prejudice.

The things I *don't* have control over: a platoon always needs an assault, support, and security element when launching an ambush. I don't have support, *or* security to back me up. I'm on my own.

Also, you're supposed to split your team. One group to execute the attack and one to lay down cover fire. Not gonna happen here.

But that's fine. The kills are going to be mine alone. I don't want anyone else involved.

You reach out and flick the light switch.

Your brain refuses to take it in.

Your vision is reduced to flashes, like Polaroid pictures, images that sear into your brain, images you will never forget.

Amy, sprawled facedown on the carpet.

The T-shirt she sleeps in riding high, revealing her panties and the small tattoo over her kidney.

Her caved-in skull, hair matted and soaked with blood.

The aluminum baseball bat lying next to her.

The dark stain that has spread out over the gray carpet.

The bulge of her pregnant stomach.

You slump back against the wall. The gun falls from your fingers as you drop to the carpet, staring at your wife.

★

The most important rule of any ambush, after all the prep, all the work, is *speed*. You have to shock your enemy. Scare the shit out of them. Go in hard, shoot everyone, then get the hell out. You want your contact to last less than sixty seconds.

That's not happening tonight. I'm going to make this last as long as possible.

You don't give the investigating detectives the footage from your security camera. You tell them you'd taken the memory card out and hadn't replaced it. You get looks. What kind of cop doesn't keep their own security camera working?

You don't care what they think. You keep the footage for yourself. Watch the three men break into your home, editing the frames into a loop and playing it over and over until their faces are imprinted in your mind.

After a while, staring at the video loop, you have the weirdest feeling that you actually know them. Every curve and angle of their faces is so familiar it's like you're looking at old friends.

When your bereavement leave is over, you use the police database to ID the killers. It doesn't take long. They have rap sheets longer than your arm.

Marcus Tully, Barry Novak, and Luther Wright.

Three names.

You write down their addresses, their known associates.

Then you launch the first phase of the operation—gathering intel.

You find Marcus Tully first. He's still living with his mother in a one-bedroom apartment deep in Overtown.

Barry Novak is a veteran. That surprises you. Disappoints you. He served in Afghanistan five years before your tour. Not in Marjah. Somewhere else. He lives on his own. He visits a support group for ex-army. He sees a shrink, drinks a bottle of vodka every night. The guy has PTSD. You can see it a mile away.

Tough shit.

Luther Wright is the outsider. The guy who always hangs on the outskirts of the gang, hoping he'll gain cred just by association. He's a yes-man. Does whatever he's told.

Phase one complete. Next step is to check known associates.

As soon as you see that one of those associates is a drug dealer, the beginnings of a plan form in your head.

I'm using the M249 Paratrooper for the ambush. The Para. It's a compact version of the M249 SAW, with a shorter barrel and sliding aluminum buttstock. Easier to move around with.

I had to call in a lot of favors from an old army buddy to get it. He wanted to sell me an M27, but I never liked them. Thirty-round magazines just don't compare to the linked ammunition the M249 uses. It's older than the M27, but I like that. It's more familiar in my hands. I trained with it. I *know* it.

I'm positioned at the top of a rise above a deserted logging mill outside Overtown. It's perfect for what I need. Far enough from town that no one will hear the gunfire, and it only has one road in and out, so I don't have to cover multiple escape routes.

I stare through the rifle scope, moving it slowly across the abandoned mill. It was built in the thirties, a series of old wooden buildings with portable office cabins dumped at one end. The place shut down around two years ago when three employees died. I was part of the investigation into their deaths. It was the owner's fault. No safety protocols. No upkeep of the saws or equipment. One of the belts was so worn it flew off, took a guy's head off, sliced through the second guy's stomach right to the spine, and got stuck in the last guy's throat.

The mill itself and the road leading through the trees lie below me in a shallow valley. At the top of the opposite valley wall is an open-sided shed holding a large pile of tied-together tree trunks, obviously stored there in preparation for the mill. I placed two propane tanks against the tree trunks earlier, one on either side, right against the wire lashing them together. I checked the wood while I was placing the tanks. A lot of the trunks are rotten and damp, but that's fine for my needs. I might not even use the tanks, but preparation is key.

★

An hour before dawn is the perfect time for a shock attack. The target is usually deep in sleep, his or her body totally shut down. The victim doesn't know what the hell is going on.

You already know that the drug dealer—Elias Finch—lives alone. You go in hard with a bright flashlight shining in his face, grabbing him and throwing him to the floor. Finch lets out an unearthly moan of terror. You've heard it before on raids. Nine out of ten people you've come at like this make the same sound. Animalistic, terrified, primeval.

You hit Finch with the butt of your gun and knock him out cold. You wait, listening, controlling your breathing. A dog barks in the distance. You hear a car drive past the dingy house. The headlights shine through the curtains and swing on past.

Satisfied, you drag Finch to the living room. If you can even call it that. You've seen the same room a hundred times before. Usually bare floorboards, but sometimes a stained carpet. A couch with cigarette holes burned into it, unknown stains forming a map of spilled drink and bodily fluids. An old table, this one covered in used syringes, overflowing ashtrays, empty beer bottles, and, surprisingly, a few novels. That's a first for you. You don't think you've ever been in a drug dealer's house that had books. A TV, sure. A game console, definitely. Something to mindlessly zone out in front of while they wait for the high to kick in. But books? No.

There's a rickety table and chairs in the kitchen. You drag one of the chairs into the living room and haul Finch into it, using the rope you brought to tie him in place.

Then you wait.

He wakes up half an hour later. Sees you sitting on the couch with your gun resting on your lap. He opens his mouth to scream, but you just raise a finger to your lips.

He's not as stupid as he looks. His mouth snaps shut. He stares at you with wide, terrified eyes.

You've planned everything for today. It's Friday, and you know this is when Tully phones Finch to organize drugs for himself, Wright, and Novak.

"When Tully calls," you say to Finch, "tell him not to come here. Tell him you think the cops have been watching. Tell him you'll bring his drugs to the lumberyard tonight at seven. The abandoned one about two miles outside of town. Nod if you understand."

Finch nods.

"If you try to warn them, I'll shoot you in the eye. Understand?"

Finch nods again, more frantically this time.

You sit there for most of the day before Tully finally calls Finch's cell phone.

You hold the gun to Finch's eye and the phone to his ear. He tells Tully everything you want him to.

Tully's not happy. He's used to getting the drugs as soon as he calls, taking them to Novak's house and shooting up there before heading out to a dive bar on the outskirts of Overtown called Double Down Tavern. You've already followed them there a few times as you considered your plan. It's got blacked-out windows and plastic seats out front for when it's too crowded inside. A neon sign hangs above the door—a purple pool cue that's supposed to move back and forth. But it's broken, so all it does is flicker on and off, buzzing loudly.

Finch tells them he has no choice. It's either meet at the lumberyard or they go without. Tully reluctantly agrees.

You hang up the phone. Then you sit and stare at Finch, wondering what to do about him. You could just kill him. You'd be doing everyone a favor. You want to. You want to raze everything to the ground. Anyone and anything connected with the men who killed your family.

You stare at him. He doesn't say anything. He knows what you're thinking, is aware that the slightest move from him could push you either way.

You check your watch. It's 3 p.m. Four hours till the meet-up. You don't want to risk leaving him like this. He could get loose. Could warn Tully and the others.

You check his room, find some sleeping pills. Strong ones. One of them would knock a healthy adult out. You crush seven and put them into water. You do it in front of Finch, let him see what you're doing.

"You're going to drink this," you say. He starts to shake his head. "You either drink this or I kill you. Either way, I need you out of action for a while. Your call."

He hesitates, then nods.

You lift the glass to his mouth and he gulps it down. You wait around forty minutes before the drugs kick in. You thought they'd work a lot faster, but heavy users are used to the hard stuff. You just hope you've given him enough.

His eyes close and his head slumps forward. You slap him, but he doesn't budge.

You check your watch. Four o'clock. Three hours left.

Time to set up the ambush.

And here I am, lying at the top of the hill, watching the lumberyard through the scope on my rifle.

Waiting.

I turn my watch around so the clock face is on the underside of my wrist. A habit from the war. You don't want any reflections giving away your position. Plus, it makes it easier to check the time when you're lying in wait.

It's seven o'clock. They should be here any minute now.

In fact...

I can see lights approaching, a spectral white glow that looks like it's floating through the trees. Then I hear the engine of a pickup truck badly in need of a tune-up.

I stretch my neck from side to side, loosening my muscles, then put my eye back to the scope. I breathe in—one, two, three, pause—then out—one, two, three. In—then out. Slowing my breathing, moving into the zone.

The truck finally heaves and skids into view, bouncing and shuddering over the dirt track, its ancient suspension barely able to keep it in a straight line.

For a moment, I think they're going to do the job for me. My own car is parked lengthwise across the road right in front of the lumber mill, exactly where I want them to stop. But they don't even slow down as they approach.

I track the pickup truck through the scope, focusing on the driver. It's Tully. He's got his head turned to the side as if he's talking, but he glances back through the windshield and slams on the brakes just in time.

The truck locks up and skids across the dirt, starting to turn side-on.

I take the opportunity. I shift my aim, slowly, moving with the truck.

Crack!

One bullet takes out the rear tire. I shift aim again, steady my hand...

Crack!

Another bullet takes out the front tire. The truck's still skidding, still spinning. They must have heard the shots, felt the tires blow out. I don't move the scope to see their faces. I wait as the car spins fully around, presenting its opposite side to me.

Crack.

Crack.

Two more shots. Two more tires. I couldn't have planned it any better.

The truck slews to a stop in a cloud of dirt about five feet from my own car. I keep my eye to the scope, waiting.

The door on the passenger side opens. Someone steps out—Wright. He tries to run. I squeeze the trigger, hear the sharp crack of the rifle. A fraction of a second later, a tiny cloud of dark mist explodes from his knee and he drops to the ground.

Now they'll be panicking. I wonder what they're going to do. I've made a wager with myself. Odds-on they try to run, even if they don't know where the shooter is.

I'm right. Tully scrambles from the truck, trying to sprint into the trees. I track him for a long moment with the sight, letting him feel some hope—then I shoot his kneecap out from behind and he goes down.

Novak starts the truck up. He's going to try to escape with four blown-out tires.

I shift my aim to the lumber shed, shoot the propane tanks. I raise my eye from the scope, see the fireballs roll up into the sky, followed by a thundering explosion that shakes the ground.

The vibrations continue as the huge pile of tree trunks roll and bounce down the hill, falling and sliding into the road, blocking Novak's escape route.

He doesn't stop. Does he think he's going to drive over the tree trunks? Idiot. I know he's not going to get past them, but I open up on the front of the truck, firing bursts into the radiator, the engine block. The truck skids and slides as he veers wildly. I keep firing. A moment later, the truck coughs and dies, smoke curling up into the air.

I wait. A part of me wants to open up on them, spray the whole area with bullets, rip them to shreds. But another part of me, the part that died in the living room that day, wins out. They need to suffer for what they did. No quick deaths.

Novak finally makes his move. The door swings open and he slides out. He's on the opposite side of the truck, so I can't get a clean shot.

I glance at the ammo rail. About fifty rounds left. I wait, but Novak stays where he is. He's panicked, doesn't know where to go, has no idea where I am.

Okay. Let me take it to him. I stand up with the rifle, the ammo belt dangling to my knees. I make my way down the slope. I keep the rifle raised, ready to shoot. I know the path is free of obstacles. I cleared it myself, walked up and down a few times to get the feel of it. I don't need to look where I'm going.

I reach level ground and he still hasn't moved. I pause, then lower myself to the dirt, the rifle to my side. I peer beneath the truck. He's still there.

I leave the rifle on the ground, take out the Glock. (Not the one I'm going to finish them with. A second gun.) Wright is moaning in pain, writhing on the ground where he fell. I know the exact moment he becomes aware of me approaching. His moaning stops.

I ratchet the slide on the gun. The sound might as well be a gunshot, because it focuses all attention on me. I wait till Tully looks over his shoulder. I can even see Novak peering around the side of the truck. I carry on toward Wright. He turns, flops over on his belly like a landed fish. He manages to push himself to his feet, one leg dragging behind him as he tries to limp away. I pause a few feet from him, wait for him to look over his shoulder—

—and I shoot his other kneecap out.

He drops, screaming. I walk forward, grab his shirt, pull him over so he's lying on his back.

"What do you want?" he shouts.

My voice is flat. Dead. The way I feel inside. "Five weeks ago, you broke into my house. You killed my wife. She was pregnant. The fuck you think I want?"

Wright's eyes widen. "That...that was a mistake! I swear! We were just looking for some cash, that's all. Your wife...she walked in on us. We panicked..."

He stops talking.

There's a noise. We both hear it.

It's a car.

No, *cars*. Approaching fast.

I turn toward the dirt road and see blue and red lights flashing in the distance, brightening the darkness between the trees.

Cops?

Why the hell are the cops here?

How...?

Wright tries to crawl away. I stamp down on his leg, desperately trying to think. Wright screams as two cars burst through the trees and skid to a stop on the other side of the fallen logs.

The doors fly open. I grab the other Glock from my jeans,

the one with the special bullets, and point it at Wright, ready to shoot him in the head.

"Constantine!"

I freeze, look back to see Mason, my partner, skirting around the edge of the logs.

"Constantine, don't you dare!" she shouts.

"These are the fuckers who killed Amy!"

"I don't give a shit!"

Other cops have exited the cars. They stand behind their open doors, guns leveled at me. Mason glances back, raises her hands in the air.

"Just wait! Let me talk to him."

"There's nothing to say!" I call out.

"Constantine, please. You can still walk away from this."

I look down at Wright. Across at Tully. I laugh out loud, barely managing to stop myself when I hear the tinge of hysteria in my voice.

"Jack. Please..."

I look at Mason. Her face is twisted with grief. We've known each other for ten years. I'm her kid's godfather.

"Don't..." she starts to say.

Novak makes a run for it. He bolts from behind the pickup truck and runs toward the police cars. I act instinctively. I swivel and shoot.

The bullet hits him in the back of the neck. Mason cries out as he collapses.

I barely have time to register this before I feel a huge jolt of pain in my arm. I stagger back, the gun falling from my fingers. Mason stands there, gun leveled at me, her eyes wide with shock, as if she can't believe what she's done.

The police are all shouting, but I can hardly hear over the rushing in my ears.

I turn around. See Tully crawling away. Wright too. He's already twenty feet from me. I bend over to pick up the Glock.

Then something hits me in the side and I'm thrown to the ground.

"Don't be fucking stupid, Jack," says Mason, right in my ear.

I try to throw her off, but she grabs my wounded arm and forces it behind my back. I scream in pain.

Then more weight falls on me. I feel hands on my head, shoving my face into the dust.

The last sight I see is the cops heading toward Wright and Tully.

ADVISORY BULLETIN
Hurricane Josephine Advisory Number 5
NWS National Hurricane Center Miami FL
5 P.M. EDT FRI AUG 27 2021

DISCUSSION AND OUTLOOK
During the past several hours Josephine has been steadily gaining in strength. Josephine is on track to make landfall over the Turks and Caicos Islands this afternoon, bringing winds of up to 120 mph (193 km/h). On this track, the center of Josephine will be approaching Miami in 12 hours. The cyclone is forecast to increase from Category 4 to Category 5 by Saturday, August 28.

WARNINGS
Evacuation is mandatory. Repeat, evacuation is mandatory.
$$
Forecaster Mills

One

Friday, August 27

6:00 a.m.

Prison is all about breaking your sentence into blocks of time. That's the only way to survive. A year is too much. Half a year is depressing. Hell, even a month feels eternal.

A week, though—a week is just about manageable. Least it is if you have something to mark the passing of time. Like family coming to visit. That gives you a countdown. A reason to keep going.

I don't have that. Both my parents are dead. No kids, no brothers or sisters. A murdered wife. So...yeah. Not much to look forward to there.

But you push on. You push on until you can't anymore. Because that's life, as my old man used to say. You live, you die. Anything in between is still a steaming pile of shit, but you try to make the most of it. He made the most of it with drugs and hookers. Ended up driving off a hundred-foot-high bridge into a torrential river at three in the morning, coked up to his eyeballs and wearing nothing but his Superman boxer shorts. The hooker who leaped from the car just before it went over the edge said he was screaming about Lydia—my mother—caging him in and stopping him from flying free, that he was going to prove her wrong.

Spoiler alert: he didn't.

But he was right about one thing. You either push on or you check out. I don't have access to coke, hookers, *or* a torrential river, so the alternative is either pissing off one of the gangs so they shank me in the shower (hopefully with something nonorganic, if you catch my meaning), or going for one of the guards, try to hurt them bad enough that they use lethal force.

I think I'd rather push on, thanks very much.

Felix says it gets easier the longer you're inside, but I don't believe much of what Felix says. He's a habitual liar. Or, as he likes to term it, a "teller of tales." Plus, I've been in here for three years now. How much longer is it going to take?

I frown as I stare through the tiny scratched window in the door of our cell. Why the hell am I thinking about the passing of time? That's a bad way to start the day. Just leads to depression.

Oh yeah. Felix.

"I mean, the kid was crying again," says Felix from his bunk. "He's been here—what? Three weeks now? I *told* him. I said the only way to survive prison is not to fight it."

"That right?" I say absently.

Our cell is on the upper level of B Block. All I can see out the window is the walkway railing and the cells on the opposite side of the pod. Looks like Stevens has been banging his head against the glass again. His window is smeared with dark crimson.

"'Course it's right. Accept you're here, man. There's no three-bedroom house in our future. No wife and kids. No puppy. No sneaking off to see your mistress on a Friday afternoon after work—you know, the one who does the things your wife thinks are disgusting. That's gone. Don't even *think* about it. This is your life now. Embrace it. Own that shit."

"I thought I had," I say.

Had I, though? I wasn't really sure. It's hard to know your own mind in prison. Too many thoughts running through your head. Things tend to get distracted, confused.

"The fuck, man?" snaps Felix. "You not listening to a word I'm saying?"

Jesus. Miss Temperamental over there. You have to be careful with Felix. Normally he's pretty chill, but the weirdest thing can set him off into a flying rage. I've never been on the receiving end of it, but I've seen inmates carried to the infirmary who have.

"I'm listening," I say. Then I pause. "Just remind me again?"

"I'm *sayin'* we have to accept we're stuck in here. Look... you seen Leo, right? The old guy? Sits at the back of the cafeteria. Always holdin' his knife and fork like he's about to stab them into his head."

"Yeah."

"You know why he's like that?"

"Let me take a wild guess. Because he hasn't accepted he's here?"

"Bingo. He's always thinkin' about a way out. Always watching, planning. Guy looks eighty years old. Been here his whole life. And he *still* thinks he's going to see the outside. Always talking about digging tunnels, sneaking through storm drains. Look what it's got him. Stomach ulcers and delusions. I told that to the new kid. Pauly."

"What'd he do?"

"Started crying again."

I glance over my shoulder at Felix. He's a big guy. Six-three, solid muscle. Black skin and intense eyes. Likes to read cheesy romance novels from the prison library. Each to his own. He's currently lying on his bunk holding a pink-and-orange book. I can just see the bare chest of some pirate-type guy on the cover.

"Just so I'm clear. You think not accepting he's in prison gave Leo stomach ulcers and delusions?"

"Sure. You gotta go with the flow, man. Live life like a Zen monk. Those motherfuckers don't stress about nothin'. That's how prison breaks you. You live with hope, it's gonna kill you in the end. You gotta realize this is your life from now on. Accept that shit in your *soul*. Then everything's hunky-dory."

"Nobody says hunky-dory anymore, Felix," I say, turning back to the door.

"I do."

Fact of the matter is, I actually agree with him. Even though I struggle with time, mainly the boredom of it all, I long ago adjusted to the fact that this is it. That my life is over.

Not that I care. My life was over before I even got caught.

But what Felix says about hope is true. Even those with something to live for lose it in the end. Maybe they keep a photograph of their girlfriend on their wall, or drawings from their kids. Birthday cards, something like that. They start off as symbols of hope. Hope that they still have a life outside, hope that they're getting out someday. But as the months drag on, despair takes over. You can't keep hope alive with no pay-off. Your mind only lets you lie to yourself for so long before it turns on you.

Best not to care about anything. Or any*body*. Nothing to lose that way.

"Head count!"

I lean back as a heavy cranking sound echoes through the pod, followed by the metallic slam of forty-two doors sliding open. I step out of the cell, checking left and right as I do so. Reflex. It's the perfect time for an attack. Nobody is expecting it.

It's safe, though. Just inmates yawning and scratching their balls as they step onto the metal grating, the first part of the daily routine kicking in. The first segment of time in the never-ending spiral toward madness or death—whichever comes first.

"You were snoring again last night," says Felix as he joins me on the walkway.

"I don't snore."

"You fucking do. Like a freight train. Seriously. You need to see a doctor or something, because I am *highly* likely to suffocate you if you carry on like that."

"Whatever," I say, stifling a yawn. I'm exhausted. Everyone is. The storm that has been pummeling Florida for the past two days sounds like it's getting stronger, the raging wind a constant howling and shrieking that can be heard through the thick prison walls. It's putting everyone on edge, keeping everyone up at night.

I slept in today because of that, but I'm usually up before five. That's the quietest time in prison. Even the crazies who stay up all the hours screaming and crying tend to drift off after four. It's my private time. My few moments of relaxation before the routine of prison forces me to break the day down into smaller and smaller chunks.

This first chunk starts at quarter after six—roll call. Every inmate has to shuffle outside and stand there while the correction officers—COs—count us off with old manual clickers. If anyone sleeps in, or if someone is too slow to make it to head count, the whole process starts all over again, right from number one. And you *really* don't want to be the guy who holds up roll call. That means a delayed and rushed breakfast, and some inmates do not appreciate that kind of change to their schedule.

Not that breakfast is anything to look forward to. Oatmeal, usually. Sometimes with peanut butter. If I'm feeling rich, then maybe some honey. But that's it. The eggs make me sick and everything else tastes like cardboard.

Work starts at eight. Not everyone has a job. You have to prove yourself worthy, show that you're a model prisoner, something I've done by mostly keeping my head down and minding my own business. And trust me, that's hard to do when you're an ex-cop. Every inmate wants a piece of you. Every CO wants to make your life hell.

I work in the maintenance shed with Henry, one of those old guys who knows how to fix everything. It's Henry's job to make sure all the machinery in the prison keeps going. That's a full-time job in a dump like this.

I earn seventy dollars a month, almost double the average income of the other inmates. That means I can indulge in my vices, chocolate and coffee, both of which I buy from the commissary. The coffee is shit, though. It's instant. Not even granules, but a fine powder. I don't even think there's any caffeine in it. You could mix that stuff with hot water and inject it into your eyeballs and it wouldn't even kick.

After lunch I hang out in the yard. Just to feel the sun on my face. I used to love the beach. Would go there every weekend with Amy. We lived pretty close and I could smell the salt on the air when the wind blew in the right direction.

Not now, though. When I'm in the yard, all I can smell is the chemical stench from the laundry. Just steam escaping from the vents adding to the wet humidity that already clings to my skin like a coating of oil.

After that, it's back to work until five, supper in the mess hall, then rec time, where we play pool, watch television, chat, play cards, or use the phones in the common area below the cells.

At eight o'clock it's the final roll call before bed.

Wash, rinse, repeat.

I lean over the railing, see two guards handing mops and buckets to a few guys from the lower cells.

"The infirmary is flooding," says Nick, the guy from the next cell over. "Whole place is under a foot of water."

"So they're taking a couple of mops?" I say. "That's going to do a lot."

Nick shrugs. "Heard the storm's getting real bad."

"Yeah?"

"Was watching the news last night."

"What did it say?"

"That the storm's getting real bad," says Nick patiently.

I wait. He doesn't seem inclined to add anything else. "And?"

"And nothing. COs shut the television off before the report finished."

"Was rec time over?" asks Felix.

"Nope." Nick taps his nose. "Control the flow of information. See what I'm saying?"

I don't even bother to suppress a sigh. Nick is convinced everyone in authority is involved in some kind of conspiracy, usually directed against him personally.

"Don't need the news to tell us the storm's bad," says Felix. "You hear it last night? That wind? Jesus, I thought the whole place was going to come down on top of us."

A loud bang echoes through the wing. I look to the right and see Evans standing at the top of the metal stairs, his baton raised to strike the railing a second time.

Typical. It *would* be his shift. Right when I'm tired and not in the mood to take his shit. I hate Evans. Seriously. I'm not talking like he *irritates* me. It's deeper than that. I despise everything about him. His face, the way he breathes, the little twitch in his eyelid when he tries to intimidate prisoners. He's a bully, simple as that. A bully who managed to get himself placed in a position of power.

If I'd ever met him on the outside, I would have made it my mission to get him thrown in prison. Maybe pulled him over, "found" some coke in his car, enough that he went down for dealing, not just possession.

Most of the other screws are okay. They come in, do their jobs, they go home. But Evans... the first time I laid eyes on the guy, I knew he should be on the other side of the bars. I've seen killers. I've seen rapists. There's always something in their eyes. Evans has that look.

And he doesn't like me because... well, I'm not sure about that. I think it's because I don't back down and I don't play his games. What's the point? I'm not a career criminal. I don't see myself as a murderer. Sure, I killed someone, but killing someone who killed your wife—that's not murder. That's revenge. *Justice*. Besides that, I'm just a normal guy. I was married for two years. Wanted to start a family. My wife was a nurse. I was a cop, then I signed up for the army, then became a cop again when my tour was done. That was it. Nothing interesting. Nothing spectacular.

Until that night.

So Evans can't figure me out, and that annoys him. He pushes and pushes, trying to provoke a reaction from me. I think it's what gets him up in the morning. The desire to break me.

I watch him make his way along the walkway. He moves slowly, with a rolling gait that speaks of an old leg injury. He likes to build up a rhythm with his counting. Left foot forward, click, right foot forward, click. He hates it when anyone breaks his pattern.

No one speaks as he does his count. On the walkway opposite, I can see Martinez doing the same thing. She always finishes ahead of Evans. Evans likes to linger, staring at each inmate until they look away. Sometimes it happens fast, sometimes it doesn't.

I look straight ahead. Evans's face slides into view, his watery eyes staring directly into mine. There's a sheen of sweat covering his face. Sure, it's as humid as the ass-crack of Satan himself in here, but Evans sweats regardless of the weather. He always looks greasy, like old cooking oil.

He waits for me to look away. Or better yet, down, a sign of total subservience. Dream on, fuckface. I keep staring straight ahead, my eyes not even flickering.

We stand like this for a long moment, neither willing to back down. Nick can see where this is going. He tries to head it off.

"Hey, Evans," he says. "What's the word on the storm?"

Evans grabs the opportunity for a graceful exit and turns his attention to Nick.

"The word is mind your own business."

He moves on, clicking as he goes.

"That's not a word," says Nick. "That's five—no, wait. Four! That's four words, Evans! Four!"

After head count, we're allowed to mingle in the dayroom,

which is a fancy—and totally inaccurate—name for the un-evenly shaped wedge of floor space outside the cells. It's like calling a dingy motel in the backwaters of Alabama a five-star luxury resort.

As always, it's a mad rush for the phones. They're everyone's lifeline. Their connection to the outside world. I don't know why they bother. About seven out of ten phone calls end up with the inmate slamming the phone down in frustration.

See, that's the thing. Being in prison regresses everyone to the mentality of teenagers. Everything is blown way out of proportion. Your whole world—your whole *universe*—shrinks down to the equivalent of high school, just with killers and gangs instead of cliquey cheerleaders and jocks. A perceived slight becomes a deathly insult. A sidelong look proof that someone is going to attack. It's just the way the mind changes when you're inside.

But that change in thinking carries through to your con-nections with the outside world too. The tiniest pause on the other end of the line, the slightest hesitation, breeds paranoia and anger. Because every single inmate who's still in a rela-tionship has only two things on their mind: when is she going to leave me, and who is she cheating on me with? It could've been the strongest, most loving relationship ever on the out-side. Childhood sweethearts, the first person you had sex with—whatever. It all crumbles to fear and insecurity as soon as the prison gates close.

The six hexagonal tables bolted to the floor are already full. Inmates claiming their spots, decks of cards appearing, com-missary food changing hands to pay off debts. As with everything in prison, there's a pecking order. No one sits down until Leon, the pod boss, decides where he's going to sit. Then his lieutenants and bodyguards take up the chairs around him. Only then do the empty tables start to fill. Those currently in favor with Leon take the closest, leaving the unpopular tables next to the door for the other inmates.

I never bother with the seats. I prefer to pace the perimeter of the block, round and round. It has two benefits. It keeps me fit and sane, and it makes the others wary of me. Anything out of the ordinary singles you out, either to be taken advantage of, or to be avoided. Walking around and around—jogging sometimes, depending on how much nervous energy I've built up—not talking to anyone, for some reason marks me as unreadable. Unpredictable.

A few inmates did try to cause shit with me once, when I first came in and they found out I was a cop. I had to put them in the infirmary. One of them nearly died from internal bleeding. Another had a broken jaw, a broken wrist, and three fractured ribs. I had no choice, though. I had to make an example of them. You don't do that, you let them push you around, then you live with a target on your back. And the target on a cop's back is pretty fucking big, let me tell you.

I haven't even finished one lap of the pod before my name is called over the speaker.

"Constantine, Manuel, Perez, Stevens, Deacon, Murphy, MacLeod, Felix, and Nunes. Line up."

This gets everyone's attention. Anything different from the normal routine is a source of interest.

We line up outside the door that leads from the block. There's a loud buzz and Evans enters, standing to the side and holding the door ajar. I don't even bother asking what's going on. I know he won't answer.

Deacon is the one who speaks up. "Hey, Evans, what's up? We haven't had breakfast yet."

Evans just stares at his clipboard.

"Come on, man," says Deacon. "I got low blood sugar. I need food."

Evans finally gives him a bored look. "You'll be fed later. You got work to do."

"What work?" asks Nunes.

"Cleaning out the old prison."

"The Glasshouse? The fuck for?"

That's a very good question. The Glasshouse was put in mothballs about thirty years ago. The place is totally old-school. About seventy years old, I think. No electronic locks. All cells opened with a key. Barely any light. Cramped. Claustrophobic. More like an asylum than a prison.

"Why we being punished, man?" asks Manuel.

"You remember where you are?" says Evans. "You don't get to ask questions. You do what you're fucking told." He hesitates. "But I'll tell you why. Only because I *want* to tell you, understand?" He waits until Manuel nods in agreement. "Some of the other prisons are being evacuated because of the hurricane. We're using the Glasshouse as temporary accommodation." He turns and addresses the rest of the inmates watching us from their chairs. "Don't get too comfortable. I'll be bringing most of you across in waves. Busy day today."

He gestures with the clipboard and we all file slowly out of the pod.

ADVISORY BULLETIN
Hurricane Hannah Advisory Number 6
NWS National Hurricane Center Miami FL
2 A.M. EDT SAT AUG 28 2021

DISCUSSION AND OUTLOOK
Tropical Hurricane Hannah has fluctuated between Categories 2 and 3 for several days due to a series of eyewall replacement cycles. She has traveled through the Gulf of Mexico and has made landfall at Johnson's Bayou, Louisiana. Her path will take her through Alabama, where winds will reach 190 mph (305 km/h) as she passes into Georgia. The cyclone is forecast to increase from Category 3 to Category 4 by Saturday, August 28. Hannah will negatively impact any Josephine-related evacuation plans of the states to the east and south, including Florida. Those remaining are advised to wait for her to pass into the Atlantic before attempting evacuation.

WARNINGS
If not already evacuated, find shelter immediately.
$$
Forecaster Mills

Two
Friday, August 27
7:00 a.m.

Keira Sawyer sits in a hard plastic lawn chair, the kind usually found out in the garden. Her hands twist nervously in her lap as she listens to the wind raging outside the office window. The blinds are closed. She's not sure if it's because whoever's office this is doesn't want to see the weather, or just because they haven't settled in for the day yet.

It was a mistake to come in. She knows that now. Hell, she knew it this morning as she was driving through flooding roads, passing lines of traffic going in the opposite direction. Stupid. Dangerous. Insane.

But she had no choice.

The door opens abruptly and a short woman wearing a CO uniform enters. She's holding a clipboard and looks stressed and annoyed. Even more so when she sees Sawyer sitting there.

"I thought he was messing with me."

Sawyer hesitates. "Who?"

"Wilson. He said the new girl was here. I said don't be crazy. No one's stupid enough to start their first day during a hurricane. And yet here you are."

Sawyer lets the insult slide. The woman has a point. "I...didn't think I had a choice. I mean, no one told me *not* to come in."

The woman stares hard at her. "You must really need this job."

Sawyer nods. "I do."

The CO sighs. "Fine. I'm Martinez. Looks like I'll be your tour guide today. Come on."

Sawyer stands up. Martinez looks her up and down. Something about what she sees makes her even unhappier.

"What do you weigh? One hundred ten?"

"One-fifteen. Why?"

"Height?"

"Five-six."

"Jesus. They're going to eat you alive."

Sawyer straightens up slightly, defensive. "I'm tougher than I look." She instantly regrets saying it. Even to her own ears it sounds childish and whiny.

"For your sake, honey, I sincerely hope so. Come on."

She follows Martinez out of the office and into the corridor beyond. It's empty, lit by harsh fluorescents recessed into the ceiling.

"Stay close," says Martinez. "Seriously. Don't get within grabbing distance of any of the prisoners. You're new. You're cute. Fuck, they're going to have a field day with you. Do not, under any circumstances, show fear. Understand? Don't look uneasy. Or panicked. And don't smile. Don't try to be their friend. You do any of that, they'll remember. Word will spread and they *will* use it against you."

Sawyer hurries to keep up with her. "How am I supposed to look?"

"What?"

"You said don't show fear. Don't smile. What *am* I supposed to do?"

"I bet you get hit on a lot in bars, right?"

"I suppose."

"The look you put on when you want to show you're not interested? *That's* how you're supposed to look."

"You mean resting bitch face."

"I mean *permanent* bitch face."

Martinez leads her along the corridor, through a door and into an open-plan office area. There is staff here, some sitting, some just passing through, heading into corridors that lead into other parts of the prison complex. Martinez heads straight for a set of double doors on the far side and shoves the bar down to push them open. Sawyer follows after, letting the doors slam shut behind her. The corridor stretches far ahead of them, so far she can't even see the end of it.

"Okay, so the Ravenhill Correctional Facility is about two square miles total. It's big. Right here we're in the administrative building. It's the hub of the prison. It's way bigger than you'd normally see in modern prisons. Basically because it was left over from the army days."

"Army days?" Sawyer asks, confused.

"I'll get to that. In Admin we've got a couple religious resource rooms, a staff gym, warehouses for storing commissary and other supplies, a loading dock, an armory, an indoor firing range, the sheriff's office, staff offices, you name it."

"But—"

Martinez half turns and holds up a hand. "Just wait. Questions later. You'll need your breath." She turns back again, striding along the wide passage. "This right here is the staff corridor. It travels from Admin all the way to the staff section on the north side of the prison. We just call the building up there Northside. There's a cafeteria there. More offices. Staff changing rooms. Same thing we have on the south side of the prison. Depending on where you're assigned, you'll either park your car Northside or down here."

"You said this is the staff corridor?"

"Yeah. No inmates allowed."

"How do you transport them?"

"There's an inmate corridor on the other side of the prison. Exact duplicate of this one, travels from Admin all the way to the Northside too. Make sure they stay in the red line when you're on escort duty."

The corridor they're moving through looks like it's never-ending. It stretches into the distance, seeming to grow narrower the farther it goes. Martinez catches her look.

"Yeah, you're not gonna have any trouble getting your ten thousand steps in. Not here. I've done forty on a shift before."

"Forty?"

"Thousand."

"Steps? But that's like..." Sawyer does a quick calculation. No, that can't be right, can it? She looks at Martinez in shock.

"Twenty miles? Yeah."

"Jesus."

"Tell me about it. Okay, listen up. I'm going to explain the layout of this place. Heading north of Admin, we have seven separate living units." She gestures to the wall to their left. "They're all in there."

"Units? Not blocks?"

"No. Some of the older inmates still call them that, but no one else. The first four complexes are general population—Gen Pop. Just your average criminal doing his time. Not nice people, but they don't give us too much shit. Or if they do, they know when to reel it in, because they don't want to end up in solitary. Some of these guys—I'd say about forty percent—are working toward a GED." She throws a look over her shoulder. "That's a General Education Diploma."

Sawyer half smiles. "Yeah, I know. I'm not that green."

"Apologies. So Gen Pop holds the guys doing the GED programs, as well as the inmates who work in the industry units."

"What do they make?"

"License plates. Military armor. Fast-food uniforms. That lingerie your boyfriend likes so much? Probably made right here."

Sawyer bursts out laughing. "Fuck off."

"I'm serious. And most of them only get paid, like, fifty cents an hour. Private prisons, Sawyer. It's legalized slave labor."

A couple of COs are walking past as Martinez says this. They give her a dirty look and carry on.

"Nobody likes talking about it," she says, nodding after them. "'Cause they all know it's not right. Anyway, Gen Pop is four units, 1 to 4. They're separate buildings linked right through the middle by corridors and sally ports with their own security pods. After those four, we get to the specialist units."

"Specialist?" Sawyer is already feeling lost.

"First off is the Transitional Care Unit. The TCU. That's where inmates who need nursing care are taken. Not just injured inmates; I'm talking post surgery, maybe end-of-life care."

"Right."

"Next in the stack is the Mental Health Unit. You do *not* want to work in MHU. Seriously. Get out of any duty rosters that put you in there. Because we have special kinds of crazies here. We're supposed to have the best team of psych doctors in the country, so we get shipped the psychos from all over. If Hannibal Lecter were real, he'd be locked up here. I fucking hate that place."

They walk on in silence. Martinez seems lost in her thoughts.

"And the last unit?" presses Sawyer.

Martinez glances over in surprise, as if she forgot Sawyer was even there. "ACU. Administrative Control Unit. The inmates call it Super Seg—that's Administrative Segregation to you and me. It's where we keep the most violent offenders. The inmates who attack prisoners and staff, anyone who's shown a direct physical threat to the life of others. They're locked down in there twenty-three hours a day. They get one hour for exercise, and that's it. ACU is designed so that staff don't have to have any physical contact with the offenders at all. The cells are accessed through two sets of doors, so you have a sally port for each cell. Safest way to do it."

"What do they do in their cells for twenty-three hours?"

"Most of them go crazy. End up in MHU. Some pace. Some punch the wall. Some read. I won't lie, it's no life. I'd rather die than be put in there."

"That...sounds like hell."

"See now, that's the most sensible thing you've said since we met. This place *is* hell. Admin is like...purgatory. We're the lost souls serving our time, doing penance or whatever till we're judged. Then the deeper into the prison you go, the lower you descend through the different levels until you finally get to ACU." Martinez throws Sawyer a serious look. "ACU is where Satan would have his throne."

They fall into an uneasy silence. Sawyer's stomach is clenched with fear. She's starting to wonder if she's made a really big mistake. Sure, she needed to be here. She needed the job. There was no other way. But this...she's not sure she can do this.

She sees a door coming up on their left and stops to peer through the safety glass, looking into yet another faceless corridor. "Where are we now?"

"Unit 4."

She looks at Martinez in surprise. "We've only passed four units?"

"Haven't even got out of Gen Pop yet. Come on."

Martinez starts walking again, not waiting to see if Sawyer is following.

"I don't get it. Why is this place so big?"

"It's what happens when you repurpose something instead of starting from scratch. It used to be an army base. The old prison? The Glasshouse? It was a military prison. Apparently, it's British slang or something. Don't ask me why the name stuck."

"Seems a weird place to even build an army base, though," says Sawyer.

"You're lucky you've got me for orientation. If it was Sheriff Montoya, he'd be showing you a PowerPoint presentation right now. It's his favorite subject. Back in the day, there were these plans to build something called the Cross-Florida Barge Canal. This was in 1935, right? Government wanted a canal

network that would cut right through Florida from Jackson-
ville all the way to the Gulf of Mexico."

"Why?"

"To move goods across Florida. The canals were supposed to
be dug by the U.S. Army Corps of Engineers. The plans were
crazy expensive, though. Funding ran out. Nothing was
finished."

"And this place?"

"This was the base of operations for the Corps of Engineers.
But when the money ran out, the army decided to make the
most of what they'd already built and turned it into a military
prison. That's why the layout is so weird. It wasn't intended to
be a civilian prison. It's been an army barracks, a building site,
an army training ground, a storm-and-flood disaster management site—"

"Wait." Sawyer is getting confused. "A what?"

"Yeah. The whole canal project was resurrected in 1964, but
this time the army was told to build these huge storm tunnels
underneath the Glasshouse. This site is close to the ocean. All
the other dams and canals they were building would feed
through here. The storm tunnels were supposed to handle the
overflow if they flooded."

"Have they ever been used?"

"Nah. Nixon canceled the whole project again in '71. Some
environmentalists were getting pissy about it. Bad publicity.
He had other things to worry about, so he just scrapped the
whole thing."

"And the flood system?"

"They didn't finish it. There are miles of tunnels about a hundred and fifty feet underneath us. Huge flood chambers. I'm
talking thirty, forty feet high. Must have cost a fucking fortune."

"So what happened to this place in '71?"

"The army thought *fuck it* and ditched the whole plot. They
sold everything to a private company owned by some guy
called Ravenhill and it was turned into a civilian prison. They

stopped using the Glasshouse in the late eighties. It was too old. No electronics or anything. It's all manual. You know? Massive levers to open the cell doors, that kind of thing. So fucking claustrophobic. You're actually lucky. It used to be an initiation for new COs to sleep a night in that place."

"Did you?"

"Yeah." Martinez shivers. "Feels like the walls are closing in on you. You hear all these noises..." She trails off, lost in her memories.

Sawyer has been counting the doors as they walk. Number seven is coming up, and the staff corridor comes to an end about three hundred feet in front of them.

Martinez stops walking. "End of the road," she says. "That's ACU to our left." She points at the double doors straight ahead. "Through there is Northside. Staff and admin. Changing rooms, kitchen, that kind of thing." She hands Sawyer two electronic keycards. "These are temps. This one will let you through the doors on either end of this corridor. The other one will let you out of the Northside staff room. My advice? Use it and leave now. Good luck. I'll catch you when this hurricane has blown over." She turns and starts retracing their steps.

"Wait," calls Sawyer, suddenly realizing what Martinez said. "What do you mean? You're not staying?"

"Fuck no. We're being subbed by the National Guard later on today. The COs are leaving in shifts, starting now. Seriously, you should just get back in your car and go. Head north. This storm is going to get real bad before it gets any better." She looks around. "Here's hoping the place is still standing by the end of it. I need this job. Got bills to pay."

She starts walking again, leaving Sawyer standing alone in the wide corridor. She can hear a weird sound coming from the door into ACU. She steps hesitantly forward and listens.

It's the sound of inmates screaming.

Three

7:30 a.m.

All the inmates called by Evans line up in the narrow corridor outside our block. The corridor is painted in that institutional yellow-green color that hospitals, mental institutions, and prisons all have in common. My theory is that someone in government got a bulk deal in the early eighties when everyone realized that the previous decade's fad for decorating your house in mustard and avocado really wasn't a good idea. Solution? Mix the colors and sell it off to government.

The corridor ends at a heavy door. To the right is a wire-reinforced window looking into the security room. We wait up against the wall while Evans counts us off on his clipboard. A younger officer, a guy named Gonzalez, stands just ahead of us, a dirty sack sitting at his feet.

Gonzalez is new, only been on the job about a year. He's still pretty decent to the inmates. Seems like a good guy. But you can already see the effect the job is having on him. Obligatory overtime means the COs work fourteen-hour shifts, and the dark rings that live permanently beneath his eyes show he's taking strain. It won't be long before he becomes just like the others. Minimum effort put in. Just watching the clock until it's time to go home.

Evans finishes his head count and picks up the sack, tipping its contents onto the floor. Belly chains spill out, curling at his feet like iron snakes. Great. Nobody likes belly chains. They restrict arm movement so much you can't even scratch your nose.

Gonzalez and Evans head down the line attaching the chains. Evans does mine, cinching it so tight it digs into my waist. Rookie mistake on my part. You're supposed to push out your stomach when they put on the chain. That way, when you relax again, it isn't so tight that it actually cuts off your breathing.

"You might want to loosen that a bit," I say to Evans.

"Might I now?"

"Yeah. It's a bit tight."

"Sure. My apologies."

He loosens the chain. I try to push my stomach out, but he jabs me hard in the side with his elbow. I wince and double up. He takes the opportunity to yank the chain even harder, locking it in place with a smile on his lips. He grabs the handcuffs attached to the chain and snaps them over my wrists, making sure they're as tight as possible.

"How's that, sir? To your liking?"

He chuckles and moves down the line, checking all the locks, tightening the cuffs that, in his opinion, Gonzalez left too loose. He then bangs on the metal door leading out of the corridor.

"Open B."

"Opening B," comes the muffled voice from the security room.

The security room is positioned as the central hub, while A, B, and C blocks are the chunky spokes radiating outward. Inside are the computers that activate all the locks in the wing. The room is protected by bulletproof glass, a solid three-inch door. It contains a gun locker in case the inmates get out of hand. Shotguns, live rounds, rubber bullets, beanbag rounds, anything a CO might need to put down any trouble.

There's a loud buzz and the door clicks open. Evans leads us into the corridor on the other side. Same color paint, but the floor is covered with gray screed that has a red line painted on it two feet from the wall.

"Stay in the line!" shouts Evans.

"Nice to get out," says Felix conversationally as everyone

shuffles to the right side of the red line. "Break from the old routine. Just like a family vacation."

I look around the corridor. Fluorescent lights are recessed in the ceiling, their glow dimmed by thick safety glass. Exposed pipes, their top halves coated black with years of accumulated dust, snake along the walls just below the ceiling. There's an old rust-colored bloodstain smeared on the wall.

"Where the hell did you go on vacation?" I ask.

Gonzalez stops at the door at the far end of the corridor. We stand there while the guards in a booth on the other side scope us out through the camera.

"Come on!" shouts Gonzalez. "Cleaning crew for the Glasshouse."

The door buzzes and releases. Gonzalez yanks it open and we file through. Guards stare at us as we pass, their faces cold and impassive.

"What you lookin' at?" calls out someone from farther down the line.

I glance over my shoulder. Nunes is giving the guards the finger as he passes the booth. "Yeah, fuck you, man. Come out here and look at me like that."

Felix, ever the unpredictable one, turns and grabs Nunes, shoving him up against the wall. "You want to shut the fuck up? You trying to get us sent back to our cells?"

"N-no, man. I was just—"

Felix pulls him away and slams him hard up against the wall again. "You was just nothing. Understand? Shut the fuck up before I shut you up."

Evans appears at Felix's side. "Let him go."

If it had been any other prisoner, Evans would have laid into him with his baton. But because it's Felix, he gives him a chance to back down on his own. Everyone knows Felix can be...impulsive.

Felix lets go and gets back in line. Evans then takes his place, ramming his baton against Nunes's larynx.

"Now—wanna say that again?"

Evans pushes harder. Nunes can't speak. Hell, he can hardly breathe.

"Can't hear you, smart mouth. I said, you wanna say that again?"

Nunes shakes his head. Evans glares at him a moment longer, then steps back. Nunes folds over, coughing and wheezing for breath.

Evans yanks him up by his collar. "No delays!" he shouts. "Keep moving."

We move on, nobody talking now. We make our way through the rest of the wing, passing the staff rec room, offices, the prison cafeteria, the corridor to the staff gym, before finally stopping at a reinforced door that opens onto a thirty-yard-long upward-slanting corridor leading into the main administrative section of Ravenhill, called, in a dazzling display of creativity, Admin.

Where we're standing now, this is the offices and support network that deals with A Wing. A Wing is a newer addition to the prison complex, built in the nineties when the four Gen Pop units in Ravenhill became too full. Only problem is, the actual prison, as well as the Glasshouse itself, takes up all the level space at the top of the hill. So A Wing had to be built on a section of flattened land cut out of the hill itself, making it about thirty yards lower than the rest of the prison.

Evans uses his keys to unlock the doors and we climb the uphill corridor. He unlocks another door at the top and we enter the reception area of Admin. Its age shows everywhere you look. The reception hall is a massive room with an ornate ceiling. The huge space looks like it belongs in a hotel instead of a prison. The walls are paneled in dark wood. Against the far wall is an antique wooden desk on which sit five computer monitors—only three of them are in use by the staff at this hour. To the right are two metal detectors leading into the waiting area and the front entrance of the prison. There are no civilians there yet. Visiting hours are in the afternoon.

Evans leads us through reception, then into a corridor that skirts the front of the prison before turning left into another long passage and finally into Receiving and Release.

R&R is where the inmates arrive for processing. Where we're signed out once we've done our time. Some prisons have R&R open to the air. Just a straight road from the outside gate to a fenced-off area where the inmates disembark. But Ravenhill's R&R is an actual depot. A roofed-over space with automatic steel doors controlled from inside.

We exit the prison. A correctional bus is waiting for us. It's a Blue Bird All American, about twenty years old. Not bad. The bus that brought me here was a converted school bus from the fifties. Windows sealed shut and no AC. This is luxury in comparison.

The driver is already in his seat, his fingers locked tightly around the wheel. He looks nervous. We climb the steps and file through the metal gate that will be locked to keep us from messing with him. I take a window seat about two thirds from the front. Felix sits next to me, shifting around on the cracked leather to get comfortable.

"I remember one time I was on a bus like this. It was going across the border. South, y'know…?"

I stop listening, filtering out the chatter. I sometimes find it best to do that with Felix. It becomes white noise, like an electric fan. I've trained myself to pick up on repeated phrases like "You hearing me?" or "You listening?" and I nod and mumble yeah. Felix never really notices. Or if he does, he doesn't care. Not that I have anything against Felix, you understand. He just talks a lot.

Gonzalez makes his way down the aisle between the seats. "Hold on tight," he says. "It's rough out there." He enters the guard cage at the rear of the bus. He and Evans both slam their gates shut and lock them, then take their seats and put on their seat belts.

"Hey!" yells MacLeod. "How come you guys get belts?"

"'Cause your life ain't worth shit, MacLeod!" shouts Evans. "I tell you that every day. You never listen."

"You lucky you behind that cage, Evans. I'd beat the shit out of you if you wasn't."

"And that's you up on report, asshole. Threatening a CO with violence."

"Can you guys shut up back there?" shouts the driver. "We're heading out."

The engine starts with a dull rumble, the seats vibrating. The driver speaks into a radio transmitter mounted on the dash. A loud buzz sounds and then the metal gates at the other end of the depot start to slide open.

It feels like the doors to hell are opening up.

The wind slams into the bus, rocking it on its wheels. Rain explodes into the depot, gushing as if a water tank has been ruptured. The inmates cry out in shock, gripping hold of the seats in front of them. Leaves and debris fly through the air, an old sheet of newspaper slapping against the windscreen.

I peer through the window, watching the gates open all the way. The morning light is yellow, an apocalyptic taint I've never seen before.

The bus starts moving.

"The fuck, man?" someone shouts. "You can't take us out in that!"

"Stop being a pussy!" yells Evans, almost screaming to be heard above the roaring wind. "You're not getting out of work detail, you little bitch!"

The headlights illuminate the torrential rain as we edge out of the depot. It's blowing in heavy horizontal sheets that surge and flick with the wind. The driver leans forward in his seat, squinting through the windshield.

"Move faster!" shouts Evans.

The driver doesn't even glance at him, just keeps his gaze focused outside.

The bus turns right onto a small road. I can just make out

the spotlights every ten feet or so. At night, they illuminate the prison grounds. Now they're reduced to weak halos that make the rain glow like molten metal.

I've never seen anything like this storm. The clouds look like they're boiling, bulging out into liver-colored knots, twisting away in the wind and then roiling back on themselves. It's hypnotic and terrifying at the same time.

After a few minutes, the bus edges onto the road that leads down to the perimeter fence. It descends the hill and then turns left when we reach the front gate of the prison, moving onto a smaller road and back up the hill again on the opposite side of a secondary fence that separates the Glasshouse from the rest of Ravenhill.

The ride grows bumpy as the road changes from smooth tar to a patchy potholed mess. No one has bothered with upkeep. Why would they? The old prison was abandoned years ago. The only reason it's still standing is because some social activist group claimed it was a site of interest and wanted it listed as a historical building. God knows why. The place is a dump. An eyesore that looks like it belongs in the Victorian era. Crumbling redbrick face, heavy steel bars painted with chipped gray enamel on the windows. It looms against the stormy sky like the opening scene in a horror movie.

The bus eventually stops before a set of old-fashioned iron gates. The high beams pick out a massive chain held together by a rusted padlock.

"Who's got the key?" calls out the driver.

"Gonzalez!" shouts Evans.

Gonzalez looks nervously out the window. "Why do I have to do it?"

"Number one, because you're the rookie and I'm not. And number two, because you already have the key. Move your ass."

Gonzalez sighs and unbuckles himself. He unlocks the door to the cage and heads to the front of the bus. Evans unlocks the second gate and the driver hits the button to open the bus doors.

Torrential rain and wind explode inside. Gonzalez stumbles back, his hand raised to cover his face. He squints into the storm, steadying himself with his other hand.

"Get out!" screams the driver.

Gonzalez staggers into the wind, his face turned to the side.

"Hey, Gonzalez!" shouts Felix. "You might wanna take an umbrella. Looks like it's gonna rain."

The inmates roar with laughter.

I press my head against the window and watch Gonzalez struggle to reach the gate. The road is a muddy river. The brown water breaks against him as he wades forward. Before he reaches the gate, he stumbles. He fights to keep his footing, but a fierce gust slams him from the side and he goes down. He hits the ground hard, then starts to roll, the wind shoving and bullying him until he manages to slap his hands flat against the ground, keeping low while he regains his breath.

The inmates are all laughing. Even Evans has a grin on his face. Personally, I would have preferred to see Evans out there on his ass, but there's no way he's going to get his hands dirty if he can order someone else to do it.

Gonzalez slowly pushes himself to his feet and staggers to the gate. It takes him a while to get the key to turn, but he finally manages to open the padlock and yanks the chain off. He drops it to the side and pulls open the gates, then starts to head back to the bus, but the right gate swings closed again as soon as he lets go. The driver honks his horn and gestures. Gonzalez looks back. His mouth moves in a curse and he wades back to hold the gate open while the bus edges forward.

The driver waits on the other side and Gonzalez scrambles back inside, the doors slamming shut behind him.

"Hey, Gonzalez!" shouts Perez. "You been on vacation? You look like you caught some sun, man."

The rest of the bus cracks up and Gonzalez just slumps against the side of the cage and flips Perez the bird.

We move along the road and stop before another solid metal gate recessed into the perimeter wall of the Glasshouse. It looks like the entrance to some medieval castle. Evans turns to Gonzalez.

"You're already wet," he says.

"Fuck sake." Gonzalez stumbles outside again, the doors quickly sliding closed behind him. He moves to a door set off to the side of the gate. It's unlocked, and he slips inside, slamming it shut behind him.

We wait a few seconds, then the gates part down the middle and swing inward. We edge beneath the prison wall and into a short tunnel lit by flickering orange lamps hanging from the bricks. The gates behind us slam shut and two identical gates in front open to reveal a concrete courtyard lit by bright floodlights.

Gonzalez climbs back into the bus and it shoots forward, the driver eager to get this over with. The Glasshouse towers above us. The driver doesn't go straight for the main entrance, but drives to the left and around the side of the prison. We finally turn into a tunnel that slants down beneath ground level and come to a stop in a loading bay.

Evans unlocks the cage and gestures for us to get up. "Move it. I don't have all day."

We climb reluctantly from the bus. Once we're clear, it immediately starts reversing back up the ramp, Gonzalez still on board.

"They leaving you alone with us, Evans?" Murphy asks.

"Don't get smart. They're coming back. Unless you want to clean out the cells on your own? I mean, I'm happy to let you. Might do you all some good. Learn a bit of work ethic. Just thought you'd want some company while you all bitch and complain."

He glares at us, then turns and pulls open a rusted metal door, holding it wide as we file inside the Glasshouse.

We follow Evans into a service corridor that smells of rotten cabbages. It reminds me of being a kid and going to my grandma's house on Sunday afternoons. That same pungent smell, like old wet socks and dampness. We move at a fast pace, kicking and crunching over the fragments of the past: broken lightbulbs, rotting magazines, smashed tiles.

At least some of the lights are working. Someone must have come across earlier and flipped the breaker to get this place powered up. They built these old places to last.

After about five minutes of walking through various corridors, Evans leads us into a laundry room. Massive antique washing machines line one wall, while industrial dryers take up the other. A metal table covered in black sheets travels down the center of the long room. It's only as we walk past that I notice the sheets aren't supposed to be that color. They're black with mildew, rotting away from the humidity.

We move through the room into a narrow corridor. Terracotta tiles cover the floor, half of them cracked, most of them invisible beneath mud and debris. The walls are covered in rectangular white tiles that must have once been shiny, but are now smeared in grime and dull with the passing of years.

The corridor ends at a heavy metal gate. Evans pulls out a ring of keys and jams them, one after the other, into the lock, swearing and cursing until he finds the one that fits.

"That how your wife feels, Evans?" someone calls out.

He ignores the comment, turns the key with a solid clunk, and pushes the gate open. It shifts reluctantly, with a shriek of protest.

"And that's what she sounds like when she wakes up and sees you in the morning!" shouts Perez.

This gets a few more chuckles, but Evans just pushes through the gate. We move deeper into the Glasshouse, through narrow, winding corridors, some dimly lit with old hanging bulbs, some not lit at all. Cracked tiles, flickering lights, chipped enamel paint, abandoned offices and rooms strewn with mildewed books and old rotting files.

We exit the service corridors and pass through the front area of the prison, where visitors once came to sign in. It's similar in style to the Admin reception—I think it must have been modeled on Admin. The only real difference is that this one has a massive circular desk that looks like it's made from solid mahogany. It could easily sit twenty people around it. The vast room is cut in half by a wall of metal bars with two locked gates—one to either side of the circular desk. There are no metal detectors. The visitors would have moved, one by one, through the gates to be patted down by guards before filing into waiting rooms to the right.

We move through reception and into the visiting area. Metal tables are bolted to the floor. An old, damaged vending machine lies on its side, tipped over and smashed. Someone has scrawled graffiti on the wall, which is weird seeing as the guards would be the only ones with access to spray paint. I try to read the writing as we pass through, but years of dust and mildew have made it illegible.

More twisting, dimly lit corridors follow, until finally we walk through a wide arch into the single prison block of the Glasshouse.

The Rotunda.

I've never seen anything like it. The Rotunda is a towering hollow cylinder easily a hundred feet high. The cells circle the inside, receding up into the distance and looking out over the empty central shaft. The floors all meld together the higher up I look. I try to count the levels, but give up after twenty.

Access to each floor is by metal stairs with lockable gates. There's also an old-fashioned elevator, one of those old brass-and-wood things with the metal grate you have to slam shut.

A twenty-foot tower topped with a security pod stands in the center. The pod has 360 degrees of safety glass so the COs could see everything that was going on. It must have been a really shitty assignment. Exposed to the eyes of hundreds of inmates who want to do nothing more than slit your throat.

There are cleaning utensils sitting next to the elevator doors: brooms and plastic trash bags, mops and buckets.

"I don't think I have to explain it to you," says Evans. "You guys take Level 1. Get cleaning. Sooner you finish, the sooner you get back for lunch."

"We're not doing all the levels, are we?" asks Deacon.

"You deaf as well as stupid? I said Level 1. Other inmates are being brought in to help."

I grab a broom and wait while Evans unlocks the gate to the first floor. Then we set to work, brushing out years of dust and debris.

About ten minutes after we start, another group arrives. They take Level 2. After another ten minutes, a third group enters the chamber and they take Level 3. This goes on until the first ten levels are filled with shouting and swearing inmates grudgingly cleaning out cells that haven't been looked at in years.

"Yo!" someone shouts from somewhere above. "How the hell does a used condom get in here? The place is supposed to be abandoned!"

Evans is sitting on the floor below with his eyes closed, his back against the central pillar, cradling his shotgun against his shoulder. "Just pick it up!" he shouts, without even opening his eyes.

"I ain't touchin' that thing! There's black stuff inside it."

We've been working for about two hours. The joking and shouting has died down. Everyone just wants to finish up and get back to their cells.

Felix and I have a good system going. I sweep the shit out onto the walkway. Felix carts in a bucket of water and throws it down, then mops up while I gather all the crap into plastic bags before moving on to the next cell. It's killing my back, though. The next time Felix heads out to refill the bucket, I lean the broom against the wall and stretch, hearing my spine crack and pop as I do so.

"Hey there, Jack," says a voice from behind me. "Long time no see."

I turn around.

Malcolm Kincaid stands in the door to the cell.

Malcolm fucking Kincaid.

Shit...

Four

Four years ago

The day Malcolm Kincaid's case goes before the judge, a drizzle the temperature of warm piss falls from the sky. It makes the heat of the day even worse, creating a damp, cloying blanket that shrouds Miami, turning the whole city into the equivalent of a steam room at a back-alley gym.

Mason and I sit in the car outside the courthouse, waiting for an update from Captain Mendes. The AC doesn't work. Sweat prickles my skin, makes my shirt stick to the cracked vinyl seat.

"How long you think he'll get?" asks Mason.

"Fuck knows." I chew nervously on a nail. "Not long. Too many people owe him favors. But a couple years at least."

"It's not enough."

It's *definitely* not enough. Malcolm Kincaid deserves to be put away for life. He's one of the nastiest pieces of work I've ever come across, and that includes my tour in Afghanistan.

It's the casual nature of his villainy that gets to me. It's an old-fashioned word, villainy. I felt like an idiot the first time it entered my head. But it fits him perfectly. Kincaid isn't the typical Hollywood-type bad guy you usually find on the streets. All show. All bark. Doing everything for the look of it. Making sure everyone knows exactly how mean he really is.

No. Kincaid lets the reputation he's built up over the decades speak for itself. He's the top of the criminal food chain in Miami, and he lives a life that reflects that. Beachfront villas. Fingers in the property market—all legit, of course, so he can prove he's an honest-to-God businessman.

But it's all a front. The guy is legit psycho. Not a raging, go-on-a-killing-spree psycho, but an I'll-wait-three-years-for-revenge-then-slit-your-throat-at-your-kid's-ballet-recital psycho.

The only problem with being top dog is that everyone wants to challenge you. The younger generation, those just getting into the game, they all think they're better than Kincaid. Stronger. They see what he has and they want it, without necessarily putting in the time. When they challenge him—and they always do—Kincaid likes to show them personally how dumb an idea that was.

That's how I caught him. His arrogance. His ego. It's the weak spot I always knew would bring him down.

"What the actual *fuck*?" says Mason.

I look up. Malcolm Kincaid stands at the top of the courthouse stairs, shaking hands with his lawyers.

My stomach sinks. I watch as they share a joke, Kincaid laughing and slapping one of them on the back.

Once again Malcolm fucking Kincaid has dodged the charges.

I was so sure this time. A witness literally placed him at the scene of the crime. A necklacing—something I'd read about in South African history books—where a car tire is placed around the victim's neck and set alight. The aftermath was one of the most horrific things I'd ever seen. Skin and tendon burned away, rubber fused to blackened vertebrae, weeping red burns crawling up the victim's face like bloody ivy creeping up a wall.

I always knew Kincaid was powerful, but I thought this time it would be different. The case Mason and I had built up was airtight. I was convinced he was going down.

I was wrong.

He descends the stairs, heading toward a black Mercedes. His wife is waiting for him, leaning against the car. She's the same age as Kincaid, late fifties, but looking good for it. Black hair, tanned skin, slim figure. A wide smile on her face as Kincaid pulls her into a kiss.

I shove open the car door, but Mason grabs my arm.

"Don't," she says.

I resist briefly, but then sink back into the seat. I slam the door, harder than necessary.

The noise alerts Kincaid. He looks up, says something to his wife, then approaches the car.

"Stay cool," warns Mason.

"I'm always cool," I mutter.

The side window's already down. Kincaid crouches and nods to Mason.

"Detective."

She ignores him, so he turns his attention to me, a sympathetic look on his face.

"Jackie-boy," he says. "How you feeling?"

I don't answer.

"I'm thinking not too good. Bet you thought you had me, huh?"

"Go fuck yourself."

"Don't feel bad. Better cops than you have tried to put me away. They all gave up in the end." He leans close and lowers his voice so only I can hear. "Either that or they ended up dead." He pats my arm, then straightens up and strolls back to his car.

I throw the door open. I'm out of the car before Mason can stop me. Kincaid hears me coming, starts to turn around.

He's too late. I grab him by the shirt, slam my fist into his face. We both fall to the ground. He gets his hands around my neck, flips me over so I'm lying on the wet asphalt with his grinning face above me, blood from his lip dripping onto my shirt.

Mason appears behind him, yanking him off, pulling him to his feet. He lets her do her thing, moving away a couple of steps without resisting.

"I'm gonna give you that one, Detective," he says. "I understand. It's hard failing like that." He wipes his mouth on his sleeve and shakes his head. "Pussy punch anyway."

He gets in the car with his wife and drives off.

I watch him go, realizing in a moment of icy clarity that he's never going to prison. Ever. He has too many city officials in his pockets.

That's the exact moment I decide to frame him.

Whatever I do, it has to be ironclad. However good I thought the case was last time, this one has to be ten times stronger. So strong that even the most corrupt judge can't let him go.

First things first. I take the shirt Kincaid bled on and I hide it in the garage. After a few days I carefully scrape the dried blood into an evidence bag. It's not much. A few flakes. But it's all I need. I have his DNA now and I sure as fuck am going to make sure I put it to good use.

The actual plan, though. *How* I'm going to frame him. I'm not too sure about that. I can't rush it. Not if I want it to work. That means biding my time. But all the while I'm planning, thinking, watching for an opportunity.

Preparing.

Over the next few months, I shake down every dealer I can find and confiscate their wares. I don't arrest them. I take their stash and tell them to count themselves lucky I'm not taking them in. Doesn't matter what they're holding—meth, Ecstasy, coke, PCP, LSD, fentanyl, methamphetamine, heroin, oxy. Doesn't matter how much they have, either—a bag, a bundle, ten pills, a single rock, I don't care. I take it all and I add it to my collection. I take a gun from one of them too, an old Beretta that's seen better days. Untraceable. On top of that, I buy myself a burner phone. I know I'll need it eventually.

After four months I have enough drugs to fill a backpack. It weighs about four kilograms. More than enough to nail someone on drug-trafficking charges.

And that includes me. Federal trafficking charges are ten years to life for holding a kilo of heroin. I've got 1.2 kilos. I've also got 2.8 kilos of cocaine. That's a minimum of five years. That means what I have in the bag is enough to put someone away for a fifteen stretch. The grass, the Molly, the oxy, that's all small-scale stuff. Icing on the cake. It's the coke and the heroin that will do the job.

Least it would if Kincaid was anyone else. As it stands, I don't think it's anywhere near enough. Evidence goes missing from the station all the time. Even a massive backpack of drugs.

That's fine, because the drugs aren't my whole plan. All that—the gun, the phone, the backpack—it's just groundwork. I'm still not sure how I'm going to nail Kincaid. I'm waiting for inspiration to strike.

Which it does one day in winter.

Not that you can really call it winter in Miami. Seventy-three degrees, and I've had my sleeves rolled up all day. It's about six in the evening now. The sun is low, shining directly into my eyes as I drive home from a malicious-damage call-out. Some disgruntled employee trashing a factory in the Hialeah warehouse district.

I almost miss it. As I sit at a red light I happen to glance to my left, where a narrow alley sits between two abandoned buildings. I see two guys struggling. One wearing a football jersey, baggy pants, and high-tops that look like they're just out of the box; the other wearing dirty jeans and a stained T-shirt. I recognize the guy in the high-tops. He's a dealer I've already shaken down. Devon, I think he's called.

The guy with the dirty jeans throws Devon against the wall and yanks a knife out of his back pocket. He lunges forward, his arm a blur as he stabs Devon again and again in the chest.

It's over before I've even registered what's happening. Devon slumps to the ground and the other guy rummages through his clothes, grabbing money and bags of drugs before running for the opposite end of the alley.

I look around. The place is deserted. There's an old Cadillac parked about twenty feet from the alley, but that's it.

When the light turns green, I swing around and park directly in front of the alley entrance. I drum my fingers on the wheel, pondering. Is this it? The final piece of the puzzle I've been waiting for?

I grab a pair of latex gloves from the cubby. I pull them on as I enter the alley and crouch down by Devon. I feel for a pulse.

Nothing.

I search his pockets and find a set of car keys. I leave the body where it is, slumped between sodden cardboard boxes and mildewed packing crates, and exit the alley. I test the keys in the Cadillac parked on the street. They fit. I make sure the doors are locked, then get back into my own car and head home.

The way I see it, if no one reports the body in the next few hours, the plan is a go. If someone *does* report it, then it wasn't meant to be.

But I have a feeling this is it. This is what I've been waiting for.

I make a call. This has been part of my plan since the beginning. I researched everyone who works behind the computers at the alarm company Kincaid uses. A surprisingly high number of employees have some kind of criminal record, but there was one guy in particular I was drawn to. I knew his face. I'd bust him myself a couple times already. Only thing is, his record didn't show any of that. Which means he had someone on the inside wipe it clean.

"Simon?" I say.

"Who's this?"

"You still at work?"

"What? Yeah, who is this?"

"Doesn't matter. What *does* matter is that I know about your past. I know you paid someone to wipe your record."

I hear his breathing speed up.

"Simon?"

"What do you want?"

"Nothing big. Just the floor plans and access code to one of your properties."

"I can't do that."

"You sure? I mean, this climate we're in. Tough to get a job, you know? Especially when you've got a record."

"Why you want that stuff?"

"None of your business. And relax. Nobody's going to get hurt. All you have to ask yourself is how much you need your job. I'll call back in one minute. Give you time to think about it."

I hang up, pacing the garage for the full minute before calling him back.

"I'll do it," he says grudgingly.

"Smart guy."

I give him a burner email address. He sends the code and the plans while I have him on the phone. I check. It's what I need.

"I've written an email to your employers," I say. "With details of your arrests. It's scheduled to go out tomorrow morning unless I stop it. You tell anyone about this, if anything happens to me, you're going down. Got it?"

"Yeah, man. I got it."

I hang up, feeling sick in my stomach. This isn't me. It doesn't sit well. My whole career I've been around cops who cut corners. Nothing big. At least not to start with. But I've seen how it affects them. Once they cross that line, it's easier to do it again. Easier to let things slide. Then it becomes a simple progression to pocketing evidence. Looking the other way when they owe people favors.

That was never me.

Until now.

Later that night, I gather up all the items I've prepared and drive back to the alley. I park a hundred feet down the street and take a stroll along the sidewalk, checking the buildings as I go. There are some security cameras, but if no crime has been reported, they won't be checked.

I glance into the alley as I pass. The body is still there. I can just see Devon's foot.

Nobody's reported it.

Am I really going to do this? I can still back out. I haven't done anything I can't make go away. The drugs can be flushed. The email deleted.

And Kincaid is free to kill again. To corrupt how many more lives? Destroy how many more families?

No. I'm not backing out now.

I use Devon's keys and get into the driver's seat of his Cadillac. I wait for ten minutes, just to be sure. In that time I see three cars, but none of them show any interest in me.

After the ten minutes are up, I start the car and reverse into the mouth of the alley. I pop the trunk and get out.

Rigor mortis is setting in, Devon's neck and upper arms already seizing up. I take out the new toothbrush I bought and poke it around inside the evidence bag that holds Kincaid's blood. I gently scrape the bristles beneath Devon's fingernails, making sure the flakes go deep.

I put the toothbrush and evidence bag away. I pause, still crouching. Why not just leave him here? Call in an anonymous tip-off? Kincaid's blood and DNA are on the body now.

No. It won't be enough. His lawyers would just come up with some story about Devon attacking him in the street.

I grab Devon's feet and drag him across the asphalt, heaving him headfirst into the trunk.

Then I climb into the driver's seat and start the engine.

I park down the street from Kincaid's mansion. There are lights everywhere, halogen floods chasing away the shadows. That makes it trickier. Not impossible. Just...tricky. I can't even see the house from where I am. The grounds are too big.

Kincaid bought the five properties surrounding his and knocked them down for the land.

There's something going on. Expensive cars arriving in ones and twos, stopping outside the gates to show the guards something before being let inside. I recognize a few of the faces. Heavy hitters in the Miami underworld.

Shit. Is he having a party or something? What do I do? Cancel?

No, don't be stupid. I'm driving around with a corpse in the car. The hell am I supposed to do with it? Put it back?

Actually, this might be good for me. A distraction. I might not even need the alarm codes now. Why would he activate the security system when people are coming and going?

I drive around the back of the house. The rear of the property faces onto a park. I drive slowly over the grass and stop next to Kincaid's wall. I pull on the balaclava I brought with me, get out of the car, pop the trunk, and drag Devon out onto the grass. I grab his legs, look up—

—and realize there's a problem.

The wall is ten feet high. How the hell am I supposed to get him over?

I drop him onto the grass again, then maneuver the car as close to the wall as I can get it. I grab his feet and climb up the bumper onto the trunk. I try to pull him up with me, but I'm not far enough back. I can't get any leverage to lift him off the ground.

This is just fucking perfect.

I keep hold of the ankles and slide up the back window to sit on the car roof. I shuffle back and pull the body up, but Devon's stupid baggy pants get caught on the bumper.

"Honest to God, Devon. If you were alive, I'd fucking arrest you for wearing those things."

I have to let the body slide back down to free the material. I pull him up again, so now he looks like he's doing a handstand against the car. I shuffle back all the way to the front windshield, then get to my knees and pull him up. First by the legs, then the waist, until I finally have him sprawled on the roof next to me.

I pat him on the head. "Could do with losing a few pounds there, bud."

I stand up and survey the distance between the car and the wall. It's about a foot. At least I didn't screw that up. I check Kincaid's yard. No one around this side of the house. Plenty of lights, but no people.

I push Devon's legs over the wall. They drop down, almost pulling him out of my grasp. I just manage to grab him, then wonder what the hell I'm doing and let go. The body slithers noisily over the wall, hitting the ground on the other side with a heavy thud.

I jump down, grabbing the backpack of drugs from inside the Cadillac and shrugging it over my shoulders. Then I clamber back up onto the car and climb over the wall into Kincaid's yard.

I drag Devon across the dew-wet grass, dumping him behind a gazebo close to the rear of the house. That's phase one.

Next: the drugs. This is the part I've been stuck on. There were too many variables to plan it out in advance. But now I'm here, I need to just pick an approach and go with it.

So—what do I have? I have the alarm codes and floor plans. I have a major distraction already going on, with Kincaid having some kind of meeting or party or whatever the hell it is. And I have lots of drugs I need to plant.

I *could* just dump the bag next to his car. Or maybe hide it beneath a bush. But once again it doesn't tie the drugs directly to Kincaid. He could just say it belongs to one of his guests. I want something definitive.

Which means I need to get inside the house.

Glass doors look out onto a stone veranda about fifteen feet to my right. I approach, finding a tiny gap in the floor-to-ceiling blinds. A dark dining room lies beyond. Thanks to the floor plan, I know there's a hallway directly outside the dining room. Left leads toward the front of the house and the enter-tainment area, where I assume Kincaid will be. Right leads toward a set of stairs to the second floor. That's the way I need to go.

I need a distraction, though. Separate from whatever is going on inside the house. Something that will cover the sound of me breaking the glass.

I move along the wall and check the front of the house. There are about ten expensive cars parked on the gravel drive-way. Two guards lounge against a small building separate from the main house. They don't look too alert. Why would they? Kincaid has the whole city under his thumb, and from what I've seen, most of the heavy hitters are here. Who would the guards be watching out *for*?

I came prepared for this. I shrug the backpack off my shoul-ders and unzip the pouch at the front. I take out a can of lighter fluid and move at a crouch toward the closest car. I spray the fluid all over the vehicle. Over the roof, the tires, the wind-shield. Once the can is empty, I stuff it in my pocket and take out a box of matches. I strike one and flick it toward the car, slipping back around the house and stopping once I get to the glass doors.

I wait until the shouting starts and slam my elbow into the glass. I clear the shards away and reach through to unlock the door, pulling it open and stepping into the dining room.

I pause, all my senses straining. I can't hear the beeping of an alarm system that needs to be deactivated. That's good. I wasn't sure, but I didn't think they'd put the alarm on with all those people here.

I hurry through the dining room and into the passage. No one around. I move quickly, heading to the rear of the house and up the back stairs. Another corridor. Spare rooms, bath-rooms, and then the main bedroom. I head straight for the walk-in closet. It's huge, about the size of my living room. I shrug off the backpack and push it high onto one of the shelves.

I take a deep breath. That's it. My plan is nearly done. I head back into the bedroom, but freeze before I reach the door.

A brand-new Rolex Daytona sits on the nightstand next to the bed. I stare at it. It's easily worth thirty-five grand. It would be so easy to just slip it into my pocket.

But I don't. That's the line I was thinking about. Nobody would know, especially not if my plan works out. But...I'm not a thief. I'm not a criminal. I'm a cop, and what I'm doing right now is getting justice, saving future lives.

I tear my eyes away from the watch and slip out of the bedroom. I can hear more shouting now. It's louder, more frantic. My heart thuds heavily in my chest as I take the stairs and head back along the passage. Nearly there. Nearly out.

I turn into the dining room—

—and find myself standing face-to-face with a startled man. He's young, barely out of his teens. Mediterranean looks, eyes wide with fear.

He raises his hands in the air. "I don't want trouble," he says.

"Bit late for that."

"Seriously, I just want to leave."

"I can't let you do that. You step out that—"

He doesn't let me finish. He rushes me, but it's a clumsy attack. I step aside and grab his arm, using the kid's own momentum to ram his face into the wall.

He drops to the floor and doesn't move. I feel his neck. Pulse is strong. He'll wake up with a killer headache, but that's it.

I reach inside my jacket as I exit the house, taking out the old Beretta I confiscated from one of the drug dealers. I fire it into the air, emptying the magazine as I run toward the garden wall. Then I throw the gun aside and take the burner phone out, dialing 911.

"Hello? I can hear gunfire! 147 Plantation Boulevard. Please hurry. There are people screaming."

I kill the call, stuff the phone into my pocket, and launch myself at the wall, hauling myself over the top. I drop to the grass and climb behind the wheel of the Cadillac, starting the engine and driving back to the alley. The street is still deserted. I grab the jerry can of gasoline I placed on the backseat and pour it over the car, then toss another match.

The Cadillac bursts into flames and I hurry to my own car. I peel the gloves and balaclava off, stuffing them beneath the seat. I turn the police radio up.

"...*repeat, more units needed at 147 Plantation Boulevard. Multiple suspects on site resisting arrest.*"

After that, things pretty much take care of themselves. By the time I get back to Kincaid's house, there are squad cars everywhere, red and blue flashing, wailing sirens bringing down property values.

I hang back on the periphery, letting others take the lead. It doesn't take long before the body and the drugs are discovered.

I watch as Mason leads a cuffed Kincaid to her car. His wife watches from the front door, a kid to either side of her. Kincaid says something to Mason and she shakes her head.

He pulls away from her and runs back to his wife. He kisses her, then crouches down next to his kids, laying his forehead against theirs. First the girl, then the boy.

I look away. I don't want to see that. Kincaid is not a father. He's not a husband.

He's a killer.

And this time he's going to prison.

Five

8:15 a.m.

That was four years ago now.

Kincaid was charged with murder. The blood under Devon's fingernails nailed him. The drugs were secondary charges, not really worth pursuing. Bit of a waste of time on my part, but I wasn't complaining.

I'd known he was serving time at Ravenhill, but our paths had never crossed. I was in A Wing and he was in Unit 4 of Gen Pop. Don't ask me how he managed to swing that—he should have been in ACU right from the beginning. But money talks, even in here.

He doesn't look too different. Still has the thick gray hair swept back from his forehead.

I force a smile onto my face as he enters the cell. "How you doing, Malcolm? You look good. Lost some weight. You on a diet?"

Yup. Bravado and cockiness. My instinctive responses to everything. It's a defense mechanism. Most cops have it. Most veterans too. Even at Amy's funeral I'd cracked a tasteless joke when I was giving her eulogy. Something about her at least not having to kill herself now when we got stuck in the rut of middle-age life and she started hating the sight of me.

Everyone thought I'd gone crazy, but Amy would have found it funny. That was enough for me.

Two of Kincaid's men enter the cell and lean against the walls, on either side of him. "This is Veitch and Cassidy," he says in a friendly tone of voice.

Two more come in and grab me by the arms. They shove me back onto the concrete slab that serves as a bed.

Kincaid nods to the left. "That's Adler." Then to the right. "That's Sullivan."

One guy waits outside the cell, taking up position to keep an eye open for interruptions. Kincaid gestures vaguely behind him. "That's West."

The cell is seriously cramped now and I realize I'm in deep shit. Evans is probably asleep, and no one else is going to do anything. Where the hell is Felix? I'm not sure he'd step in, but it might make Kincaid think twice.

"Is this about me punching you? Because—"

"Don't be stupid. You know it's not about that."

Shit and fuck. "So you know?"

"That you framed me? Yeah, I know."

"How?"

"Wasn't difficult. I had my people look into it. Spoke to someone at the alarm company. He had an interesting story to tell. Didn't take me long to figure out who wanted me put away so bad they'd break the law."

Fucking Simon. What a prick.

Kincaid strolls toward me. "I always wondered if I'd get a crack at you," he says.

"Must be your lucky day."

"Must be," he agrees thoughtfully. "You know, life has been gray lately, Jack. I don't mind admitting that. The doc gave me pills—antidepressants. I don't think that shit works, but seeing you has really given me a boost." He takes a deep breath. "Fact is, I feel better right now than I have in years."

"Happy to help out."

He stares at me for a long moment. "You look at me, what do you see?"

"A killer," I say without hesitation. "A drug dealer. Someone who would do anything to get what he wanted."

He nods as if I've just confirmed his suspicions. "You know what I see when I look at *you*?"

"I'm sure you're going to tell me."

"A coward. A corrupt cop who couldn't do his job properly, so had to break the law. A man who couldn't protect his own wife and child."

I try to lunge forward, but Adler and Sullivan keep a strong grip on me. "Don't you fucking *dare* talk about them."

Kincaid smiles. "Found a little chink in the armor there, have we? See, that's what I'm talkin' about. Perception is not reality. I don't look at myself as a criminal. Same way you don't look at yourself as a corrupt cop. *Or* a coward. You know why? Because in your own head, you did your best. You did what you thought was right."

I stare at him, waiting for the punch line. It doesn't come. "So...what? You're saying we're the same?"

"That's exactly what I'm saying. Everything I did, I did for the right reasons. For my family."

"Bullshit."

"You don't know me, boy. You might think you do, but you don't. I grew up poor. In the slums. My old man died, my ma, God rest her soul, made sure I stayed in school. All she wanted was for me to graduate and make an honest living. She died when I was fourteen. And I sat there with her body in that...*shack* I grew up in and I thought: Why? What has staying honest got me? What did it get my mother? She died because we couldn't afford medicine. Because she used all her money to feed me. To keep me in school. So I thought, fuck that. And I started to take what I wanted. I dropped out of school and I figured out how to make my life livable, because I was *not* going to end up like my ma."

"Shh," I say. "Listen."

Kincaid cocks his head to one side. "What?"

"Nah, it's okay. Thought I heard a violin playing."

He chuckles. "You're a funny guy. Ain't he funny?" He looks around at his goons. They all nod and grin.

Kincaid turns back to face me. "But the thing is, while I was living in that squalor, I met someone. A girl. We were both seventeen by then. And she gave me a reason to take more care. See, before her, I didn't give a shit what I was doing, who I was stealing from. But when I met her, I changed. *Everything* changed. I started doing it all for her. Everything I stole, every plan I made, was to raise that woman out of the ghetto, to make me worthy of her. And you know what? I did it. I got us out. I got us a home, I built my empire, we had two kids. And those two kids...man...You a parent? Oh, shit. No. Course you're not."

I surge to my feet, this time managing to pull away from Adler and Sullivan. Kincaid steps back just as they grab me again. I struggle, lash out, hit Sullivan in the face. Adler balls a fist and punches me hard between the ribs, right in the lungs. I fold over, wheezing for breath as they shove me back onto the bed. I try to regain my breath, while Kincaid carries on talking as if nothing had happened.

"I'm telling you, when those kids appear in your life, there isn't a single thing you wouldn't do to protect them. To protect your family. It becomes...like a primeval need. An *instinct*. They're your tribe and you'd do anything for them. *Anything.* You know that already, though. Your kid wasn't even born yet, but you did what you had to for revenge." He pauses for a moment. "You loved your wife, right?"

I don't answer.

"'Course you did. See, I'm gonna give you some credit. I don't think you're some big bad cop, someone who shoots first and asks questions later. I actually think you had the same thing with your wife that I had with mine. When you find the one...I mean, I'm not talking about all that 'you complete me' bullshit, you know? But when you find the one, she sure as shit makes life worth living."

He leans forward, his passive face turning dark. "You took that from me. You separated me from my family. My wife. My kids." He stares hard at me for a long moment, jaw clenching. Then he turns away, walks to the door of the cell, turns back again. When he speaks, his voice is shaking. "That's not even the worst of it. I'd been with my wife thirty years. I've been in here four." He pauses, takes a deep breath. "She died three years ago, Constantine. Cancer. And I didn't get to see her. I didn't get to say good-bye. I wasn't *with* her. All. Because. Of *you*."

Oh fuck...

Kincaid gestures. The goon waiting outside the cell—West, I think—takes something out of his orange jumpsuit pocket and hands it to Kincaid. It's a shank. Razor blades melted into a toothbrush.

Kincaid nods at Adler and Sullivan. Before I can do anything, they grip me tight, pushing me down, making sure I can't move.

I still struggle, trying to pull away. I'm not going down without a fight. Adler punches me in the face. I grunt in pain. Bursts of light flash across my vision. I blink, shake my head. Look up to see Kincaid standing in front of me.

"Hold him tight."

The fingers tighten on my shoulders and arms. Kincaid smiles. "Don't worry, I'm not going to kill you right away. This is just for starters." He taps the shank against my chin. "You know those fans with the red ribbons tied to the front? When they're switched off and the ribbons just sort of...hang there? That's what your face is going to look like five minutes from now." He leans closer so his mouth is only an inch from my ear. "After that," he says softly, "I'm gonna do something else, and it'll hurt so bad you'll be begging me to slit your throat."

"Boss!" West, at the door, quickly steps in and holds his hand out. Kincaid passes the shank to him and everyone straightens up just as Evans appears, peering at them all through the cell bars.

"The fuck is going on in here?"

"Prayer session," says Kincaid. "We're discussing our Lord the Savior and how he can save our friend Jack's life. Isn't that right, Jack?"

"Yeah," I mutter. "Hallelujah." Because no matter what happens in prison, you don't snitch.

"Pray on your own time, dickwads. We're done here. Line up downstairs."

No one moves. They all glance at Kincaid, and only when he gives a small nod do they all file out of the cell.

As he leaves, he looks at me. "We'll pick this up later."

It's around one o'clock by the time we all gather at ground level. I make sure to stay as far away from Kincaid and his guys as I can.

"Are we coming back?" asks Nunes.

"No," says Evans. "We're done. The evacuees are on their way."

"Thank Christ for that," says Perez.

Evans leads us back along the corridors and into reception. But instead of taking us through the back hallways and the laundry, he opens a door into a new corridor, this one much cleaner than the ones we used to get to the Rotunda.

As we walk, I can't help thinking about Kincaid's words. Can't help wondering if I did the wrong thing. I took away a husband and wife's last moments together. Kincaid has every right to be pissed at me.

But…come on. No. Not my problem. Kincaid is a piece of shit. He's a murderer. Why the hell am I even feeling sorry for him?

Because you know what it feels like to lose someone you love without getting a chance to say good-bye.

I push the thought away. I'm not wasting my sympathy on him.

The storm is much louder now. The wind shrieks and howls around the old building, whistling through gaps in the brickwork. I glance out the windows as we pass, but I can't see anything. The rain batters and streams across the glass in twisting rivulets.

"What category is she?" someone calls out.

Evans doesn't answer.

"Have they named her?" asks Felix.

"Josephine," says Evans eventually. He hesitates. "Category Four."

Questions are instantly thrown at him, voices raised in fear and panic.

"Four?" shouts Murphy. "Are you fucking serious? Shouldn't people be evacuated?"

"The whole of Florida's already been evacuated."

"What about us?" asks Felix.

"State figures Ravenhill has a solid chance of making it through the hurricane. This place was built to last. Plus, it's high enough above sea level to avoid the flooding."

Nobody seems convinced. I don't blame them. Category 4 is high up on the Saffir–Simpson scale. It means winds of up to 156 miles an hour. A Cat 5 is anything above 157. You get to know these things if you live in Florida.

"What was Hurricane Irma?" I ask Felix, who's walking beside me.

"Category Five. Hundred and eighty miles an hour. Katrina was one seventy-five."

A few of the inmates overhear and exchange worried looks.

Evans senses the mood changing and quickens his step. He pushes through a set of swing doors, leading us into a large tiled room. It looks like it was the Glasshouse's receiving and release area. It isn't like the new R&R over at Ravenhill. There's no sheltered depot here. Just a door opening into an outside area that might have once been fenced off. I peer through the windows. There are a couple of buses out there, but I barely notice them. My gaze is fixed on the sky. The clouds have become so dark and heavy that it looks like the middle of the night.

The outside door suddenly bursts open, slamming hard against the wall. The wind surges in, knocking Perez and Deacon off their feet. They push themselves up as a dark figure sprints and slips over the threshold, followed by a line of drenched inmates in orange jumpsuits, all chained together.

"Shut the door!" screams Evans.

But they can't. More inmates are coming in, ten, then twenty, then thirty, then even more, all of them barging into R&R until everyone is standing shoulder to shoulder.

This is a CO's worst nightmare. Prisoners in close proximity to each other usually means trouble. It's the perfect time to settle scores.

I look nervously around for Kincaid as more officers rush in, pushing the inmates forward so they can close the door behind them.

There's chaos everywhere. Inmates and officers are swearing, snapping at each other as they try to shake the rain off. Evans is still shouting, ordering the prisoners to line up around the walls and give the guards room to move.

And that's when I see them.

Two faces.

Two faces that haunt my dreams. Every. Single. Night.

Marcus Tully and Luther Wright.

Two of the three men who murdered my wife.

I can't believe it. A hurricane is smashing through the Eastern Seaboard. People are losing their homes, their lives. Cities and towns are being evacuated. The hurricane is taking from everyone it touches. But it's giving me something it's not giving anyone else.

A second chance. A single moment in time when I can get justice.

They're fifteen feet away. Too far for me to reach. I feel my pulse thudding in my throat. Blood surges in my ears as I stare at those faces, the last thing my wife ever saw. A hatred deep and pure fans to life inside my soul. The same anger that got me through the weeks after Amy's death.

The COs are screaming for quiet. Some have their day sticks out and are shoving a few of the louder inmates into orderly lines so they can be taken to the cells.

My attention is wholly focused on Tully and Wright. Three

years in prison has aged them. Tully is thinner, his wrinkles more pronounced, a road map of his time behind bars. Wright has picked up a lot of weight.

I have to be careful. I'll never get another chance like this. All I need to do is be patient. Wait for them to walk by. Evans is keeping me and the others to the side while the evacuees move through the room. I'm standing by the door. They'll walk right past me.

I'll have to take them both at the same time. I can't let either one get away. Not again.

"Okay, move it!" shouts one of the new COs. "Single file. Keep it slow!"

The inmates start to file past me as they head into the Glasshouse. Tully and Wright are ten feet away now. Felix is talking to me, muttering about inhumane conditions. I ignore him and he gives me a shove in the back.

"Hey. You hearin' me?"

I don't answer. Tully is first. I stare at his scrawny neck. Like a bird's. I can snap it quick, then turn on Wright.

Six feet...

Tully looks in my direction. I quickly bow my head, but I know it's too late. I look up again. His eyes are wide, his mouth open as if to say something.

I lunge forward, barging past the other inmates. Cries and shouts of protest ring out. I ignore them. I grab Tully's wrist. He tries to pull away. I can feel him slipping through my grasp. I knee him in the stomach and he doubles over, coming within reach of my cuffed hands. I grab his collar, trying to get hold of his throat. There's shouting all around me. I shove him off his feet. He hits the ground and I drop onto his chest, hands around his neck. He's shouting something at me, but I can't hear above the roaring in my ears.

Someone grabs my shoulder, pulls me back. I lash out with my elbow, hear a howl of rage. I recognize the voice. Evans. I wrap my hands around Tully's throat again.

Then everything inside me shuts down as fifty thousand volts surge through my body. I arch back, every muscle in my body stiffening in shock. Pain explodes across my entire being, slicing through me like splinters of glass cutting through my veins.

My vision goes completely black, then slowly fades back into color.

Another surge of agony as Evans shoves his stun gun into my neck.

The floor flies up to meet me.

Then nothing.

ADVISORY BULLETIN
Hurricanes Hannah and Josephine Advisory Number 1
NWS National Hurricane Center Miami FL
12 A.M. EDT SAT AUG 28 2021

DISCUSSION AND OUTLOOK
Tropical hurricanes Hannah and Josephine have changed paths and are due to intercept each other by 6 a.m. this morning. It is anticipated that these Category 5 hurricanes will form together, undergoing a Fujiwhara phenomenon, wherein vortices will join to form a rare and dangerous superstorm.

Maximum sustained winds for this forecast period are near 200 mph (321 km/h) with higher winds possible.

HAZARDS AFFECTING LAND
The combined hurricanes are anticipated to bring unprecedented damage to the Eastern Seaboard, as well as into Florida, Georgia, Alabama, Mississippi, Louisiana, and Texas.

WARNINGS
All must evacuate.
$$
Forecaster Mills

Six

Friday, August 27

3:30 p.m.

Sheriff Montoya picks up the phone for the third time in ten minutes.

Still dead.

He's been out of contact with the outside world for two hours now. He was talking to Jefferson over at State, checking what was happening with the hurricane.

No—*hurricanes.*

Because one isn't enough. Oh no. They have to get *two* hurricanes, Hannah and Josephine, forming into one monster storm—something called the Fujiwara effect—that's going to hit with full force sometime in the next few hours. And *obviously* it's Cat 5. Because that is the kind of luck Montoya is cursed with.

Miami has been evacuated. Place is a ghost town, no one left behind. Same with most of Florida, Alabama, and Georgia. Buildings are being ripped apart. There's major flooding, fires. One hundred and eighty-seven people have already died.

The last thing Jefferson said before the line went dead was that the plans had changed. The Glasshouse was supposed to be a safe haven for evacuated prisoners, but with the hurricane being what it is, they were going to have to move *everyone*. There was even talk of storm surges coming in off the ocean, forming mini tsunamis. Jefferson said he'd be sending the National Guard to help them evacuate. That they'd be there by two.

Montoya checks his watch. Half past three. He is slowly starting to realize that the National Guard might not be coming at all.

He can't even find out what's going on out there. They're completely cut off. No TV signal. No cell reception, no landlines, nothing. The only information he has are the printouts on his desk that Jefferson forwarded from the National Hurricane Center tracking the paths of the hurricanes. When they'll arrive, when the eye of the storm will pass over them, when the winds should die down, that kind of thing.

None of it looks promising. And it's only going to get worse over the next eighteen hours.

He sits at his desk and listens to the storm. The noise is relentless, a constant barrage of howling and screaming. The heavy slam of rain on the roof. The constant creak of the building, like it's about to collapse at any moment.

He gets up and peers through the small window. It looks like the middle of the night. Something is sparking and flashing in the distance. A fallen electric cable? Fuck. That's all they need. For the power to trip. They have generators that would keep them going for...what? Twelve hours if they're lucky. Emergency lighting would work, air circulation, that kind of thing. But after that? Everyone would be screwed.

What the hell is he supposed to do? Just wait? For help that isn't going to come? Have they been abandoned? Forgotten in the chaos? It's entirely possible. But where does that leave them?

Fuck.

Montoya has gotten through his life by avoiding making big decisions. Big decisions mean big risks, and big risks mean lots of blame if something goes wrong.

What should he do? There's no way they can evacuate everyone. Hell, they only have one bus. The rest had been taken to fetch inmates from the other prisons. It will be a tight squeeze to fit just the skeleton staff that is still here.

He keeps skirting around his thoughts, not liking where they want to go. But he can't avoid it any longer.

He stares at his desk. Not blinking. Not moving. He's scared that if he moves, the idea will become real. That it will mean acknowledging he is capable of such thoughts.

But it's there. Waiting. An insidious root that crawls through his mind, pushing its way forward.

He can leave the inmates behind.

Abandon them to their fate.

If the hurricane passes and the prison is still standing, no harm done. Really, his duty is to his officers. They're innocent of any crimes, whereas the inmates—they're murderers, rapists, child-killers, drug dealers.

Why should he risk his life for them? He deserves more. His *staff* deserves more. And it's not as if he's just abandoning them to die. Of course not. He'll evacuate the staff, then once they're out of the hurricane path he'll inform the National Guard that the prisoners still need help. Hell, he might even get a medal. *Everyone* could die if he doesn't take the brave step and leave, exposing himself to the elements to get word out. He's doing the right thing here.

He pushes the button on his desk mic. "This is Sheriff Montoya. All staff is directed to meet in the cafeteria. Repeat, all staff to the cafeteria right now."

He grabs his car keys, then pauses. Habit. None of them can just drive out in their cars. They won't make it twenty feet. The bus is their only hope. He drops the keys back on the desk and leaves the office.

The cafeteria is full by the time he arrives. Lots of annoyed and worried uniforms all talking at the same time. He holds up his hands for silence. It doesn't make a difference.

"Settle down!" he shouts. He waits till he has their attention. "Here's the situation. You all know about the hurricane. Well, it's gotten worse. Hannah and Josephine have joined together and formed some kind of mutant superstorm. Category Five.

They say it's going to be bigger than Irma. Which means we need to evacuate."

"How the hell are we going to do that?" asks Bright, a young woman from New Orleans. "We have eight hundred prisoners here."

"I'm not talking about the inmates." Keep it cool, he thinks. Sell it like your life depends on it. "The staff that is still here is evacuating in the bus now. Jefferson says the Federal Emergency Management Agency is working with the National Guard and are going to evacuate the prisoners as soon as they can."

"Who's staying behind to keep an eye on things?" asks someone.

"No one."

"But there are people in the infirmary—"

"I understand that. But we've got no choice here. Everyone will be locked in their cells till help comes." He looks around. "Any other questions?"

Nothing. He was expecting *some* argument, but everyone stays silent. He's not sure whether he should be happy that it makes things easier for him, or disappointed in their lack of commitment to the job.

"Where are we going?" asks Bright.

"We'll get onto the I-95 and head north. We keep going till we hit Dade City."

"That's nearly three hundred miles away!"

"Yeah, three hundred miles away from the hurricane."

"Unless it heads north too."

"We're not going to think about that," says Montoya. "Anyway, last I heard it's going to keep moving west and taper out over the Gulf of Mexico in a couple of days. Let's just focus on putting miles between us and this place. Okay?"

A few nods from the staff. Not everyone looks comfortable, but no one is complaining.

"Okay...Make sure everyone is in their cells and meet me in R&R in twenty minutes. Go."

The COs spring into action, filing out of the cafeteria to make sure all the prisoners are locked down. As soon as he's alone, Montoya sags into a chair and wipes the sweat from his face.

The bus is parked outside R&R in the roofed-over depot, left there after bringing the inmates back from cleaning the old prison. Jesus. How the hell is *that* place going to survive the coming storm?

Don't think about it. Not your problem.

He wasn't the one who volunteered the place as a refuge in the first place. That's on Jefferson. In fact, he needs to start seeding that as soon as they get to safety. Jefferson planned all this.

He waits as the staff files into the foyer, arriving in ones and twos. He ticks off their names on his clipboard as they step outside into the depot. The bus slowly fills up, the nervous staff taking their seats, squashing together, some forced to stand and hold on to the seat backs for support. Finally, after about another ten minutes, everyone seems to be accounted for.

He has to check, though. Montoya ducks back inside the prison, moving through the empty corridors, looking into abandoned offices. It's...eerie. That's the only word to describe it. All the years he's been here, the prison has never been empty. There has always been movement, life, plus an overwhelming sense of desperation that he's always attributed to the inmates. Except that feeling isn't there anymore. Which kind of means it must have come from the staff instead.

It's all clear. He heads back to the bus and climbs inside. The driver scowls at him. It's Hicks. Montoya doesn't like the look of him. Never has. Young, skinny, greasy skin and a tattoo on his forearm, visible below his rolled-up sleeve.

"We need to get going," Hicks says.

"The hell you waiting for, then?" growls Montoya. He surveys the bus. It's filled to bursting point. Everyone looks worried. Scared.

"The gate," says Hicks.

"What?"

"Someone has to open the gate."

"Jesus! Louis. Open the gate."

Louis looks up from his seat. He's another young kid. Barely into his twenties. "Why me?"

"Because you're young. You can run faster. Move it."

Louis hurriedly heaves himself up from his seat and squeezes past Montoya.

"Wait."

Louis pauses and Montoya unclips the huge key ring he carries on his belt. It's got all the universal keys he uses to get around the prison. They're the symbol of his position, his power. He hands it over reluctantly. "You'll need them to get into the security room."

Louis grabs the keys and runs back inside the prison. Montoya watches him go, feeling suddenly small and unimportant.

Louis moves quickly through R&R, using Montoya's keys to get through the locked doors. He heads straight for the closest security room, the one beyond reception that guards the sally port into Unit 1 of General Population. He unlocks the door and pulls a chair over to sit down at the computer, then grabs the mouse and hovers the pointer over the gate leading out of the depot.

He hesitates, eyes drawn to the cells clearly visible on the five computer screens to his left. All the doors are marked red, showing that they're locked tight.

Christ. He stares guiltily at the screens. They're running away. What's the point in pretending? They're bailing on their responsibilities, saving their own hides because the storm is going to take them out.

If they leave the inmates like this, they're all going to die. Drown. Trapped in their cells as the water slowly rises.

But is what he's contemplating any better?

Yes. It is.

If he was an inmate, he knows what he'd want. He'd want a chance, however small it might be.

He hesitates one last second, then thinks, fuck it, and uses the mouse to open all the cell doors in the prison. Then he opens the doors and sally ports leading between the various units. Obviously he doesn't unlock the outside doors. He doesn't want anyone actually escaping. But at least this way the inmates might survive any flooding until help gets to them.

Last thing he does is open the gate, then he sprints back to the bus. He's done the right thing, surely? The inmates in A Wing would *definitely* have drowned if he'd left them in their cells. That whole wing sits close to the bottom of the hill, and the prison is already starting to flood.

Yeah, he did the right thing.

About five minutes after the kid heads inside, the depot gate slides open.

As soon as it does so, the shrieking begins.

When Montoya was a kid, he used to stay at his grandma's house. She had a fireplace she never used, but when the storms came rolling in, the wind would howl and whistle down the chimney, the noise impossible to block out. This noise is the same, only magnified by a thousand—a *hundred* thousand.

The wind whistles through the slowly widening gap. It hammers the gate, slamming it back and forth in its guide rails. Rain and debris surge into the hangar, slapping into the windshield of the bus.

Something hits hard and cracks the glass. A few of the guards cry out. Everyone grabs hold of the seats. Louis comes barreling back onto the bus, his face pale, eyes wide with fear.

"Keys?" snaps Montoya.

Louis looks confused; then a look of alarm crosses his face.

Jesus Christ, the idiot has lost your keys.

"You want me to go—"

"Just sit the fuck down and shut up." The keys aren't important anymore. Staying alive is all that matters.

As the gate opens wider, the depth and pitch of the wailing wind changes, shifting from a shrill whistle to a scream, then to a long-drawn-out thunderous roar.

The bus shudders and rocks as the gate finally trundles to a stop. Hicks just sits there, staring through the windshield, his fingers curling and uncurling around the wheel, his knuckles white.

"Hicks."

He doesn't move. Just stares straight ahead.

"Hicks!"

He jerks and turns panicked eyes to Montoya.

"We move, we drive away from the hurricane. We sit here, the hurricane comes to us. Got it?"

Hicks licks his lips, then nods. He revs the engine and the bus edges slowly forward, heading out into an afternoon that is as dark as night.

As soon as they leave the hangar, the wind slams into the side of the bus, lifting it up onto two wheels. This time everyone cries out, Montoya included. He falls back against the doors, the back of his head slamming painfully into the glass.

This is it, he thinks. The bus is going to flip. We're all going to die.

But then the wind eases slightly and the vehicle slowly heaves back down onto all four wheels. Hicks has frozen again, his knuckles white as he clenches the wheel.

"Move," says Montoya. "Get up."

Hicks blinks up at him. "What?"

"You're a liability. I'll drive."

"But...you're not authorized. I could lose my job."

"Get out of the fucking seat, Hicks!" shouts Evans, appearing suddenly from behind Montoya and grabbing Hicks by the shirt. Hicks scrambles to his feet and Evans yanks him back toward the passenger seats.

Montoya takes his place, buckling the safety belt over his fat stomach and checking the controls. It's been a while since he drove a bus, but nothing much has changed. He's got this.

He puts his foot down and the vehicle surges forward. No time for pussyfooting around now. He wants out of this dump, to get on the road and head north as fast as they can.

He accelerates down the hill, speeding toward the prison gates. The Glasshouse is somewhere on their left, but he can't even see the lights. It feels like he's driving in a slowly constricting tunnel. He can't see anything. Just sheets of rain illuminated by the bus headlights.

The perimeter gate looms suddenly out of the darkness. Montoya slams on the brakes. The bus skids, slewing sideways through the mud before finally rocking to a stop, side-on to the gates. The headlights shine directly on the gatehouse.

If it wasn't for the electrified fence, he would have just driven through. But he can't risk it. He doesn't know if it's still live. He needs to open the gates properly.

He glances over his shoulder. No one is looking at him. Everyone is staring down, avoiding his gaze. They know what he's going to ask.

"Evans?" he says hopefully.

Evans looks up, but shakes his head.

Cowards. Fine. He'll do it himself. He undoes the buckle and pulls the lever to open the doors. He's instantly drenched, rain surging in and soaking him through, shoving him back with a wet slap.

He staggers outside. The wind punches him as soon as he sets foot on the asphalt. Once, twice, over and over, pummeling him from all sides. He slips and falls to his knees. The wind slams against his back and tries to lay him out flat, but he manages to push himself to his feet and stagger toward the gatehouse. The rain feels like shards of metal against his skin. The roar of the wind deafens him to everything.

Montoya pulls open the door and falls inside. He grabs hold of the desk and pulls himself up. He takes a few deep breaths, then fumbles in his pocket for his keycard and holds it in front of the scanner, unlocking the computer. He scrolls to the front gate controls and clicks on *Unlock*.

He peers through the window, but can't see if the gates are opening. He staggers outside, making his way back to the bus. Someone is waiting just inside to open the doors, and he staggers up the steps and drops into the cracked leather seat.

He takes a few steadying breaths, rubs the water from his face. The wipers are on, but aren't doing a thing. He still can't see if the gate is open.

He puts the bus into reverse and spins the wheel to the right, the bus slowly coming around to face front. The gates stand wide open. He lets out a sigh of relief. He hits the gas and the bus surges forward. He hunches close to the windshield, trying to see as the bus vibrates and slides along the asphalt.

He eventually stops at the bottom of the road leading up to the prison complex. Two options. The 95 goes straight north, but it runs close to the coast. The 75 will take them west for about a hundred miles before turning north, but will add another hour onto the trip. Left takes him toward the 75. Right to the 95.

He hesitates, but he really doesn't want to spend any longer than necessary driving in this.

He turns right.

He can't go fast. He wants to. His foot is itching to jam the pedal right down. But there's too much debris. Palm trees have fallen into their path. Cars are skewed and abandoned randomly in the road. Some have flipped, others have crashed into each other. The asphalt itself is hidden beneath about a foot of water. He has to be careful. Too much power and they'll hydroplane.

This trip is going to take longer than he thought. Thank God he didn't choose the 75.

It takes them twenty minutes to travel the four miles to the 95. He turns onto the interstate with a feeling of relief. Relief mingled with nervousness, because the water is deeper here. Easily two or three feet. Plus, the ocean is just to his right. He can't see it, but he can hear it above the storm, the roaring of the water surging and breaking against the sea barrier. And if he can hear it from inside the bus, it must be crazy out there.

He keeps telling himself it's okay. He has time. The hurricane hasn't even hit yet. Jefferson told him landfall would only be at 6 or 7 p.m. As long as he's far enough north by then—

And then the bus is floating, sliding sideways off the interstate. Montoya hears screaming from behind him, but his attention is focused out the windshield. All he can see is foamy seawater. A huge wave has broken over the barrier and is pushing them off the road.

The water slowly recedes and the wheels touch the ground again. He unclenches his hands from the wheel. They're shaking. He clenches them into fists to try to steady them. It doesn't work.

Louis is using the comms, talking to someone. Montoya thinks he hears something about the National Guard, but he can't focus.

The engine has cut out. He tries to start it up again, but all he hears is a throaty growl that won't catch. Questions are being thrown at him; he ignores them as he focuses on the engine.

Come on. Start, you piece of shit. Start!

The engine finally coughs reluctantly to life and the demands and questions behind him turn to cries of relief.

He puts his foot down and the bus inches forward.

The sea barrier cracks and falls away, miles of concrete crumbling and washing out into the ocean.

A massive wave hits the bus full on, rolling it onto its side and slamming it up against the lane divider. The water keeps coming, surging through the breach in the barrier, pummeling the vehicle until it's completely underwater.

Then the bus is pulled back with the current and dumped unceremoniously into the ocean, where it fills with water and sinks slowly to the seafloor.

Seven

3:45 p.m.

"This is Sheriff Montoya. All staff is directed to meet in the cafeteria. Repeat, all staff to the cafeteria right now."

The voice is scratchy and tinny as it issues from the speaker. Sawyer barely hears it. She's sitting in the staff room in Northside, her stomach in knots as she watches the storm through the reinforced glass.

Everything is dark. Lightning flickers every few seconds, illuminating the churning clouds, lighting up the torrential rain as it's thrown from the sky. Debris flies through the air and tumbles hard to the ground. She's already seen a car bumper, a street sign, and random pieces of wood. She tracks all the wood and timber, doing a mental jigsaw in her head as she tries to identify its origin. She thinks it must have been a shed or a hut that's been ripped apart.

What the hell is she doing here? She must have been insane to fight her way to work this morning. Was it even worth it? Nobody has really noticed she's come in. She could easily have postponed her first day, skipped town with the other evacuees and come in once everything had returned to normal.

But no. She had to stick to her plan. Her *timeline*. That was all that mattered to her. Making sure everything was done properly. It was stupid. She can see that now. Her stubbornness has a very real chance of getting her killed. But she had to do it. For her brother.

She blinks and looks away from the window. What had the sheriff said? To meet in the cafeteria? Right.

She stands up and uses the keycard Martinez gave her to exit the room. She hasn't come across the cafeteria yet. She's not sure where it is. She moves along the silent corridors, peering through doors as she passes. Lots of offices, some empty rooms, some storage closets, a small gym with bikes and treadmills squashed inside, but no cafeteria.

She eventually finds it close to the door into the long staff corridor that leads to Admin. But it's empty. Just a few tables and two vending machines, one with drinks, one with junk food.

That's when she realizes how much of an idiot she is. Martinez said there was a staff cafeteria in Admin. That's where everyone will be. That's where all their offices are.

She swears under her breath and uses the keycard to open the door leading into the staff corridor. She pauses briefly at the daunting sight of it stretching ahead of her. She knows she's going to come to hate this corridor. She hates it already and she's only used it once.

She sighs and sets off at a fast walk.

When Sawyer finally arrives in Admin, it's completely deserted. All the desks in the open-plan office are empty.

Soft music comes from somewhere; a hidden radio tuned to a seventies station. *"Well I don't know why I came here tonight..."*

You and me both, she thinks. She shivers, glancing around the empty bull pen. She feels odd, like she's trespassing. Like she shouldn't be here.

She picks one of the corridors leading out of the office space. She has no idea where she's going, so one corridor is as good as another. It leads her deeper into the large building Martinez called Admin. She moves silently, her ears straining, but she doesn't pick up any sounds other than those of the storm.

She's about to turn back, intending to take another of the passages, when she spots an evacuation plan on the wall. She hurries over to inspect it, finds the "You are here" mark, then searches outward for the cafeteria.

There. Back through the bull pen and along a corridor to the left. She takes the map out of the Lucite frame and folds it up, placing it in her back pocket. She might need it if she gets lost again.

She retraces her steps to the passage indicated on the map. It doesn't take long to find the cafeteria. It's a large space with tables and benches bolted to the floor and a long food pass-through on the opposite side of the room. Off to the left there's an open doorway leading into what she assumes is the kitchen.

The cafeteria is empty.

Sawyer feels a growing sense of alarm.

"Hello?"

She waits, but there's no answer.

"Hello?" She shouts this time. Still, nothing.

She pulls out the map and unfolds it. She finds what she's looking for—Sheriff Montoya's office. She needs to find him. Find out what's going on.

She heads through the cafeteria and into the kitchen. Both walls are lined with huge ovens and gas cooktops. She exits into a narrower corridor, then turns right, making her way along the hallway until she enters one of the main passages of Admin. It's much wider than the others, easily ten feet across; according to the map, it travels from one side of the building to the other.

She counts the doors as she walks until she finds the sheriff's office. She knocks, but there's no answer.

She pushes the door open and peers inside. Empty.

She's about to close the door again when her eyes are drawn to the desk. It's covered with charts and printouts. Satellite imagery of the hurricane. She moves closer, glancing through the various pieces of paper. They're all from the National Hurricane Center. The first page is dated three days ago, and each one is an update on the path and severity of the hurricane as it gathers strength and approaches land.

No... *hurricanes*. She reads the reports with growing horror. Josephine and Hannah. Coming together to form a superstorm.

She flicks back to the first page. It's a projected timeline of the superstorm as it passes over Florida. The tail end of the hurricane is only going to pass them around midday tomorrow, but the projections are all saying Florida will be totally flooded by then.

One particular sentence catches her eye. It gives the projected time of the eye of the hurricane arriving over the Miami coastline, 5:05 a.m.

And scribbled next to it in red ink: *5:40–6:20.*

That must be when the eye passes over the prison. The eye of the hurricane—an area of calm, usually about a mile wide.

She hears a door slamming shut somewhere farther up the corridor. She exits the office, searching for the origin of the sound. She's starting to panic now. She has a growing suspicion about what's happened, but she doesn't want to admit it to herself. Because if it's true, it means she's in serious shit.

She spots something that pulls her up short.

A door stands wide open, a ring bristling with keys dangling in the lock.

She approaches cautiously and peers into the corridor beyond. According to her map, this corridor is a sally port that leads into the first of the prison units. Unit 1 of Gen Pop. There's no one around. She pulls the keys from the lock and steps into the corridor.

"Hello?"

She follows the passage until she comes to another open door on her left. This one leads into a security control room. She steps inside. It's empty, but there are monitors and computers everywhere, camera feeds showing various shots from the prison blocks.

Sawyer stops moving, her eyes wide with shock as she attempts to take in what's happening on the screens.

There's a riot going on in Unit 1. All the cell doors are standing wide open. Every single one.

The inmates are free.

Sawyer's eyes flick among the security monitors. It's just...it's just people killing each other: inmates fighting, stabbing, breaking necks, mobs chasing down lone figures, throwing them to the ground and kicking the life out of them, stomping on faces and skulls.

She tries to look away, but every monitor holds something similar. Scenes of death, the floors and walls covered in blood.

Three of the monitors show an outside feed. She stares in shock as a bus passes the camera. Her eyes widen. It looks like the bus is filled with COs.

They're leaving. Abandoning the inmates.

Abandoning *her*.

She turns to the desks. Five computer screens show electronic blueprints of the prison. All the cell doors that are supposed to be locked and marked red are currently green.

She pulls out a chair and sits down. She uses the mouse to pull back the view. It's not just Unit 1. It's the entire prison. Even the Mental Health and Administrative Control units— the two blocks where the psychopaths are kept.

They're all loose. Eight hundred inmates.

And they have the run of the prison.

Sawyer feels panic well up inside her. Her neck prickles, like someone is standing behind her blowing on it. She hesitates, not wanting to turn.

Her stomach twists. She lunges to her feet, shoves the chair back and whirls around.

There's no one there. She takes a deep breath, her eyes fixed on the open door leading out into the corridor. Jesus Christ. If she's found wandering around...

She darts forward and slams the door shut.

She needs to get out of here. *Now*. Her thoughts are racing. How? What can she do?

The bus. They obviously didn't know she was here when they left. Martinez said she wasn't on the employee list yet.

That's why she had to give her a temp keycard. They'll come back for her, surely? She just needs to tell them she's still here.

Next to the monitors is a small box with an LCD screen and a transmitter hooked to the side. She grabs the transmitter and pushes the button. "Hello?"

Nothing.

She checks the box. The screen isn't even lit up. She finds the power button. Static bursts out of the speaker. She pushes the button again. "Hello? Anyone there?" She releases the button. Still, no answer.

This isn't going to work. She needs to know what channel the bus communications are on.

She searches around the desk until she finds a binder with laminated pages inside. She starts to flick through it when she hears a shout outside the room.

She ducks down, then crawls to the window. She peers through the thick safety glass, sees an inmate sprinting down the corridor chased by two other men. None of them try to get into the security room, but she uses the keys she found to lock the door anyway.

She stays low and crawls back to the binder, paging through it until she finds the channels for the prison buses. There are only four. She types in the first number.

"Sheriff Montoya? Are you there?"

Nothing. Just static.

She tries the next code, then the next and the next, before going back to the beginning and trying them again, one after the other, until finally someone answers.

"H . . . hello?"

"Who is this?" she demands.

"Uh . . . Louis."

Sawyer hears a loud screeching over the speaker, then someone shouting.

"Louis? You still there?"

"Who is this? Is this the National Guard? We need help."

She's about to answer when she hears a sudden crashing and a scream of fear. "Watch out! Watch—"

Then a burst of static.

"Louis? Hey, Louis, talk to me."

No answer. She pushes the button again. "Louis? You there?"

Static.

Jesus Christ. Sawyer slumps down onto the floor. Was that really what it sounded like? She can't escape the thought.

That was the transport bus crashing.

She throws the transmitter back on the desk in a fit of rage. What the hell were they thinking? Abandoning their duties like that? Leaving the prisoners to fend for themselves while they made a run for it? Why would they do something like that?

Her thoughts race. The only possible reason—the only thing that makes the slightest bit of sense—is that Montoya didn't think this place was going to survive the coming storm. Obviously they thought the Glasshouse would; they wouldn't be using it for the evacuated prisoners if they didn't. But it wasn't looking good for the Ravenhill Correctional Facility itself.

Or for the prisoners inside.

Or, in fact, for her.

She can hear the inmates screaming and shouting now. The volume has been steadily increasing over the past few minutes, but she's tried her best to ignore it.

She can't. Not anymore. She blinks and looks around as if seeing her surroundings for the first time. What is she going to do? She has to adapt her plan. She can't just abandon it altogether. This might very well be the last chance she has. If she's going to die, she's at least going to die doing what she came here for.

She crawls to the window and peers out into the corridor. She presses her forehead against the glass, trying to see into Unit 1. But she can't. The angle is all wrong.

She hesitates, wondering what to do. Wait and hide? Or take a chance?

She already knows the answer. She was never one to play it safe.

She puts one hand on the keys still sitting in the lock, the other on the handle. She slowly unlocks, then opens the door, slipping the key out, then back into the lock on the other side of the door.

She hesitates one last time. Once she steps into the passage, she can't stop again. She'll have to keep moving or she'll be eaten alive.

Sawyer takes a deep breath, then moves out into the corridor. She pulls the door closed behind her, locks it and pulls out the keys...

...Then she runs.

She feels an instant wave of panic. She stumbles, almost turns back. This is stupid. Suicidal. She's going to die. She's going to be caught. Fuck knows what they'll do to her.

But what else can she do? Hide underneath the desk for...how long? Hours? Days? Until the hurricane strips the roof away and takes her out? No. She has to move forward. Staying still—stopping—means death.

She pushes on, forcing one foot in front of the other. She can hear screaming, shouting, shrill laughter coming from the open units behind her. God knows what's going on in the seven complexes that make up Ravenhill. All those inmates roaming around, free to settle scores, free to do whatever they want. It's going to be a bloodbath.

Her thoughts keep going back to what would happen if they caught her. She can't help it. She glances over her shoulder. Nothing there. But she can't shake the feeling that someone is going to just reach out and grab her, yank her back and drag her into a room.

And then—

"*Hey!*"

She throws a look over her shoulder. There are two guys standing at the other end of the corridor, back toward the security room. They glance at each other, then start to run.

Sawyer stifles a sob and sprints along the corridor, emerging back into the open-plan bull pen. She heads straight across the floor, into a random passage, running until she finds herself in the entrance and reception area of the prison. There's a door on the opposite side of the room. She makes for it, yanking it open and sprinting through. She almost falls flat on her face, suddenly finding herself in a downward-sloping corridor. She regains her balance and glances back, thinking she has time to lock the doors. She doesn't. The men are too close.

"Where you running to?" shouts one of them. "Come on. We just wanna have some fun."

Sawyer puts her head down and wills every last ounce of energy from her body, using the downward slope of the corridor to gain extra speed. She collides with the door at the bottom and pushes down on the handle at the same time, throwing it open and swinging around in a circle as it opens. She slams it shut behind her and grabs the keys, sobbing in frustration as she rams them, one by one, into the lock. None of them fit.

One of the inmates hits the door. The handle goes down and the door opens slightly. Sawyer throws her weight against it, using her shoulder to try to ram it closed.

A flash of pain surges through her arm. She cries out and pushes the door closed, seeing a blade withdraw back through the gap. She tries to ignore the pain and keep the door handle pulled up while she fumbles another key into the lock.

This one fits. She yanks it to the right, sobbing with relief as she hears the tumblers click into place.

She lets out a shaky breath and turns around, sliding down onto the floor as the inmates pound on the door. She can feel it vibrating through her skin.

She examines her shoulder. There's a gouge there, easily two inches long and about half an inch deep. Blood wells from it, soaking into her shirt. She holds the material down over the wound, hoping it will stop the flow. It won't be enough. She needs to find the infirmary. She can get wound glue, or maybe surgical staples.

She pushes herself to her feet, pulls the map out of her pocket. She traces her path and realizes she's in A Wing, the newer part of the prison that was built lower down on the hill. She checks over the evacuation map until she finds the infirmary for this wing. It's not far from where she is now.

She sets off. There's nobody around, but she can hear screaming and shouting coming from somewhere in the distance. She pauses at the end of the passage and peers around the corner. She freezes. There are three inmates moving away from her. One of them jumps up and smashes the overhead light with a long piece of metal. They laugh and disappear around the corner.

Sawyer takes a deep breath and slips into the passage, making her way toward the infirmary. Every step she takes is like walking through mud. Her whole being screams at her to run in the opposite direction, to hide, to make herself as small as possible. She feels the panic rising in her again, an urge—a *need*—to just flee. It's almost impossible to fight. Every fiber of her soul screams out that she's walking toward her death.

But all she can do is keep going forward. She's trapped either way. She tries to block out the screams of pain, the shouts of triumph, the calling of gang names.

"Woods!"

"Chicanos!"

"East Bloods, motherfucker!"

She doesn't know what's going on. A standoff between gangs for control of the wing? For weapons? What? She feels tears well up and angrily wipes them away. *No. Fuck you. I will not cry.*

She keeps going. It's the hardest thing she has ever done in her life, but she makes it to the infirmary door and finds the correct key.

She has just pushed the door open when something slams against the back of her head.

She cries out in pain, staggers. She holds herself up by the door as her vision swims. The nurse's station in the infirmary fades in and out of view as she tries to pull herself around again. Her hands aren't working properly. Her feet get tangled and she drops to her knees.

There's a loud ringing in her ears. Echoing shouts come from down the hallway. She grips the door and tries to look into the corridor. An inmate is running toward her. Her head drops. She finds herself looking at the screed floor. Something there doesn't make sense. It's a pool ball, covered in blood. It has the number 7 on it.

Lucky number seven, she thinks woozily.

She lifts her eyes to the inmate. He's only a few feet away. He's going to get her.

But then he skids to a stop, his eyes moving along the corridor to her right.

Someone shouts. The inmate turns to run, but four figures bolt past the infirmary door and grab him. He goes down screaming, and the figures pile on him with metal pipes and knives.

Sawyer manages to pull the keys out and close the door. She fumbles, trying to put the key in the lock to secure the door from this side. She feels her vision fading. Everything is turning hazy and gray.

The last thing she hears before she passes out and falls to the floor is the click of the lock sliding into place.

Eight

11:00 p.m.

I'm trapped by a cloying web, suffocating in the darkness. I struggle against it, trying to pull myself up to the tiny light glimmering far above me. I start to panic. Jesus, I'm going to die. I need to get away—

My eyes snap open.

My whole body aches. My muscles are stiff and tight. Like I've run a marathon in my sleep.

I attempt to sit up. I hear the sound of clinking metal and my arm jolts to a stop. I squint down in the dim light, trying to focus eyes that feel too big for my head.

My left wrist is handcuffed to a bed.

I look around in confusion, struggling to figure out what's going on. There's a dark shape against the wall to my right. I lean closer. It's an old ECG machine. Unplugged. Dead.

I'm in the infirmary.

What...?

And then I remember. Wright. Tully. Fighting to get to them. Having my fingers around Tully's neck. The COs coming for me, Evans using his stun gun...

I squeeze my eyes shut and let out a scream of frustration and rage. I *had* him. I had Tully in my hands and I let him get away.

I thrash around on the bed, pulling against the cuff, straining to get free. My vision swims. My head pulses with the effort, throbbing against my skull.

I drop back onto the bed, fighting down a surge of nausea. I take slow, deep breaths.

Keep calm. Don't freak out...

My eyes slide closed. I drift for a while, fading in and out of consciousness. I dream that I'm standing in a river, the water lapping around my legs...

My eyes open again. I stare up at the old white roofing tiles.

I'm not dreaming. I really can hear a lapping sound.

I lean over the bed.

The floor is hidden beneath about two feet of water.

The room is flooding. For a moment, I'm puzzled, wondering if the toilets and showers have backed up. But then I realize. The hurricane...

"*Hey!*" I shout.

No answer.

I pull on the cuff again, hoping to break the metal frame it's hooked around. I jam my feet against the bed and heave with everything I have. My vision swims with blackness. A wave of dizziness washes over me and I flop back onto the thin mattress.

I close my eyes again...just for a minute.

Just to stop everything from spinning...

...and then something cold wakes me up. Something... wet?

I look down. The water now laps gently over the bed, touching the back of my legs.

I tense my muscles and pull against the cuff. My tendons and veins stand out. My wrist pulses with sharp pain as the cuff cuts into my skin. The metal bars of the bed groan. I grit my teeth, putting every last ounce of strength into the effort.

The frame finally pops out of the join where it curves down to form the legs of the bed. I pause to take a few breaths, then slide the cuff over the end of the rail and drop into the water.

It's surprisingly warm. Almost unpleasantly so. I wade to the door, try to push it open.

It doesn't budge.

I peer through the wire-reinforced window. There's a light coming from somewhere down the corridor, but all it reveals is an empty flooded passage.

I do a quick check of the room. There's a metal drip stand in the corner. I grab it and try to wedge it between the door and the frame. It doesn't work. The gap isn't even wide enough to insert a knife.

I ram the bottom of the stand against the small window, but all I manage to do is bend the metal. The glass is way too thick.

I pause to catch my breath, fighting off waves of dizziness. I realize this isn't just the aftereffects of the stun gun. I'm actually struggling to get air into my lungs. I glance up at the air vent. If the power is down, that means the ventilation system won't be working, either. I'm just breathing my own recycled air.

I kick the door over and over. But it's hopeless. It's not like whoever designed the prison *wanted* the inmates to get out.

I slump back against the wall. Is this it? Is this how I go? Drowning in prison? Or slowly suffocating to death?

There's a metallic clicking sound to my left. I turn in surprise just as the door opens, pulled slowly outward against the floodwater.

A woman moves hesitantly around the door and stands in the entrance. She's holding a red fire ax in her hand. In the faint light from the passage, I can see she's young. Still in her twenties. Tanned features, possibly Mediterranean. A delicate face and hazel eyes with crinkles underneath that make it look like she's going to break into laughter. Amy had that. It was what first drew me to her.

We stare at each other for a long moment.

"Hey," she says. It's almost a challenge.

"Uh...hey."

Another drawn-out silence.

"I saw you earlier today when you were brought here. One of the COs said you used to be a cop." She says it accusingly.

"Yeah. I was."

"They said you're in here because you killed the guy who murdered your wife."

"And my baby."

"What?"

"My wife was pregnant. And I only killed one of them. Two got away."

"Oh...okay. Um...serious question. You're not, like... psycho, are you? I mean, you're not a mass murderer or a rapist or anything like that."

"No."

"So...you're not going to cut my throat? Or bash my head in?"

"The day's young."

Her eyes narrow.

"Sorry," I say. "Bad joke."

"Right. Great timing. Way to read a room."

Her fingers curl and uncurl around the ax. She still looks like she's trying to decide between ramming it into my head or running away.

"I'm Jack Constantine."

"Keira Sawyer." She pauses. "I'm new here. First day."

"That's...unfortunate. Mind telling me what's going on here, Keira?"

"Nobody calls me Keira. It's Sawyer."

"Okay. Sawyer. I've been out since around two. Can you fill in the few gaps?"

She takes a deep breath. "Right. Strap yourself in. It's around midnight now. Hurricanes Josephine and Hannah have joined up to form some kind of superstorm. You may have noticed that the infirmary is flooding, which doesn't bode well for the rest of the prison. And the hurricane hasn't even reached full strength yet."

"Jesus..."

"Yeah, hold that thought. It gets worse. All the cell doors have been opened. Every single one in the prison. Which means all the inmates are free. I sincerely doubt that's going to end well. So...to sum up. Inmates running around killing each other. Prison flooding. Category Five super hurricane hitting us... What else? Oh yeah. The COs are all gone and I don't think anybody on the outside actually knows about us, so no help is coming."

"Wait. What? Back up. What the hell are you talking about?"

"The National Guard was supposed to come and relieve the staff. Watch over you guys until the hurricane passed. They didn't turn up. My guess is they're dead. Montoya decided all the staff should leave when the Guard didn't show. Now *they're* dead too."

I open my mouth to speak, but she cuts me off.

"I heard it on the radio. Trust me, they're dead. So..." She shrugs. "We're well and truly on our own. Or to put it another way—fucked."

"So why are *you* still here?"

Sawyer looks embarrassed. "I... got lost. They left without me." Her hand rises to touch her head. Her hair is matted at the back with what looks like blood. "One of the inmates hit me. I made it in here, locked the door with my keys. But I passed out. Only just woke up."

"So... you haven't been out into the prison again?"

"Not for a few hours."

"How do we know anyone's still alive?"

"We don't."

I glance away from her, my thoughts racing. Think about it logically, I tell myself. Take it step by step. Obviously the first thing to do is get out of the infirmary. The whole place is going to be underwater within an hour.

"You still got the keys?" I ask.

She shakes her hip slightly. Metal jingles and I see the keys attached to her jeans.

"Good. We need to get out of here."

She looks at me like I just said the stupidest thing she has ever heard. "Good idea. Wish I'd thought of that." Then she turns and starts wading through the water.

I follow after, letting her lead the way through the infirmary.

As we move away from the cells, drawing closer to the outside walls of the prison, the sound of the hurricane increases in volume until it gradually overwhelms everything. The thundering of the wind ratchets up so it seems like it's slamming through the bricks themselves, enveloping us in an earsplitting scream.

And the rain...it smashes and hammers the roof, sounding like a million stones being thrown against metal.

How the hell do we survive this? The water is past my waist. If it carries on rising as fast as it is, then the whole of Ravenhill will most likely be underwater by dawn. We need to get to higher ground. Somewhere to hole up until the hurricane passes.

As we wade through the water, I find my thoughts returning over and over to the Glasshouse. I'm not sure if it's because Wright and Tully are locked up there or because it's the highest ground in the area, but either way, I come to realize it's probably our best shot. It's even shielded on one side by the bank of a hill. It's old. Sturdy. And the authorities obviously thought it was strong enough if they were shipping inmates there.

Except...how the hell do we cross the open ground to even *get* to it? If the hurricane is as bad as this woman says it is, we'll be ripped apart if we step outside.

We leave the corridor behind and enter an open ward. There are hospital beds all around the walls, just visible beneath the water. In the center of the room is a bank of ruined ECG and EEG monitors.

Sawyer stops moving, staring off to the left. I follow her gaze. There's a large shape bobbing gently in the water. I move closer. It's a body. The guy's arm is pulled out to the side, still handcuffed to a bed that's bolted to the floor. The figure is facedown, hospital gown hanging obscenely open at the back.

Sawyer hesitates, then tears her gaze away. There's nothing we can do for the poor bastard, so we start moving again, heading through the door into the corridor beyond. Bandages and wound dressings, still sealed in their sterile bags, float past us. Sawyer grabs one and stuffs it down her shirt. I don't ask why.

Sodden sheets blossom out across the surface of the water. Various machines line the corridor, their cables and attachments drifting around like the limbs of a jellyfish. Defibrillation paddles, blood pressure machines, oxygen masks.

As we draw closer to the end of the passage, the hurricane grows even louder, a horrific roaring and screaming that doesn't let up. It pummels my senses until I can hardly think straight. I can actually *feel* the wind now. It barrels down the corridor, whipping the floodwater into miniature whitecaps. We struggle against it, pulling ourselves along the walls, fingers scrabbling for purchase on machines or door frames.

It gets worse the closer we get to the nurse's station, until we finally emerge from the corridor into a scene of utter chaos.

The windows are gone. Empty, gaping maws that now spew floodwater into the infirmary. I try to shield my face from the worst of the storm, but it's impossible. The screaming wind whips the water up into a stinging rain that lashes my skin like tiny needles. The wind batters us, shoving us sideways into the walls. It overwhelms everything, blocks out all rational thought.

We unconsciously grab hold of each other's arms, wading forward against the storm, heading for the locked door that leads out of the infirmary and into the prison.

I try to shield Sawyer as she uses her keys in the door. When she finally manages to unlock it, we both pull on the handle, using all our weight. The force of the floodwater makes it difficult, but we heave it slowly toward us. Water surges past our legs and through the gap, frothing and pouring into the lit corridor beyond. Sawyer slips through the gap and I follow, letting the weight of the water slam the door shut behind us.

The noise of the hurricane dies down slightly. Not a lot, but enough that I can hear myself think again. There's power out here, light.

I know we're in my unit, A Wing, but it looks different. I glance around at surroundings that appear simultaneously familiar and alien. There are blood smears all over the walls. Some of the lights hang loose from the ceiling, dangling from red and blue wires.

A body lies a few feet away. It's almost completely submerged in the water, arms floating up above its head. I check left, then right, but there's no one else around.

I squat down and turn the corpse over. The guy is Puerto Rican. I've seen him around the yard, a member of the Ñetas. The guy's stomach is a mass of puncture wounds. The numbers 031—the sign of the Bloods—have been carved into his chest with a knife.

I feel around under the body, checking for a weapon. Wishful thinking. A scream echoes in the distance. It's the kind of scream you make when your life is being taken forcefully.

"We need a plan," says Sawyer nervously.

"You think?"

There's a second door to the right of the infirmary entrance. A freight entrance, where medicine gets delivered. I stand up and peer through the glass. There's a short corridor beyond and an exit at the far end.

"Give me your keys," I say.

"Why?"

"Just give them to me."

"No!"

I snatch them from her belt, ignoring her angry protest, and turn back to the door, ramming each key into the lock until I find the one that works. I push the door open and hurry to the exit at the end of the passage.

"What the hell are you doing?" says Sawyer, trailing behind me. "Those keys are for internal doors only. You need a key-card to get out."

I cup my hands against the glass, peering outside. At first I can't see anything. Just utter darkness. But then a bolt of lightning arcs across the clouds, illuminating the outside of the prison.

It's like looking into hell.

I thought it had been bad earlier in the day when we were in the bus. But looking outside now, I know instantly that a bus wouldn't make it five feet before being plucked up by the hurricane.

Outside the door is a small staff parking lot. Most of it is under water, and all the cars have been blown and tossed into the retaining wall that was built into the side of the hill. In the brief flash of light, it looks like they've been sitting in a scrapyard for years. Twisted and destroyed, smashed up and ripped apart.

There's another flash of lightning, and this time I see that a telephone pole has been thrown into the ground like a javelin. It's cut right through the asphalt and buried itself about ten feet deep.

"They say the winds are going to push one ninety," says Sawyer softly. "Maybe even two hundred."

"Jesus..."

"Can I have my keys back?"

I hand them over wordlessly. Any hopes I had of reaching the Glasshouse, whether for safety or to get Wright and Tully, are gone.

"We need to get out of here," says Sawyer.

"What's the point?" I say softly, still staring out the window. "You think Ravenhill is going to survive this?"

"I'm not talking about Ravenhill. I've been thinking about this. I'm talking about the Glasshouse."

"Are you blind? If we step outside, we're dead. There's no way we can get to the Glasshouse."

"Not now. But in about five hours we can."

I look at her in confusion.

"I was in the sheriff's office. I saw the storm reports from the National Hurricane Center. The eye of the hurricane passes over the prison at five forty a.m."

"The..." I glance sharply out the window. The eye of the hurricane. Of course. It will be totally calm outside. A hurricane this big, the eye will last at least half an hour before it passes over. Maybe even longer. "Shit...I didn't even think of that."

"Well, don't beat yourself up too much. I hadn't thought about it, either. Not until I saw the reports." She fishes around in her jeans pocket and pulls out a keycard. "Plus, I can get us out the Northside staff entrance."

I reach for the card, but she snatches her hand away and slips it back into her pocket. "Uh-uh. We stick together. You watch my back, I watch yours. Think about it. I'm a woman trapped in an all-male prison. You're an ex-cop trapped in...well, prison. We need each other if we want to get through this in one piece."

I briefly consider just taking the keys and card from her. Leaving her here to fend for herself. But the thought vanishes almost as fast as it comes. I couldn't do that. To be honest, I'm surprised at this realization. I thought this place had killed any compassion I had left. I mean, there wasn't much in there anyway, not after Amy died, but still...it's nice to realize I'm still *slightly* human.

"That keycard, does it open any other exits?"

"I don't think so. Martinez said it was for the Northside staff room door. That's where I have my locker."

She must have seen the look of disappointment on my face. "What?"

"Well...here's the thing. You said all the inmates are loose. That all the cell doors in this place are open?"

"Yeah."

"Well, I hate to break it to you, but there's only one way to get to the Northside staff room. And that's past seven prison units. Through about eight hundred pissed-off, blood-crazed inmates. I'm talking psychopaths, rapists, pedophiles, murderers, child-killers, wife-killers, bank robbers, animal-fuckers, cannibals, and serial killers." I smile humorlessly. "Welcome to the Ravenhill Correctional Facility. Abandon hope, all who enter here. Bed and breakfast included."

"Oh," says Sawyer. Then, "Shit."

"Shit indeed."

Nine

11:30 p.m.

The water in A Wing is just below my calves, but that's definitely not from us opening the infirmary door just now. It's getting in somewhere else, which means it's going to keep rising. It's not as bad as in the infirmary, but that's like saying having a blowout where three tires explode is not as bad as all four tires going.

I wade to a door about six feet away and peer through the window into the corridor beyond. Most of the lights have been destroyed. The thick Plexiglas coverings have been ripped away, the globes smashed or stolen. Some of the casings have been ripped right out of the ceiling, the wires dangling from circular holes. Paper and torn books float on the surface of the water like leaves in a lake. There are more blood smears on the walls.

My stomach clenches up. This is reminding me too much of Afghanistan. My whole body is screaming at me not to go any farther. To find a place to hide, to find weapons, anything except go forward.

But just like then, I've got no choice. I have to stop thinking. Just act.

I take a deep breath and pull the door open. I half expect to hear someone shout out. Or jump at me brandishing a knife. But nothing happens.

I step into the passage. The light above the door is gone. The area surrounding me is cloaked in shadows. Sawyer follows. I wonder how *she* must feel. If she gets caught by the inmates...

I can't help glancing over my shoulder at her. Christ, if they get hold of her...

"What?" she says softly.

I shake my head. "Listen, I don't want to sound patronizing here, but you need to stay out of sight, okay? Even if someone attacks me...you need to keep hidden."

"A gallant murderer. How sweet."

"I'm not a murderer," I snap. "Don't call me that. I punished someone who killed my wife and baby. And I'd do it again. I *will* do it again. Soon as I get to the Glasshouse."

She looks at me, surprised. "I thought we were going to the Glasshouse to find shelter. Are the men who killed your wife there?"

"They are now. And there's no reason I can't do both."

She gives me a long look, but doesn't respond. There's nothing to say.

We start moving again, wading slowly along the passage, making our way toward the corridor that connects A Wing to Admin and Ravenhill itself.

There's a faint rumbling sound that's bothering me. It's just on the edge of hearing, but it seems to be getting stronger. It's not the wind. It sounds different. Somehow...*deeper.* I'm about to ask Sawyer if she can hear it, when we hear frantic splashing coming from up ahead. Then:

"*No...!*" A shout trailing off into a scream.

I grab Sawyer and push her through the closest door. I catch a brief glimpse of shelves of books—the library—then turn and quickly close the door. Not all the way. I keep it open just enough so I can see through the gap.

A figure sprints into view, his face twisted with fear. A wolf-like howling echoes from the passage behind him, trailing away into a series of yips.

The guy sees the library door. He leaps forward and tries to push it open.

I don't let him.

"What the hell are you doing?" Sawyer whispers fiercely. She tries to pull the door open, but I hold it firm.

"Let him in!"

"Don't be stupid."

I use my hip to shove her aside and put all my weight on the door. The guy on the other side is pushing hard, forcing the small gap wider. He realizes that someone is actually holding the door closed, and he peers inward, locking eyes with me.

"Let me in!"

"I can't."

"They're going to—"

Four figures suddenly appear in the corridor, ululating in triumph. They leap through the water. One grabs the terrified inmate by the neck, slamming his face against the door. I jerk back, trying to hold it steady.

The attackers throw the guy to the floor, then lay into him. Kicking him in the face, the ribs, stamping on his head. He starts out screaming and moaning, but it's only a few moments before he falls silent.

Still, the beating continues. Then one of the figures pulls out a long bread knife that must have been stolen from the kitchen. He leans down and slices it across the unconscious figure's throat. Blood pools out, slowly spreading and darkening the water.

The four inmates watch for a few moments, then stroll off, laughing and joking as they go.

I turn—

—straight into Sawyer's slap.

I stagger back, eyes wide with amazement. "The fuck?"

"The fuck? The *fuck*? You just let that man die!"

"There was nothing I could do!"

"You could have let him in!"

"And then what? Those four would have come after him. We'd *all* be dead now. I was *protecting* us."

She opens her mouth to argue, but I cut her off.

"Save it. Look, I'm sorry you feel shit, but it was him or us."

"You're responsible for his death!"

I frown, but not because of what she said. There's
something...

"All you had to do—"

I hold up my hand. "Shut up."

Sawyer actually takes a step back to get a full look at me, as
if she's not sure she heard correctly. "Did you just...?"

"...tell you to shut up? Yes! Now shut the fuck up!
Listen!"

She stops. We both stand in silence, surrounded by books
and water that I suddenly notice is almost up to my knees.

"What...?" she says.

"Look."

I point to the water. Ripples are spreading toward the center
of the room. I put my hand on the wall. I can feel it thrum-
ming, a vibration that's growing stronger by the second.

Sawyer and I lock eyes. I can hear a noise now, a low roar
that rises above and beyond the constant background cry of the
hurricane. It hits me like a heavy bass beat in the chest.

Something is coming.

I feel a primeval fear in the very depth of my being, the fear
of being at the mercy of something I have no control over.

"What *is* that?" whispers Sawyer.

The ripples in the water are growing larger, faster, lapping
up against my legs. I can feel the vibration through my feet
now. The roaring sound is growing louder and louder.

I look around desperately, but there's nowhere to go.
Nowhere to hide. We're trapped.

The noise increases in volume, a roar that is shaking everything. Books fall from the shelves, splashing into the water.

I pull the library door open. The water in the passage outside surges back and forth in waves, whitecaps breaking against
the walls and surging up into the air.

I think I can hear the sounds of screaming above the roar.

I lean out and peer along the corridor just as the door we
used to enter this part of the prison bursts inward, pulled from

its hinges, flying through the air and banging against the wall. Water explodes into the passage, a torrential flood that pummels and slams into every corner. The walls themselves start to buckle, then sag. Holes open up, jets of water spraying through before the walls give way under the pressure and collapse.

I slam the library door shut. Sawyer and I move back against the far wall, but we're trapped. No way out.

The door slams open like it's been hit by a battering ram. Water roars inside, a gushing, surging flood that instantly engulfs and swallows us.

My feet fly out from under me. I go under, the crosscurrents tossing me around as if I'm a leaf in a gale. I'm thrown against the wall. My head cracks into a shelf, then I'm yanked away and thrown sideways as the floodwater surges into every corner of the library.

I try to right myself, try to fight the raging currents. My lungs strain for air. I need to climb, to break the surface. I try to swim upward, but I can't get anywhere. I can't escape the water. I stop fighting, whirl around in confusion. I think I can make out lights beneath me, on the floor. But that can't be right. Why would there be lights on the floor?

No. I realize I've been turned around. I've been swimming in the wrong direction.

I kick off toward the lights, clawing with my hands, trying to fight the swirling currents. I finally break the surface, gasping in lungfuls of air. I'm about three feet from the ceiling, and the water is still pouring inside.

I turn in a frantic circle, searching for Sawyer. I can't see her anywhere.

The water surges over my head again. This time it goes in my mouth, up my nose. I cough and splutter, feeling my lungs constrict. I panic, take another huge breath, swallowing more water as I'm pulled under. Dim pools of light flash and flicker behind my eyes as I try to find my way back to the surface. I've been tossed around again. I can't tell what's up and what's down.

I try to force the water from my lungs, but I just end up coughing, sucking more in. My throat constricts. I gag, but there's no air. My lungs spasm. Panic wells up and I frantically pull myself in any direction I can, hoping it might lead me to the surface.

Something grabs me by the hair. Instinctively I lash out, trying to escape, but then I realize it's someone trying to pull me up. I stop fighting and push off with my legs and arms, finally able to figure out which way is up.

I burst through the water and slam my head against the ceiling tiles. I suck in air and reach up, trying to stabilize myself against the roof. The water swirls fiercely around me. I wipe my eyes and see Sawyer treading water next to me, trying to steady herself against the wall and the ceiling.

I look around desperately. The water is boiling and frothing by the door, although the doorway itself is now completely submerged. There's no way we can fight the current and get out. And even if we could, so what? Where can we go? The water is everywhere. A Wing is the lowest set of buildings in the prison compound. It's being swallowed up by the hurricane.

Then something catches my eye. Where my head hit the ceiling tile, there's a small gap. My eyes widen. Of course, the library is supposed to be staff only. No need for concrete ceilings in here. I push up, shoving the ceiling tile in. A dark space greets me. I wave at Sawyer, gesturing upward. She clambers through first, then I pull myself up after her.

The actual roof of the prison is about four feet above us, forcing us to stay hunched over. Pipes and cable-tied electrical wires cover the walls. I balance on the metal support struts so I don't fall back into the room below.

The sound of the hurricane is deafening up here. The screaming of the wind, the rattling and pounding on the roof itself, the roaring of the water below. It's hard to even think straight. Adrenaline surges through my body. It feels exactly like it did when I was in Marjah. That urge to act, that need to keep moving, to fight. To survive at all costs.

Sawyer and I start to move. It's not totally dark. Some of the downlights are still working, their illumination shining back up into the ceiling space. It won't last long. The water is going to trip the electrics soon enough.

I think we've been moving for about a full minute when Sawyer stops. I get close to her, shout in her ear.

"What are you doing?"

"Listen!" she shouts back.

I tilt my head, trying to hear anything different in the sounds of the hurricane. I think I can hear screaming coming from down below, almost hidden beneath the thunderous boom of the water.

Sawyer kneels down on the struts and slams a few of the ceiling tiles out. They drop a foot into the water and are swept away by the current. Through the gap I can see some inmates struggling to stay afloat in a room. I think I recognize one of them. Castillo. A lieutenant in the Latin Kings gang.

"Leave them!" I shout.

"No!" she screams. "We can't."

She leans down even farther and holds her arm out.

"Hey!"

Castillo turns in her direction. Sawyer gestures for him to swim toward us. He looks confused at first, then spots me next to her.

I sigh and lean down, holding my arm out too. Castillo tries to swim toward us, but the surging water keeps pulling him back. He eventually stops fighting the current and just relaxes, letting the water take him round in circles until he's passing directly below us.

He grabs Sawyer's hand. I shift over and take hold of him too, the both of us dragging him up into the ceiling. Other members of the Kings have seen what we're doing and are trying to swim toward us. But one guy—Silas, I think his name is, one of the biggest guys I've ever seen—decides not to even bother trying. He jabs upward with a meat cleaver he's holding, pushing out a ceiling tile about ten feet away.

I straighten up. Castillo hesitates, his gaze lingering on Sawyer. Then he turns and moves across to where Silas is now struggling to pull himself up into the ceiling space.

Sawyer kicks in more ceiling tiles, leaning over and pulling up any of the Kings she can grab from the room below. I hesitate. I should just keep moving. I don't owe Castillo anything. He'd kill me as soon as look at me any other day. And Sawyer... well, it's becoming obvious that's she's actually insane. Or terminally naïve. Either way, she's going to get me killed eventually.

But I don't move on. I sigh and join her. The quicker it's done, the quicker we can get moving.

When it's clear there are no more inmates in the room below, I gesture to Sawyer that we need to go. We managed to rescue nine inmates in all. I'm not sure how many there were to start with. Sawyer pauses, but then nods. Good. So she's not entirely stupid. We set off. I leap from strut to strut, heading in the general direction of the uphill corridor that leads into Admin.

I know I'm close when we reach a brick wall in the roof space that blocks any way through. That means we're moving out of the staff areas and into the prison proper. I kick in the ceiling tiles below me. The water doesn't look as high here. Maybe just above my chest. There must be a few closed doors stopping the flood. They won't last long, though.

I drop into the water, Sawyer following right behind me. Castillo's men do the same, sticking with us in the hope that we have some kind of plan. Joke's on them. I'm probably leading us all to our deaths.

I start swimming and wading, pulling myself toward the doors that lead into the corridor. Sawyer is right next to me, her hair plastered to her head. I look behind me and see

Castillo and his men still coming. There are others too. Inmates from A Wing taken by surprise by the flood, all following us in the hope that we're heading to safety. The water is rising fast. It's almost up to my shoulders now. The roaring is growing louder again, like we're standing beneath a massive waterfall. I wipe my eyes as we arrive at the door and I try to open it.

It's locked.

Sawyer moves in front of me and fumbles with her keys. The inmates are crowding behind us now, pushing us against the door, shouting panicked questions.

I try to shove them back, but they're too tightly packed. I have to turn and lash out. Punching those closest to us, yanking them by the hair, just to give Sawyer room to try to get the keys into the lock.

She's fumbling beneath the water, trying to insert the keys by touch. I hear a deafening crash from somewhere behind us, followed by screams and a sudden increase in the sounds of surging water. What the hell was that? Another wall going down? The roof caving in?

I look at Sawyer. She is pale and struggling with the lock. Then her face clears and she nods in my direction. She tries to pull the door open. It doesn't budge. I grab the handle with her. Pull. Nothing. Other inmates grab hold, all of us trying to fight against the weight of the water.

The door finally shifts. Water surges into the corridor as we slowly pull it open. It's absolute chaos as everyone rushes through, clambering over each other, fighting to get away from the rising water.

We're all swept up in the rush. Nobody can stop. It's either move forward or be crushed underfoot. I try to find Sawyer. I catch a glimpse of her up ahead, helping someone who must have been knocked over in the stampede.

We all move as fast as we can up the slanted corridor. It feels like it's never-ending. I look back and see that even more inmates have joined the exodus. Jesus, there must be at least eighty now, all trying to funnel into the narrow passage leading up to Admin.

The door ahead is only about twenty feet away, but it doesn't seem to be drawing any closer. The water level is rising rapidly, the floodwater entering the corridor and surging up the incline. The inmates are shoulder to shoulder. It's getting difficult to even move.

Then the water starts to lap over the heads of those at the bottom of the corridor.

I can feel the shift, the rise of sudden panic. Inmates start to flail around, desperate to leave A Wing behind. We're pushed forward by those at the back, some tripping and plunging beneath the water, trampled underfoot.

I'm shoved up against one of the small windows. A flash of lightning outside draws my attention. At first I can't figure out what I'm looking at. The lighting seems to be reflecting off a wall about thirty feet high.

Another flash. I see a car tumble past, lifting into the air and skimming across the surface of the water like a skipping stone.

And behind it, lit by the lightning...a wave...a storm surge that looks like a tsunami, thirty feet high, cresting, coming straight for the prison.

Others see it too. Panicked screams break out. Shouts, swearing, people fighting to get to the top of the passage, trying to get away from the windows.

I look around for Sawyer, see her about six feet away. I barge my way through the inmates, grabbing hold of her and half dragging, half pushing her toward the door.

"Get out of the fucking way!" I shout. "Move!

We reach the front of the crowd and shove the door open. At least it wasn't locked. The surge behind us almost gets us both trampled. We manage to dodge to the side as the inmates cascade through the door into the reception area like sand through a funnel.

The water in here is only up to my ankles. There are gasps and cries all around as people trip or are pushed to the floor. Some of the inmates rush toward the huge desk against the far wall, climbing on top of it in fear that the water will keep rising.

I wait by the heavy door while the others spill through. I peer through a window in the corridor and watch the wave coming. There are still inmates struggling toward Admin. There's no way they're going to make it.

The storm surge hits, slamming into Ravenhill.

The whole building shakes. The lights flicker, dim, switch off, then struggle back to life again. I can hear the groaning of tortured stone, the distant crashing of something collapsing.

The inmates still in the corridor stand frozen. They're all hoping it will pass over, wash over them like the tide washing over rocks at the beach.

But it doesn't. One of the windows in the passage cracks, splinters, then bursts inward. Leaks spring up all along the walls. Water pours in through the rapidly expanding holes, rising to fill the corridor.

The inmates scramble over each other to get to the door. They're not going to make it. The water is rising too fast. As I watch, part of the wall by the bottom door collapses. Water and wind surge in. Another section of wall crumbles away. The wind screams through the now exposed passage. A few stragglers are immediately plucked up and sucked into the boiling clouds.

There's no choice. We have to close the door. I try to push it shut, but a fierce gust of wind slams straight into it and sends us all flying back to land on our asses in the water.

The scream of the wind and the storm is deafening. Lightning flashes. I can hear distant explosions. Collapsing metal, grinding concrete.

The lights flicker one last time and go out, plunging the reception area—and, I assume, the entire prison—into darkness.

I get up and pull myself to the door. Others join me and we

try to shove it closed against the wind. I'm looking straight into the storm. Straight outside. The entire A Wing is totally destroyed. Just...gone.

The inmates who made it through before the hurricane flattened the corridor push themselves to their feet and put their weight against the door. We push against the wind until we finally manage to shove it closed.

The screaming wind drops slightly in volume. Sawyer hands me the keys, one of them already selected. I ram it home and turn it in the lock. I can hear ragged breathing behind me, the splashing of water.

Someone farther into the reception says, *"Fuck..."* in an awed voice.

I lean my head back against the door. All that stands between us and the hurricane is about three inches of metal. I really don't think it's going to be enough.

I doubt this place will hold for *three* hours, let alone five.

Ten

Saturday, August 28

12:30 a.m.

The prison generators kick in. The lights flicker to reluctant life, but none of them are at full strength. They cast a thin, watery glow that fails to chase away the darkness. The generators are at least thirty years old and the last time they were serviced was about eighteen months ago. I know that because Henry and I were the ones who did it. The prison was too cheap to hire actual contractors.

There's a heavy silence inside the reception as we all listen to the raging of the hurricane. It overpowers everything, a constant booming and crashing, waves of rain slamming against thick windows, random objects pummeling into the roof—I figure road signs, trees, fences, parts of houses, anything that can be plucked from the ground.

And now we have to deal with the storm surges. I'm not sure how they work. If that even was a storm surge. Maybe it was just floodwater pushed into a wave by the wind? I have no idea if they're going to keep coming. The whole building is vibrating and creaking under the strain.

Some of the inmates are already leaving, moving deeper into the prison to get away from the crowds. Probably a smart move. Others are still distracted, staring through windows at the hurricane outside. But as soon as they realize they're not about to die, old grudges are going to be settled.

"Gotta admit, I'm not feeling a hundred percent safe hanging around in here," says Sawyer.

Jesus. Sawyer...

I glance around the room. No one is paying any attention to us—to *her*. But it won't be long before they remember she's here. Probably best for me to hide my face too. Cops, ex or not, aren't well liked in prison.

We move around the wall, staying in the shadows, sticking to the outskirts of the crowd. I keep my eyes on the inmates, trying to block Sawyer from view with my body.

I catch a glimpse of Castillo. He's talking to two huge men: Silas, and another guy who looks like he's around six-five, a solid mix of bulk and muscle.

They stop talking and turn to look at the door we all just came through. Then they start scanning the inmates, searching for something.

Searching for some*one*...

Shit...

I speed up my pace, heading for the closest door. Sawyer keeps up and we exit the reception area into a short hallway that ends at a T-junction about fifteen feet ahead.

"Where are we going?" she asks.

"Somewhere to hole up. We need to plan our way forward." And hide, in case Castillo *is* after Sawyer.

We move as fast as we can while trying to stay out of sight of the other inmates. I check the doors as we pass, opening them and peering into the rooms. Most of them are offices filled with desks and computers, others used to store old PCs and broken monitors. None of them are suitable because all the doors are cheap wood and would cave in with one kick.

I finally find somewhere that will work. I can feel the door is heavy and reinforced even as I push it open.

"In here," I say, stepping inside.

It's a supply room, about thirty feet long and fifteen wide, separated by five rows of floor-to-ceiling shelves. Toilet paper, laundry detergent, and hand sanitizer lie scattered across the floor. The inmates have already ransacked the room, taking anything edible or dangerous.

"Lock the door."

Sawyer finds the right key while I do a quick check to make sure there isn't another entrance.

It's clear.

I sigh and slump down onto an eighteen-pack of toilet paper, leaning my head back against the wall.

Jesus. I can't believe it's only been about an hour since I woke up. My body feels like it's been run over by a truck.

Sawyer sits down opposite me. "You okay?"

I open my eyes, looking at her in surprise. "Me? Yeah," I lie. "I'm fine. Hundred percent. What about you?"

She shrugs. "I've been better."

Understatement of the year. I let my eyes drift closed again. We sit in silence for a few minutes, letting the adrenaline wash through us. I keep seeing flashes of those poor bastards taken out by the storm surge. The panic in their eyes, the fear when they realized they were about to die and there was absolutely nothing they could do to save themselves.

I shiver and open my eyes. Not a good idea to dwell on that. "Can I ask you a question?"

"Shoot."

"What was with you punching out those ceiling tiles?"

She frowns. "What do you mean?"

"Why'd you do it?"

She looks at me like I'm stupid. "Because those men would have died otherwise."

"Well... sure, but they probably deserve it."

"Nobody deserves that."

"You don't know what they're in here for."

"So? Makes no difference to me."

"You put yourself in danger, though. And me. We could have died."

"But we didn't. It's called decency, Constantine. You must remember what that is. Being human?"

I shrug. "Whatever happens happens. There's nothing we can do to change it. All we can do is fight to stay alive as long as possible. *That's* being human."

"You don't really believe that. You used to be a cop."

"*Used* to. I'm telling you this now: don't put yourself in danger like that again. Nobody in here is worth saving."

"Not even you?"

"Especially not me."

"Come on," she says. "Are you seriously saying you don't have anything to live for?"

"Not anymore."

"Nothing? No one? No parents? Brothers or sisters?"

I shake my head. "Just me."

"Friends?"

I think about it. "I suppose Felix is an okay guy. He's my cellmate."

"Jesus. That's one miserable life you live."

"I try my best."

"Well, here's the thing. I *do* have people to live for. I want—"

I cut in. "Who?"

She pauses, her train of thought derailed. "What?"

"Who do you have to live for? A husband? Kids?"

"No kids. I've got an ex-husband. He's all right, I guess. But I've got family. Friends. People I'm responsible for."

I can sense her reluctance to talk. But if she's going to judge me, I have a right to ask. "Who?"

She hesitates. "My brother, Mike. He...looks up to me. And...he kind of hates me."

I frown. "Which one is it?"

"Both, I guess. He hasn't talked to me for a couple of years now."

"Why?"

"Long story. Our mother died when he was ten. I was thirteen. Cancer. Long. Drawn out."

"Sorry."

"Not your fault. That's on God."

"You still believe in God?" I say, surprised. "After seeing your mother suffer like that?"

Sawyer thinks about it, then shrugs. "Sometimes." She pauses for a moment, her eyes drifting back through the years. "She refused treatment in the end. She knew it wasn't going to do any good. Died at home. But it took over a month. Every morning Mike woke up and waited at the foot of my bed—never went on his own. We'd go to our mom's room and knock. We'd never just walk in. We were too scared of what we'd find. We waited till we heard her call out. Or she'd push her book onto the floor. Something just to tell us she was still alive. Then we'd go in and she'd get us to pray with her."

"*She* still believed?"

"Right till the end. She was hardcore. Used to read us the Bible as our bedtime story. I could probably recite the whole thing from memory. She always said whatever happened was God's plan."

I snort my disgust. "Fuck that shit. If that kind of thing is God's plan, then he's the bad guy."

"So I take it you haven't been saved by our Lord and Savior?" Her tone is light. She's joking.

"Nope. I was forced to go to Sunday school when I was a kid. My grandparents took me. The teacher—he was what you would call a traditionalist. Fire and brimstone. Screaming and shouting. Think I was about six at the time. From that moment on, I kind of took offense to people trying to tell me what to do."

"And your wife?"

"What about her?"

"Was she religious?"

"She called herself a weekend Christian. But not even that. She went to Midnight Mass on Christmas Eve, maybe on Easter. That's about it."

"You ever go with her? To Midnight Mass?"

I laugh. "No. She wouldn't let me. Said I'd burst into flames if I set foot inside the church."

Sawyer smiles.

"So..." I say. "Your mom?"

Her smile fades. "One morning we stood at her door and knocked. She didn't reply. It was just...silent. We didn't know what to do."

"Where was your dad?"

"We weren't sure. We looked for him, but...eventually I just pushed the door open..." She glances away, her face clouding. "I saw my dad first, lying on the bed next to my mom. She was dead. My dad was just...crying. Silently. Her hand was on his cheek. I don't know if he put it there or if it was her last act. I remember thinking how weird it looked. The pale white of my mom's dead skin against his face. When he saw us watching, he freaked out. Started screaming and shouting for us to get out. To shut our eyes."

"He didn't want you seeing your mother like that."

"That's what I thought at first. But when I got older, I got to thinking he didn't want us seeing *him* like that. Showing emotion. First time we'd ever seen him cry. He wasn't big on hugs and kisses, you know?"

I nod.

"After that, it was never the same between us. He would never look us in the eyes. It's like he was ashamed."

"Your dad's old man, your grandfather. Was he one of those old-school tough guys?"

"Yeah. Spare the rod, spoil the child. He beat our gran too. I found that out later, at my dad's funeral. His sister told us. Kind of made me understand my dad a bit better."

"He ever hit you?"

"No. He was never like that."

"That's how it goes. You either become your parents or you push so far away from what they were, you become the total opposite." I pause. "Most people just become them. It's easier."

Sawyer nods.

"What about your brother? How did he turn out?"

She hesitates. "I...had to pretty much raise him myself. Our dad didn't have a great job, so he couldn't afford babysitters or anything. I did the best I could, but he fell in with a bad crowd. They got him involved in crime. Delivering parcels on his bike when he was still a kid. Then dealing drugs."

"Where is he now?"

"Bellevue. Possession and dealing."

"Shit, I'm sorry."

"Yeah."

"It's not your fault, though. You did your best, right?"

"Yeah," she says softly. "I did my best."

We trail off into an awkward silence. Sawyer winces and rolls her shoulder. Then she takes out the sealed wound dressing she picked up in the infirmary.

"Can you help me with this?" she asks.

She hands me the dressing and pulls her shirt down over her shoulder to expose a deep cut.

"Try and pull the lips together and make sure the seal is tight," she says.

I open up the packet and take out a square dressing. I peel off the backing, exposing the adhesive around the edges, and carefully place it over her shoulder, making sure it sticks all the way around.

I have to force myself to smooth the dressing down. It's the first time I've touched a woman's skin in three years. First time I've touched a woman other than Amy in ten. It feels like I'm cheating, which is stupid. How do you cheat on a ghost?

I crumple up the packaging and drop it into the water. "Done."

"Thanks." She pulls her shirt up again. "We need to plan our route," she says, taking something out of her pocket. She unfolds it on her lap and I see it's an evacuation plan—a map of the prison.

I lean forward, glad to be distracted from thoughts of Amy.

I point to the large rectangular block at the bottom of the map. "We're somewhere in here. The admin building."

"Right." Sawyer points to the very top of the map. "And that's the Northside staff room. Where we need to get to. I think we should try for the staff corridor."

She points to the long corridor traveling up along the right side of the prison map, heading directly to the block at the north end of the prison. I've never been to that side. Like she says, it's staff only.

"It's a straight path, see?"

"Sure, except for the fact that there are eight hundred inmates somewhere between us and the exit. It could be overrun already."

"Could be...The other option is the inmate corridor." She points to the corridor on the left side of the map. It exactly mirrors the staff corridor, with all the prison units, 1 to 4, then Transitional, Mental Health, and Administrative Control all nestled between the two passages.

"Either one could be blocked."

"We won't know till we check."

"I suppose." She's right. We need to get to the north end of the prison as fast as possible. Which means we try the direct route first.

"Okay. Staff corridor it is."

We get up. The keys are still hanging in the door. "What's with those keys?" I ask. "Is there one for every lock in the prison?"

"Nah. They're the sheriff's keys. See?" She shows me the name tag hanging from the key ring. "I think he has universal keys for the storerooms, staff rooms, the doors between the different prison units." She turns the key in the lock, then pulls it out and clips the ring back onto her belt. "If there was a separate key for every door, this thing would weigh a hundred pounds."

She cracks the door slightly. We wait, listening. I can hear noises in the distance. Shouting. Screaming. Laughing. It sounds like an asylum.

No noises come from the corridor directly outside the

storeroom, though. Sawyer opens the door wider and I peer out, checking both ways.

"Clear."

We slip outside and move quickly along the passage, splashing through the ankle-deep water. There's a lot of noise coming from up ahead. I'm nervous every time we reach the end of a corridor or turn into a new passage. We need to avoid confrontations as much as possible. Sure, Sawyer still has her ax—she looped it down through her belt when we were in the library—but I don't have any weapons. I don't rate my chances against knives and metal poles or whatever the hell else the inmates are arming themselves with.

We have to duck into hiding around ten times as we make our way to the staff corridor, pausing at each turn, listening for sounds of approach, then doubling back and ducking into storerooms and offices until the coast is clear again. I'm not a coward, but I'm not stupid. Trying to get past inmates when they're hyped up on blood and freedom would be like trying to reason with a kid on a sugar high. It's not happening.

"This is it," says Sawyer finally, nodding at a reinforced door.

"That leads into the staff corridor?" I ask. "You sure?"

"I was here just a few hours ago."

"Okay. So we get in there and we run. We just keep going, right? All the way to the north end of the prison. Then we find a place to lay low for a few hours."

"Think you can keep up?" she says. "It's a pretty long corridor."

There's a lightness to her tone. I look at her and see a tentative smile on her face, a look of excitement in her eyes. I get it. We're close to getting out of this. Close to reaching safety. All we have to do is make it to the other end of this corridor and then wait until the eye of the storm comes. Simple.

"I'll be fine," I say. "Don't worry about me."

She takes a deep breath and unlocks the door, then hooks the keys back on her belt and pulls the door slightly open, just enough that we can see into the corridor beyond.

Most of the lights are gone. One or two still work, casting small pools of radiance down into the darkness. The roaring of the hurricane is even louder in here. The right wall of the passage is all that stands between us and the outside world.

This isn't what I was imagining. I was thinking an empty corridor, brightly lit, still locked off from the inmates.

Stupid me.

There are entrances to each of the units along the left side of the corridor, and it looks like they've all been opened. There've definitely been inmates here. There's trash strewn everywhere, floating around in two and a half feet of water. Plants from the COs' offices, photographs, food packaging, shredded mattresses. Toilet rolls that are now mushed-up islands drift slowly around the corridor.

"So...I'm thinking maybe we don't run," I say. "Maybe a stealthy approach is called for."

"Yeah. I think you're right."

We enter the long corridor, sticking to the left wall. I can hear shouts and screams coming from inside the units, the sounds drifting back to us through the sally ports. They must all still be open. We wouldn't be able to hear so much if they were sealed tight like they should be.

We reach the door leading into Unit 1. I gently try the handle, just to check. The door moves slightly but doesn't open. It looks like it's been barricaded on the other side. There's a plastic-covered mattress blocking the window.

We keep moving. A huge expanse of darkness stretches ahead of us. The next pool of light is about a hundred yards away, a strip light that dangles from the ceiling. After that, there's a light outside what looks like Unit 3, and then another one illuminating the door that leads into the Northside section far ahead.

We keep walking. We reach the first pool of light, and as we do so, there's a shout up ahead. It isn't the usual screaming we can hear coming from the units. This is much closer. We stop moving as a man stumbles out of the door and into the light outside Unit 4. He's holding his stomach, hunched over as he tries to keep his balance.

He falls to his knees. A figure emerges behind him and wades through the water toward him.

Even from this distance, I recognize the features of Malcolm Kincaid.

"Don't move," I whisper.

We stand still. We're directly beneath the light, but I'm hoping if we don't move, we won't draw any attention.

Kincaid glances back over his shoulder. Adler and Sullivan, two of his goons from the Glasshouse, emerge into the corridor. They're followed by a guy who stands about two feet taller than them. His name's Carter. I've seen him around the prison, but have always kept my distance. The guy's got a bad rep.

Carter is holding something heavy in his hands. A hammer? No, a meat tenderizer.

Without pausing, he swings it around in a wide arc. Even from here we can hear the wet, meaty thud as it connects with the face of the man on his knees. He drops instantly into the water.

Sawyer tries to stifle a cry of shock, but she doesn't quite succeed.

Kincaid, Adler, Carter, and Sullivan all turn toward us.

Even from this distance, I lock eyes with Kincaid.

He smiles coldly, then turns his head to say something to the three men standing by his side.

I grab Sawyer's arm and shove her back toward the door. "*Now* we run."

I glance back once and see Adler, Carter, and Sullivan sprinting out of the pool of light and into the darkness. Sawyer and I run as fast as we can back to the entrance to the staff corridor, exploding back into the admin building. Sawyer pauses to fumble with her keys, but there's no time for that. I grab her and pull her after me.

Eleven
1:00 a.m.

Sawyer and I sprint back through the admin complex, once again ducking into offices and empty rooms to avoid any prisoners wandering around. Every single one of them is armed with some kind of weapon: knives and sharpened pieces of wood, metal poles salvaged from the gyms or office desks, pieces of broken glass wrapped with tape or orange material torn from prison uniforms.

We weave randomly through passages as we try to shake off Adler, Carter, and Sullivan. I'm hoping the inmates we manage to dodge will at the very least delay Kincaid's men. I'm not sure, though. Kincaid has a reputation. I don't know if any of the inmates will want to cross him.

"You think we lost them yet?" gasps Sawyer.

"No..." I wince and press on my side. I've got a killer stitch going on. "Believe me. Kincaid wants me dead. Now he's seen me, he's not going to let it go."

"Why? What's he got against you?"

"I...put him in here. When I was a cop."

"Ah...Okay. I get it."

She really doesn't.

I peer around the corner into the next corridor. Looks clear. We start moving again, splashing through the water. I keep looking over my shoulder. We've been running for a few minutes, but there's not many places to go in the admin building. Kincaid's guys can't be far behind us.

"Where are we actually going?" asks Sawyer.

"I'm thinking we head over to the inmate corridor on the west side of the building. Hopefully it's not blocked off like—"

I stop talking as we round a corner into another passage. I hear loud voices up ahead, laughing and talking in Spanish.

I grab Sawyer and rush to the closest door. It opens into a staff bathroom. We duck inside and I push the door until it's almost closed. They walk past our hiding place, joking around with each other. They're still wearing their orange prison uniforms. Two of them have white T-shirts on, while the others are bare-chested. I scan the exposed skin. Among all the other tattoos they sport, they all have ink showing a five-pointed crown. That's the symbol of the Latin Kings.

Castillo's men.

"Who is it?" whispers Sawyer.

I gently close the door. There's no point in hiding it from her. I kept quiet back in the reception so she wouldn't freak out, but she needs to know the danger we're in.

"Latin Kings," I whisper. "Castillo's men."

"Castillo?"

"The guy we pulled out of the water."

"Oh...Why are we running from him?"

"What do you mean, *why*? You think he's our friend now because we saved him?"

"Isn't he?"

"Jesus—are you really that naïve?"

"*No!*" Her voice is defensive.

"Look, any inmate in this prison is going to be after you. Either for your keys or because of...other reasons."

I look at her, make sure she understands. She does. She folds her arms over her T-shirt, trying vainly to disguise any hint of a female figure.

"Exactly. You need to stay out of sight. We both do."

I wait until the sound of Castillo's men fades away; then we exit the bathroom and keep moving west. The admin building itself isn't too wide. We should be close to the inmate corridor by now.

We're passing a corridor that branches off to our right when I hear a shout. I look over and see the massive form of Carter standing about thirty yards away. He looks to his left and shouts again.

"Over here!"

Fuck. I push Sawyer and we start to run. We only make it a few steps before the lights flicker, then suddenly wink off.

We're plunged into darkness. Sounds seem to grow louder. Sawyer's breathing. The sudden slowing of Carter splashing through the water. I hear shouts echoing around other parts of the prison.

I reach out and put my hand on Sawyer's forearm. She stiffens, almost jerks away, but I tighten my fingers and lean close to where I think her ear is.

"Move slowly."

We wade through the water carefully, so as not to make any noise. I remember the layout of the corridor. It travels ahead of us for about thirty feet, then turns right. We angle slightly until we bump up against the right wall, then use our hands to guide us to the turn.

I hear Carter shouting behind us, calling out to Adler. There's an answering call even farther into Admin, back toward the staff corridor. I'm not sure if Carter is waiting for backup, but the more distance we can put between us and them, the better.

We're moving in what I think is the general direction of the inmate corridor. It's hard to tell. We've made a few turns already, right then left, then right again. We need to keep track so we don't end up back where we started.

"You think the generator has run out of gas?" asks Sawyer.

"Shouldn't have. It's supposed to last at least twelve hours."

I've barely finished speaking when the lights flare to life. A few of the strip lights pop at the surge of power, dropping sections of the corridor back into darkness. I hear Carter shouting again. Voices respond—Adler and Sullivan, I assume. All three are much closer than I want them to be, and I hear the sounds of splashing feet as they give chase again.

We run. There are doors all along the hallway, but I skip the first couple, not wanting to make it obvious where we've gone.

"Next one!"

Sawyer grabs the door and shoves it open. I follow her in and slam it shut behind me, quickly turning around to see where we are.

It's a staff cafeteria. Tables and benches are bolted to the floor. On the far side of the room are serving counters, and just to the left of them, the door into the kitchen.

Felix sits at one of the tables, calmly eating a huge plate of fries. I look at him in amazement.

"Felix?"

"Constantine! My man. Glad to see you're alive. Wasn't sure you were gonna make it." He points a sauce-covered fry at me. "But you're a survivor. I always said that."

Felix's orange jumpsuit is torn, covered in blood. He has cuts and bruises on his face and makeshift bandages around his forearm and bicep.

"You okay there?"

He glances down at his wounds and shrugs. "It got a bit dicey, I won't lie to you. I had to kill a couple of people. Protection, you know? Had to do it in front of some of the others too. Show them I'm not to be fucked with. Seems a few of them forgot in all the excitement." He dips a fry in a dessert bowl of ketchup, then pops it into his mouth. He leans back and looks appraisingly at Sawyer. "You going to introduce me to your friend?"

"Sawyer, this is Felix."

She looks at me with wide eyes. "This is the guy you said was your only friend?"

Felix throws a surprised look in my direction. "You said that?"

"Uh...yeah. But I'd nearly just died. You can't hold me to it."

"You soft motherfucker."

"Listen," I say urgently, "we're heading to the Glasshouse. Sawyer has a keycard to get out of the Northside staff room. We're going to wait till the eye of the storm passes over, then head for shelter. You in? Because I really don't think this place is going to last."

"This is very true." He squints at me thoughtfully. "How you planning on getting to the staff room?"

"The inmate corridor," says Sawyer quickly.

Felix shakes his head. "No chance. It's gone."

My stomach sinks. "Gone? What do you mean, gone?"

"Gone. As in absent. Not there. Vanished. Kaput. It has ceased to be."

"How?" asks Sawyer.

"How you think? Same reason you saying this place isn't going to last. The hurricane destroyed it. Heard some people talking. They said it came down the same time A Wing was taken out."

Shit. My mind races. There has to be another way.

"Constantine."

I glance over at Sawyer.

"Kincaid's guys?"

Christ, yeah. "Felix, we need to get out of here. Kincaid and his boys are after me."

"Right. Just let me finish these."

"Felix. For fuck's sake..."

"Calm your pants, man. *Fine.*"

He gets to his feet just as the door slams open and Adler, Carter, and Sullivan enter the cafeteria.

I exchange a brief glance with Felix and Sawyer; then we all turn and sprint toward the kitchen at the back of the cafeteria. I leap over the closest table, sliding across the top and landing in the water, still moving.

We burst through the open doorway. The kitchen is a large square room, red bricks laid into the floor, black-and-white tiles, stainless-steel worktops and huge ovens with gas stovetops around the walls.

I grab Sawyer's ax from her. She doesn't protest, but keeps moving. I take a step to the side of the door and swing the ax in a wide arc. It connects with Adler's midriff as he sprints into the kitchen. I feel it cut through his jumpsuit, slice through the skin, and dig deep into his stomach. I twist and pull it out again.

Adler gives out a weird burp, an expulsion of air and pain, and staggers to a stop, staring down at his own intestines as they loop slowly out of his stomach, spooling in the water like sausages thrown into a pot.

Carter and Sullivan barge into the back of him, shoving him forward. Adler drops to his knees. I swing the ax over my head, aiming for Carter, but he sees it coming and raises his arm, blocking the shaft before it can connect.

I hold on. We stand frozen, both pulling as hard as we can. Carter raises his other hand and hits me in the face. He loosens his grip on the ax as he does so, but so do I. It splashes into the water as I stagger back, trying to evade Carter's punches.

We move deeper into the kitchen. I keep my arms raised to protect my face, but more and more blows are landing. I hit up against the kitchen counter and attempt to fight back, but every time I lash out, Carter uses the gap to land a blow. The guy has boxing training. I haven't.

Then suddenly Carter stiffens, his eyes going wide. I straighten up, see Felix standing to the side. He's just rammed a knife into Carter's ribs. I'm not sure if he had it all this time or found it in the kitchen.

Doesn't matter either way. Carter roars and slams his elbow into Felix's face. Carter is big, even bigger than Felix, and Felix goes down, hitting the water and slamming his head hard on the tiles.

Carter lumbers toward Felix. I go after him, reaching out to twist the knife still sticking out of his side. But just as my fingers graze the handle, Sullivan grabs the collar of my prison uniform and yanks me back. The material digs sharply into my throat. It feels like someone has rabbit-punched me in the larynx. I'm jerked off my feet and land on my back, breath exploding from my lungs.

Sullivan drops to the ground behind me, wrapping his arms almost gently around my throat.

I gasp for breath, but I can't get any air into my lungs. I reach up and grab Sullivan's head, pull him closer by his ears. He tries to jerk away, but I hold on, crabbing my fingers around his face until I find his eyes.

I dig my thumbs in, pushing as hard as I can. Sullivan screams, his grip loosening. I smash my head back into his face. He cries out again and lets go. I lunge forward and stagger to my feet.

Sullivan is on his feet too, lurching around blindly. I grab him and slam his head as hard as I can into the metal countertop. He drops immediately.

I turn around and see Sawyer trying to pull Carter away from Felix. She looks tiny next to him. Carter turns casually toward her, grabs her hair and uses it to toss her sideways. She slams into the oven. She tries to steady herself, then cries out in pain and snatches her hands away. The gas rings are burning and a pot of oil still sits on the heat. Felix and his French fries.

Sawyer grabs the pot and spins around with it, throwing the whole lot into Carter's face.

Carter screams in agony as the boiling oil coats his skin. His face and neck instantly turn red, angry welts and blisters flaring up. He staggers back. His eyes have gray-white films over them. He carries on screaming, arms outstretched, flailing around. Sawyer is pressed up against the counter, trying to avoid his swinging arms.

I dart forward and pull the knife out of Carter's ribs, then jam it into the back of his neck. His screams stop and he drops into the water.

I grab Sawyer. By this time Felix is back on his feet, and we hurry back to the cafeteria.

We lurch to a stop in the kitchen doorway. More inmates have entered the cafeteria. Latin Kings. Fuck. I turn back, Felix and Sawyer following suit, and head for the door that leads out of the kitchen.

The Kings come after us. I let Felix and Sawyer move ahead; then I lean behind one of the ovens and grab the gas hose. I yank it out of the canister, hearing the hiss of escaping gas.

I sprint after Felix and Sawyer. They've already vanished through the door into the corridor beyond. I skid out of the kitchen, slamming up against the wall, then turning back and yanking the door shut.

"Run!"

We make it about ten paces before the escaping gas meets the lit stove burners and the explosion hits.

The kitchen door flies off and slams against the wall, embedding itself into the concrete. A fireball explodes out of the room, rolling into the hallway and surging both ways along the corridor, stopping just short of us. Smoke billows out after the flames, thick clouds rising to the ceiling.

Then the sprinklers kick off, drenching us even more than we already are, pattering softly into the calf-deep water, falling from the ceiling like a fine spring shower.

We move away from the kitchen, looking for a place to regroup. If both corridors are out of action, it means the only way we can get to the north side of the facility is to go directly *through* each of the prison units. The four Gen Pop units will be bad enough, but what about the Mental Health Unit? The Administrative Control Unit? What the hell has been going on in there since the cell doors were opened?

There's a lot of mess around us. Toilet paper floating on the water, blood, even what looks like shit smeared on the wall.

Up ahead we hear the sound of splashing feet. Jesus Christ. Not again.

"Fight?" asks Felix.

"I don't have any weapons. You?"

He clenches his fists and raises them. "Only these babies."

"Jesus, Felix. Seriously?"

"What? You don't think these are lethal weapons?"

"I think even you would have a hard time stopping a knife with your fist."

Sawyer has already pulled open the closest door. We head inside and I listen through the wood. And it *is* wood. Thin. Cheap. Not reinforced. Pointless even bothering to lock it.

I hear the splashing sounds approaching. Then people speaking.

"I'm telling you, I heard voices."

"Could have been anyone."

"Yeah. And it could have been them."

There's a pause, and then the sound of someone approaching through the water. "Castillo wants an update," says another voice.

"Ramirez, this is impossible, man. We've had to fight off, like, five ambushes already. There's no way we'll find them."

"Castillo wants them, so you keep looking. I don't give a shit how many motherfuckers you have to fight. Understand?"

"Waste of fucking time." The voice sounds sullen.

There's a splash and a cry of surprise. Then something slams into the door, throwing it open so it slams into my head. I stagger back and look up in shock. The massive guy I saw back in reception talking to Castillo and Silas is standing in the doorway, holding one of the Kings up by his neck. He must have slammed the guy into the door.

I'm assuming this is Ramirez. He smiles at me, showing uncomfortably small teeth.

"Hey there," he says.

★

There are seven other Latin Kings with Ramirez. Even Felix knows those are bad odds. We allow—well, we don't have much choice, do we?—them to lead us through the corridors until we reach a set of double doors.

Ramirez pushes them open and steps inside. We follow and find ourselves in one of the staff gyms.

It doesn't look like it has ever been state-of-the-art, but right now it's a mess. Rusted dumbbells are strewn across the floor, some of them sitting in pools of blood that blossom around them like ink stains in the water. The benches have been pulled apart, the legs and metal supports probably used for weapons. There are a few old weight machines scattered around, a shoulder press, a rowing machine, that kind of thing.

The changing rooms are off to the left. Two separate doors for men and women.

"Boss!" shouts Ramirez.

A moment later, Castillo emerges from the men's changing room. He breaks into a grin when he sees us.

"My friends! I'm so happy to see you all. You ran off without giving me a chance to say thank you."

More of his men exit the changing rooms and join the others who escorted us here. They're all carrying weapons: knives, poles, pieces of broken wood. By the time the stream of bodies stops, twenty or so Latin Kings surround us. I glance nervously at Sawyer. She's looking scared. Her face is pale, eyes cast down to the water. I can feel the tension in the air, see the inmates throwing hungry looks at her. Felix, God bless his twisted soul, steps closer to her, glares around at the Kings. I said he was an okay guy. He's never hurt a woman, as far as I know. Only three cops and a hotshot hostage who tried to rush him when he was robbing a bank.

"No need to thank us," I say. "Just doing our civic duty."

Castillo doesn't answer me. He's looking straight at Sawyer. "I think congratulations are in order. I don't know how you've managed to avoid the attentions of some of the...*hungrier* inmates, but here you are. Still walking and breathing."

Sawyer tenses up even more. Castillo senses it. "Relax. I'm not after you. But I have to admit, those keys you've got there. They *really* caught my attention."

I glance down at Sawyer's belt, at the sheriff's keys. Castillo steps forward. I try to get in front of him, but Ramirez grabs me from behind, pushing down on my shoulders so I can't move.

Sawyer finally looks up, holding Castillo's gaze.

"I saw you use them when you opened up A Wing," says Castillo. He reaches out and slowly unclips the keys from Sawyer's belt. She stiffens, but doesn't otherwise move.

Castillo holds eye contact with her the entire time. There's something obscene about it. Something in his expression. I struggle against Ramirez, but he just digs his fingers deeper into my shoulders. Felix glances at me, unsure. I give a small shake of the head. No point in making a move yet. We'll be killed.

Castillo holds the keys up and examines them. He sees the name tag dangling from the ring. "Sheriff Montoya's keys," he says happily. Then he frowns mock seriously at Sawyer. "You shouldn't have these, young lady. They're likely to be very dangerous in the wrong hands. Tell you what, I'll hold on to them. Make sure the sheriff gets them back, okay?"

Sawyer doesn't respond.

"I said, *okay?*"

Castillo stares at Sawyer until she nods. It doesn't seem enough for him, so she clears her throat. "Okay."

"Good. Glad that's cleared up. You should actually be thanking me. After all, I'm only doing my civic duty, right, Constantine?"

"They don't operate the outside doors," says Sawyer quickly. "You can't use them to escape."

"Perhaps. But you know what they *can* do? They can open the door into the armory."

Sawyer throws a look of alarm in my direction. Fuck. I hadn't even thought of that.

Castillo nods, a huge grin on his face. "Yeah? Pretty smart, huh?"

He throws the keys at me. Ramirez lets go of my shoulder and I just manage to catch them. I look at Castillo in surprise.

"Here's what I want you to do," he says. "You and Ramirez go to the armory. Bring back everything you can carry. And for fuck's sake, lock it behind you, okay? I don't want no one else getting guns."

"Why the fuck would I do *any* of that?"

"Because I'm going to keep your friends here until you come back."

Sawyer's eyes widen.

"No," I say. "No chance."

"You either do it or I slice open both their stomachs right here and you can watch them bleed out. Then I'll start cutting off parts of your body."

I hesitate, glancing between Felix and Sawyer. Christ, I've got no choice. If I refuse, he'll just kill us all.

"If I do this, will you let us go?"

Castillo laughs. "You really think you're in a position to negotiate?"

"Not really. But what good are we to you? You want to settle grudges with guns, that's your deal. You want to wipe out the other gangs, go for it. We just want to get out of the way and ride out the storm."

Castillo thinks about it, then nods. "Okay. Sure. You get my guns and maybe I'll let you go."

"Nobody touches Sawyer," I say.

Castillo looks hurt. "My friend, what kind of a degenerate

do you take me for? The woman will be safe. As long as you bring the guns back."

Ramirez grins, showing his tiny teeth again. He gives me a gentle shove, almost sending me on my ass.

"Let's go, little man."

I follow him out of the gym, wondering if I'll see Felix or Sawyer alive again.

Twelve

1:30 a.m.

I follow a step or two behind Ramirez, making sure not to crowd him but also not falling so far back that he thinks I'm trying to lose him. There's something about the guy, a constant low-key buzz of barely suppressed violence that I do *not* want to be on the receiving end of. I could maybe defend myself, but I have the feeling if I tried to land a punch, this guy could turn my fists into Jell-O by squashing them between two fingers.

He's resting his meat cleaver casually against his shoulder as he walks. There's a genuine spring in his step, as if he's actually having a good time.

He glances back at me with a grin. "I feel like that guy. What's his name?"

I shake my head. "No idea."

"You do, man! The guy with the mask." Ramirez holds the cleaver up in the air.

"Michael Myers?" I venture. "Jason?"

"Yeah! Jason! Him." He turns and comes at me in a stiff-legged walk, the cleaver raised to strike. I'm proud of myself for not just turning and running, because that sight is pretty fucking terrifying.

He lowers the weapon and chuckles again. "Maybe when we get out of here, I'll audition. They're always remaking that shit, you know? Maybe I've got a new career ahead of me. It'll be hard not to hurt the actors, though. You get so used to finishing people off, and then you have to pretend with that shit? Play make-believe? Not gonna be easy."

We make our way through the prison toward the armory. Normally I'd be ducking between rooms, hiding from sight until other inmates pass by. But we've now encountered four or five different groups of prisoners, and they've all taken one look at Ramirez and walked the other way. I briefly consider asking him to come with Sawyer, Felix, and myself to the Glasshouse, but I don't think that's a good idea. He'll tell Castillo, and I don't want to have to deal with that bastard while we try to find our way to safety.

And while I finally get my revenge.

Sawyer's given me another chance. If she hadn't let me out of my room in the infirmary, I'd be dead. Wright and Tully would be...well, they'd still be alive. Not sure how long for. But that's not the point. I have another chance to avenge Amy. To avenge our child.

And maybe I'll even survive the night. Who knows? Maybe after the storm passes over, I can just walk out of here. I'm sure a lot of the inmates have the same idea, but none of them have Sawyer on their side.

Revenge. Survival. Freedom. Things I never thought I'd get another chance at. The hurricane has brought them all to me. They're all within my grasp.

I think about outside. Where would I go? I've never given it any thought, mainly because I didn't care. I knew I wasn't going to see the other side of the prison walls for another ten to fifteen years, but now...now the thought of the future worms its way into my mind. I can maybe live again. Once I've gotten rid of Wright and Tully, I can start over. Let Amy rest now that she's had justice.

It would mean living off the grid. Getting my hands on fake ID, a new Social Security number, that kind of thing. Shouldn't be too hard. You get to know people when you're a cop. People who can help with that kind of thing.

'Course, all that depends on me surviving the night.

I bring myself back to the present. Water trickles down the

walls, forming small rivulets and streams that add to the rising floodwater. It's above my calves now. I do a quick calculation and I don't like the answer.

"The water's rising fast," I say.

"Hadn't noticed."

"It's gone up a foot in the past half hour."

Ramirez doesn't say anything.

"If it carries on like this, we'll be under six feet of water in three hours."

"Lucky I'm six-five."

"Seriously, man. This place is flooding fast."

"Look, just shut up, okay? Castillo says we gotta get the guns, so we get the guns."

"You always do what you're told?"

Ramirez spins around, his freakishly small teeth bared. "The fuck's your problem, man? You want me to just cut your throat, tell Castillo you got taken down?"

I raise my hands in the air. "Hey, man. Chill."

"Don't fucking tell me to chill!" he shouts. "I don't like it when people tell me to chill!"

"Jesus. Okay! Fine! Just...lead the way."

I gesture ahead, hoping he'll just turn around and carry on walking. He doesn't. He stares at me for a long-drawn-out moment.

I watch warily. I can almost see the thoughts running through his head, trying to decide if it would be easier to just get rid of me now. Finally, with a muttered "*Prick*," he turns and sets off again, kicking through the water like a spoiled kid.

I need to be more careful. Especially if there's a chance I could get out of here.

Ramirez throws a look over his shoulder. "What the fuck are you waiting for?" he shouts. "You want me to come back there?"

I set off after him. Ramirez shakes his head in disgust, then turns and wades through the water again.

We've been walking for another few minutes when Ramirez

snarls suddenly and rushes into a side passage. He moves surprisingly fast for such a big guy. It reminds me of the burst of speed a hippo puts on when it attacks.

I follow him, wondering what's set him off now, and am shocked to see him dragging Henry through the water by his leg. Henry's the old guy I work with in the maintenance shed, fixing all the broken shit in the prison. He's coughing and spluttering, water washing over his face, going up his nose, into his mouth.

I rush in and shove Ramirez. It's like trying to shove a house.

"The fuck are you doing?"

"He was going to attack us."

"He's like a hundred years old!"

Ramirez looks down at Henry and reluctantly drops his leg. I help him up. Henry is almost comically pleased to see me. He grabs me by the shoulders, squinting shortsightedly into my face.

"Jack? Is that you?"

"It's me."

He pulls me into a hug. "Oh, sweet Jesus. I never thought I'd be happy to see your ugly face."

"What the hell are you doing out here?"

"Yeah." Ramirez frowns. "You sure you weren't attacking us?"

Henry glares at him. "What's your problem? Does it take a while for the blood to reach your brain? I'm seventy-seven years old." He glares at me. "Not a hundred."

"Not really important right now, Henry. What *are* you doing out here?"

"Trying to stay alive."

"And you think walking around the corridors of Admin is the best way to do that?"

"I'm looking for a place to hide. Anyway, Admin is probably the safest place in the prison."

I frown. "Explain."

"Admin is...no-man's-land. As soon as you get into the

units, it's fucking insane. The gangs are going at it, Kincaid's doing his thing, acting like Emperor Nero. Fucking Preacher and his psychopathic followers are running around everywhere cutting people's heads off. The Kings, the Bloods, the Crips, the Ñetas, they're all set on proving to each other who's the strongest."

Wonderful. Sawyer, Felix, and I have to find our way through all that. "So do you have somewhere in mind? Or are you just going to wander around until you see something that catches your eye? I mean, if you don't know where you're going, you can come with us—"

"No he fucking can't," growls Ramirez.

Henry ignores him. "I appreciate the offer, but I don't really like the company you're keeping, Jack. I think the best thing for me is to stay as far away as possible from you and your pet gorilla."

Ramirez takes a threatening step toward him. Henry yelps and runs back along the corridor. Ramirez watches him go with a look of disgust, then turns and starts walking again.

About five minutes later, we're approaching the corridor and sally port that leads into Unit 1, the first of the four General Population units.

We pause outside and listen. I can hear screaming. A *lot* of screaming. And objects hitting against metal, the sound echoing out along the passage.

It sounds like Henry was right. It's chaos in there.

We move on, heading deeper into Admin. According to Sawyer's map, the armory's only a few corridors away now. Our pace picks up. I don't know about Ramirez, but I want this over and done with as soon as possible. I feel totally exposed walking around like this. Kincaid might have sent his other goons to look for me. In fact, I'm sure he has. It's just a matter of time until they find me.

As we turn into yet another featureless corridor, Ramirez

freezes and throws a hand up for silence. I open my mouth to ask what he's doing, but his glare causes the words to wither and die on my tongue.

A moment later, I hear it. Approaching footsteps slapping through the water, accompanied by a *lot* of voices.

The corridor is empty. Nowhere to go. I run ahead and peer around the corner. Nobody there, but I can hear the voices approaching from around the next turn.

There are doors in the corridor I'm looking into. I gesture for Ramirez to follow me and run for a door about ten feet away. I hear his raspy breath behind me, hear the voices and footsteps approaching up ahead.

I grab the door handle and turn.

Locked.

"Oh, fucking *excellent*," says Ramirez.

We sprint back the way we came.

"*Hey!*"

I keep running, but throw a quick look over my shoulder. I see about five black guys with their scrubs cut off at the waist and one of their prison uniform legs rolled up. I catch a quick glimpse of the letters *MOB* tattooed on a few of them. Another has a picture of a dog paw. These guys are the Bloods, and they do *not* get on with the Latin Kings.

"Hey, man, who the fuck are you?" calls one of them.

"Keep moving," growls Ramirez.

"That's the cop!" shouts another of the voices. "Hey, come back here, little piggy. I'm talkin' to you!"

We sprint around the corner—

—and skid to a stop.

There are another ten inmates standing in front of us. They are a mixture of races—black, white, and Latino—but they all have one thing in common: a small crucifix tattoo on their necks. The man in the middle—a black guy, around fifty, bald, with a neat gray beard—is wearing a chaplain's uniform. A black shirt with the white collar and everything.

He steps forward with a disarming smile. "And what do we have here?" he says. "Visitors?" He glances at the inmates behind him. "What did I say, my people? I said ask the Lord and He will provide."

There's a noise behind us. I look back and see the Bloods sprint around the corner. They pull up short when they see what's going on, then immediately turn and run back the way they came.

Ramirez and I exchange worried looks. That can't be good.

"Ignore them," says the guy dressed up as a chaplain. "They are unbelievers. They fear me because I am armed with righteousness and holy vengeance."

"Amen," say the inmates behind him.

"Amen indeed. For is today not Judgment Day? Is today not the day when it will be determined whether you lived a life of righteousness or wickedness?"

The guys behind him all nod and murmur in agreement.

"And does it not say in Corinthians, 'Judge nothing before the appointed time; wait until the Lord comes. He will bring to light what is hidden in darkness and will expose the motives of the heart. At that time each will receive their praise from God!'"

"*Amen!*" shout the inmates behind him.

I'm starting to get a very bad feeling about this.

"And *I* must expose the darkness in the heart," he says, raising his voice with every word until he's shouting. "*For am I not the Preacher?*"

Fuck...

"Shit," mutters Ramirez.

This is the psycho serial killer who's supposed to be locked up in ACU. The one who tortured young couples in the murder room beneath his church and ate their remains.

"I see by the looks on your faces that you've heard of me," says Preacher. "This is good. It will save time. Now, will you submit to my judgment?"

"Not really a believer in an imaginary man in the clouds," I say.

"God doesn't give a flying fuck whether you believe or not, my child. And you should watch your tone, for it says in Matthew 12:36 that 'everyone will have to give account on the day of judgment for every empty word they have spoken.'"

"So we're being judged for empty words?" I say. "Like lies and shit?"

"Indeed."

"And how's that going for *you*?" I ask.

"The fuck are you doing?" mutters Ramirez.

I ignore him.

"My words are not empty. But even if they were, I am exempt," says Preacher. "For I am His instrument. All must confess to me. Lying will only bring pain. 'For God will bring every deed into judgment, including every hidden thing, whether it is good or evil.'"

"Right. And who exactly are you to judge? Didn't you spend your spare time carving up young kids and eating them?"

"I was doing God's will. 'For He has set a day when He will judge the world with justice by the man He has appointed.' Acts 17:31. *I* am that man. *I* am the tool of His righteous fury."

"Good for you. Everyone needs a hobby."

I sense a blur of movement in my peripheral vision. Then I see Ramirez's cleaver spinning through the air, heading straight for Preacher's face.

Preacher ducks to the side. The machete hits one of his followers right in the forehead, burying itself deep in his skull.

All eyes are on him as he hits the water.

There's a splashing sound behind me. I turn and see Ramirez sprinting away up the corridor.

Fuck.

I follow him, but he has a head start, and like I said before, he's fast for such a big guy. I sprint along the corridor, turn into another passage, then duck into the next. I've already lost sight of Ramirez. I can hear the sounds of pursuit close behind me, Preacher and his followers coming to...do whatever it is they do. Carve us up. Crucify us. Eat us. Sodomize our corpses. Whatever it is that priests enjoy doing on their days off.

I try the first door I pass. Locked. I try the next. It opens into a small staff break room. I duck inside and quickly close the door, listening while the running footsteps approach and then move on past. I breathe a sigh of relief, leaning my forehead against the door.

Think. What's the plan?

Ditch Ramirez? No. I can't. I can't leave Sawyer and Felix with Castillo. He'll kill them both.

Okay. First things first. A weapon. I head across the tiny room and yank open the drawers. All the cutlery is gone. I open the fridge. I don't know what I was expecting to see in there. Maybe a knife stuck in a jar of mayo or something. But it's empty.

Wait...

Ramirez's meat cleaver. It could still be there.

I open the door a crack. It's clear. I leave the staff room behind and run back to where we encountered Preacher. The body's still lying in the water, the cleaver stuck in the guy's skull. I yank it out, then move in the direction of the armory, hoping that Ramirez will find his way there and we can get this over with.

I'm almost there when I hear the shouting coming from up ahead. I round a corner to find four guys hanging off Ramirez. *Literally* hanging off him. One has his arms around the big man's neck, trying his best to cut off his air supply. Two more hang on his arms, and the other one is on the floor, trying to yank Ramirez's leg out from under him. It's like watching kids trying to tackle the Incredible Hulk.

There's no sign of Preacher or his followers. These are Crips attacking Ramirez. I can see by the tattoos. One has *211* inked onto his shoulder. Another has the numbers *3 18 9 16*. They spell out the word "Crip" in that stupid alphabet-number code you used as a kid.

The Crips hear me coming. The guy holding on to Ramirez's leg stands up, wiping water from his face. He comes right at me, arms wide as if ready to take me into a bear hug.

It's a stupid stance to take. It leaves him completely open. I've kept the cleaver behind my back, but as soon as the guy comes within reach, I lash out, cutting his hand off at the wrist.

We both stare at the stump in a split second of surprise. I didn't think the cleaver was anywhere near as sharp as that. Blood gushes into the water and the guy starts screaming,

The other three are distracted by his wailing. Ramirez shakes the two guys off his arms and then slams up against the wall, crushing the guy on his back between his body and the concrete.

The guy releases Ramirez's neck and he spins around and wraps his huge hands around the Crip's throat, squeezing until I hear the crack of breaking vertebrae.

The other two Crips overcome their shock and launch themselves at him. I run toward them. I swing the cleaver and hit the closest in the spine. He screams and arches backward. I keep hold of the handle and yank the blade free. The guy drops face-first into the water, paralyzed and drowning.

Ramirez punches the final Crip in the throat. The guy drops into the water with a crushed larynx, gurgling and gasping for breath.

Ramirez turns to me. His chest is heaving. His face is covered in blood and sweat, his eyes dark like a shark's. He holds a hand out.

I'm not arguing with that. I pass him the cleaver.

At the exact same moment, Preacher and his congregation of psychotics appear in the corridor behind us.

"This way!" I shout.

Ramirez follows me as I sprint toward the armory, Preacher and his men hot on our tail.

Ramirez might be fast, but I'm definitely quicker when we take off at the same time. I skid into the corridor where the armory is located. There are lots of doors here, but most of them stand open. Only one remains closed, and it looks heavy, made from metal.

As I reach it, I glance back and see Preacher's guys closing on Ramirez. I fumble with the keys. Jesus. Why the fuck are there so many? I try the first one. It doesn't fit. Ramirez shouts behind me. I risk a glance to my right, see Preacher's men attempting to beat him down with metal poles and...is that a crucifix? They're beating him with a fucking crucifix.

Ramirez, for his part, is flailing around with the cleaver. He hits one of his attackers in the chest. The guy drops backward into the water, blood spreading out around him. Ramirez then whirls around and slices the cleaver against another of his attackers, shearing away a thick chunk of skin from his arm. The man screams and falls back, stumbling against the wall. Ramirez roars with laughter.

"Come on, then! Get on your knees and pray to me, bitches!"

I try the next key. Nothing. Same with the next, and the next.

The next key, though. The next key opens it. Fucking finally! I yank open the heavy door and dart inside.

I'm greeted by a neat, clean room with three rows of guns mounted along the wall. The top row holds semiautomatic rifles, the second row shotguns, and the bottom row handguns. A locked cabinet covered with thick metal mesh is packed with boxes of ammunition.

I duck my head out of the room. *"Ramirez!"*

I put the key in the inside lock and wait while Ramirez sprints toward me, Preacher's men close behind. I push the heavy door, timing it so that he's just able to slide through the gap. Immediately Preacher's men slam up against the door, arms flailing around inside the room as they try to force it open.

Ramirez whirls around and swings the cleaver in a frenzied attack. I turn away as hot blood spatters my face.

The weight against the door lessens briefly and I manage to slam it shut. I quickly turn the key and then stagger back, watching Ramirez warily.

The guy is covered in blood, his face dripping. He sucks in ragged gasps of air as he stands there, still clutching the cleaver in his hand.

"You good?" I ask.

Ramirez turns to take in the rows of guns. "Yeah," he says. "I am now."

I follow his gaze. I have to admit, the sight of the guns *is* comforting. I've been around weapons most of my adult life. First as a cop, then as a soldier, then as a cop again. Seeing them now makes me feel like I'll finally be able to protect myself properly. Maybe stay alive long enough to get to Wright and Tully. To escape.

The guns are held in place by a metal rack locked down by a thick chain and padlock. Ramirez makes short work of the padlock with repeated strikes of his cleaver, doing the same for the lock holding the ammo cage shut.

I take down one of the semiautomatic rifles. A Ruger Mini-14. Not bad. I used them in training. They're pretty old now, and I much preferred the M4 carbine, or even the M16, but the Mini is okay. Looks like they come with thirty-round magazines.

I turn my attention to the shotguns: Remington 870 Magnums with magazine extension tubes mounted below the barrel to give you an extra two or three rounds. The handguns are Beretta M9s, guns I've used my whole adult life.

Ramirez yanks open the ammo cage and we start loading bullets into the Ruger magazines. He finds a couple of heavy-duty canvas bags and packs the rifles away, one after another, as we load each magazine to capacity.

We keep going until he can barely lift the bag, then start

loading the second with shotguns, sliding the cartridges in, one after another, before packing them away.

I keep back a couple of guns, ready to load up around my person. I don't know if Ramirez will have a problem with it, but I'll cross that bridge when I come to it. I keep a Ruger and shove an M9 in my pocket. It's not comfortable, but knowing what's waiting on the other side of the door, comfort is the last thing I need to worry about.

We're finally ready. Ramirez lifts the heaviest bag himself and leaves the one crammed with shotguns and M9s to me. I slip the two carry handles over my shoulders, carrying it like a backpack. Then I put the strap of one of the shotguns over my right shoulder, letting the gun rest up against the bag, and pick up the Ruger.

I can feel the adrenaline surging through my system now. My whole body is buzzing.

"You ready?" asks Ramirez.

"Ready."

I move to the door and crouch down.

"What the hell are you doing?"

"Staying low so you don't shoot me in the back of the head."

"Oh. Right."

I quietly unlock the door and take the keys out, slipping them into my pocket. Ramirez counts to three using his fingers and then yanks the door open.

I tense, but there's nobody waiting on the other side. I wait, breathing slow and calm, every sense straining to pinpoint the enemy. I can feel Ramirez's hulking form behind me. Can hear his erratic breathing, impatient, hungry for blood.

I move forward, still squatting. I edge the shotgun out and around the doorway.

The corridor is empty.

"Clear," I say.

Ramirez knees me in the back. Not too hard, but enough to push me off balance.

"Keys."

I stand up. He's holding out his hand. I hand them over and he locks the door behind us, dropping the keys into his pocket.

He brings his Ruger up to his shoulder. "Let's go kill some Bible-bashers."

Thirteen

2:00 a.m.

It feels like I'm back in Marjah.

The gun feels familiar, reassuring. It even *smells* comforting. Oil, metal, the faint tinge of gunpowder. I can almost hear the shouts of my unit, moving from burnt-out building to burnt-out building, villages hiding enemies around every corner. Shoot on sight, don't pause, keep moving. Don't look. That's the trick. Don't stop and look at what you've done. Who you shot. Because there are mistakes. There are always mistakes. But that's war. You can't stop. You do, you die.

Ramirez and I move slowly along the corridor outside the armory. I'm to the left, Ramirez to the right. I let my training take over. I've not felt this calm since Amy's death. Move slowly. Long, even strides, swing around the corner, eyes moving with the barrel. An extension of who I am. Slow breathing. Eyes focused.

Another empty corridor.

No. I can hear something. I raise my arm, palm out toward Ramirez. He stops walking. I glance sidelong at him, gesture with two fingers toward the next turn in the corridor and start to move. Slowly. Breathe in, breathe out. Calm.

I can just see Ramirez in my periphery, but I concentrate on the turn up ahead. As I get closer, I crouch down. It's a simple thing, but people expect you to be at head height. The split second it takes for them to adjust to a new target can be the difference between taking the enemy down and being shot in the face.

I pause three feet from the turn. I wait. Listening. I hear the sound of slow footsteps moving through the water. One person, trying to stay quiet.

I move to the wall, then quickly swing around the corner.

I instantly lower the gun and straighten up from my crouch. It's Henry.

"Henry? What the fuck are you doing?"

Ramirez appears around the corner, his gun still raised. I push the barrel down so it's pointed away from the old man.

"Where did you get guns?" he asks in amazement.

"Never mind that. What are you doing here?"

"Are you following us?" growls Ramirez.

"No. I'm just trying to find a good place to hole up. Like you said I should."

"Fuck this guy," says Ramirez. "Come on. We need to get back to Castillo."

He turns and moves down the corridor, heading back in the direction of the gym.

"Look, just find a room and stay hidden, okay?" I say, keeping one eye on Ramirez as he wades toward the end of the corridor.

"I will. Soon as I find..."

I'm not listening anymore. I'm staring at Ramirez.

He's stopped just before the corridor turns to the left. His head is tilted slightly. Listening.

Shit.

I start moving. Henry says something, but I don't hear it. Ramirez sprints around the corner—

—and the shooting starts.

The noise is deafening, the explosive crack of the Ruger rounds echoing back along the corridor. I pause at the corner, then quickly peer into the passage beyond.

I'm looking into a scene of chaos.

Most of Preacher's crew lie dead in the water. There's blood spatter all across the walls. Smoke drifts through the air, the smell of cordite strong in my nostrils.

Henry appears by my side. "Jesus..." he whispers. We both enter the corridor, staring in shock at what Ramirez has done.

One of the wounded pushes himself up and tries to limp away. Ramirez shoots him in the back, then ejects the clip and rams a fresh one home, turning to me with a huge grin on his face.

"You see that?" he says, slightly out of breath. "Man, they just burst. Like pumpkins or something."

Henry steps forward. "Are you fucking insane?" he shouts. "You can't just—"

Ramirez shoots him in the chest.

Henry's small body flies back about three feet and hits the water. I turn, rush toward him, but I know it's too late. His sightless eyes stare up at the ceiling.

"Call me a fucking gorilla," mutters Ramirez.

My mind blanks out. I drag my gaze away from Henry, straighten up—

—and shoot Ramirez.

I do it almost casually, firing as I lift the gun to aim. The bullets hit him in the stomach and stitch a jagged line up his chest and sideways along his neck and into the wall.

He doesn't even have time to look shocked. He tilts slowly sideways, his face hitting the wall with a wet slap. He slides downward and lands in an awkward heap in the water.

I stare at him for a long moment.

I didn't plan that. It was instinct. But as I stare at the bodies floating in the floodwater, it makes me realize something.

We're *all* going to die here tonight.

It's a gut feeling. Intuition. I don't know if it will be the inmates or the hurricane that will kill everyone, but one way or another, I don't think any of the people trapped in this prison will be alive this time tomorrow.

I'm not getting out of here. I'm not visiting Amy's grave. I'm not getting a chance to say good-bye. It was stupid to even think it would go down like that. I can see that now.

One way or another, I'm going to die tonight. We all are.

And you know what? If that's the case, fine. The only thing I care about is getting the bastards who killed my wife.

Which means I *need* to get to the Glasshouse. No matter what. Not for protection. Let Sawyer tell herself that if it helps. I need to get there to kill Wright and Tully. Before the hurricane kills us all. Before I get shot. Before a wall falls on me or I get struck by lightning. I want them dead at *my* hands. Not the storm. I'm going to be the one who kills them, and they're going to look me in the eyes as I do it. There's no being careful now. It's all about getting to Northside. Getting through anyone who tries to stop me.

I feel a surge of relief at the realization, something that surprises me. There's no fear. No existential dread. I'm going to die tonight. Yes. But not before I've accomplished my goal. There is a feeling of uncomplicated happiness at the thought. I've never had my life defined so simply, and for some reason it fills me with a joy I haven't felt in years. I'm sure my shrink would have a field day with that, but I couldn't give a shit. I feel energized. *Free.*

My eyes fall on the bag of guns Ramirez was carrying. I already have my own. I can't carry two bags and defend myself at the same time.

There are doors on either side of the corridor. I try the first. An office. I move to the second and find a small closet filled with cleaning supplies. Bleach and tile cleaner, mops and towels.

I drag Ramirez's bag into the room and heave it up onto one of the shelves. I don't want to just leave it lying out in the open. This way I can come back for it if I need to.

I exit the storeroom, closing the door behind me. I pause, hand still on the door handle. Someone's coming. I can hear voices, hurried splashing as men run through the water. Shit. Maybe Ramirez didn't get all of Preacher's men. Maybe the survivors went for reinforcements.

I wade in the opposite direction. Get back to the gym, hand

my bag of guns over, collect Sawyer and Felix, and get to the Glasshouse.

Survive. Then kill. Then die. In that order.

I stop suddenly. The keys! Sawyer's keys are still in Ramirez's pocket.

I shrug the bag of guns off my back, letting them fall into the water, and run to Ramirez's body. It's still slumped against the wall at an awkward angle. One hand floats in the water, bobbing around in the waves as if testing the temperature.

I fumble in his closest pocket. Empty. I try to slide my hand down between the body and the wall, but I can't get to the other pocket. I heave on Ramirez's orange overalls, pulling him over to the side.

He slumps over with a heavy splash. I feel around in his pocket. The keys are there. I pull them out, breathing a sigh of relief.

Something yanks hard on the Ruger slung over my shoulder. I'm pulled off my feet, falling backward. Something lands on my chest, pushing me down beneath the water. I force my eyes open, see a shadowy shape above me. Then another, off to my side. I struggle, but I can't shift the weight. Fingers scrabble for my throat, nails dig painfully into my skin.

I shove my hand into my pocket, trying to pull out the M9. It gets snagged in the material. I struggle to get it free as the fingers tighten around my throat.

I pull the handgun out of my pocket and fire upward through the water, the slugs thudding into my attacker's chest.

The weight drops backward, falling across my legs. I break the surface, drawing a deep breath and pointing the M9 quickly around the corridor.

Deserted. The second figure is gone.

I shove the deadweight off my legs and stand up. I pocket the gun, then swing the rifle around from my back, pointing it toward the end of the hallway. I wait for a few seconds, breathing heavily, but no one else appears.

I take one calming breath before realizing I've dropped the keys.

I check the floor, searching beneath the water. They're nowhere to be found. I move my attacker's body, checking to see if he's lying on them. Nothing.

The second figure. He must have grabbed the keys while I was fighting this guy.

Which means he has access to the armory.

Fuck. I wasn't even planning on giving *Castillo* the guns, but to arm a bunch of psychopaths like Preacher and his followers? That's just going to make it all but impossible to survive long enough to get Wright and Tully.

I grab the bag of guns, sling it over my back, and retrace my steps toward the armory. I pause before the final turn into the corridor. I can hear excited voices, arguments.

I'm too late.

I duck my head briefly around the corner, then pull back. No one in the passage. I look again. The armory door is standing open. The keys are in the lock.

Maybe I can just lock them all in. That would be the simplest thing all around. Get them out of the way, grab the keys, and head back to the gym.

I bring the Ruger up to my shoulder and turn into the passage. I move slowly through the water, trying not to make a sound. The door draws closer. I only have eyes for the keys. Fifteen feet.

Ten.

Five.

I can hear Preacher's men talking about the guns, about who they're going to kill first. Which unit they're going to storm. It sounds like Henry was right. The General Population units are all held by different cliques, barricaded and locked down.

I lower the rifle and reach out, grabbing hold of the keys. I'm just about to put my shoulder against the door to ram it shut and lock it when a skinny guy exits the armory, a bundle of shotguns cradled in his arms.

He freezes, staring at me with wide eyes.

Shit. Plan B. I quickly slip the keys out of the lock, back up a step and raise my rifle again.

"I don't want to shoot you," I say. "Just stay cool, okay?"

The guy's eyes shift to the left.

Goddammit.

He drops the shotguns and dives back into the armory, shouting as he does so.

Wonderful.

I shove the keys into my pocket and back up along the corridor, rifle raised to my shoulder. I fire a quick burst, hoping to keep them out of the passage.

I can hear them arguing. I lower the gun slightly, pointing it at waist height. The arguing stops, then the first guy appears exactly where I'm aiming—low. Smart guy.

Not smart enough.

I fire, hitting him in the forehead. He jerks back and slams into the water.

No one else comes. I keep moving, backing up as fast as I can. When I reach the end of the corridor, I turn and sprint, not bothering to keep quiet now. Splashing, wading through the water, just trying to get to the next T-junction to put some walls between myself and Preacher's men.

I can hear them coming, shouting, calling out for backup. My neck tingles as I run, waiting for the bullets to hit.

I sprint around the corner, slipping in the water and ramming up against the wall. As I do so, gunshots ring out and bullets pepper the wall above me, exactly at head height. I shove myself to my feet and keep running, trying doors as I pass. Most are locked, but after a few attempts I find one that opens to my touch.

Bullets cut the door frame to splinters as I duck inside. It's an office. I scramble forward, diving behind a large wooden desk. The water is easily two and a half feet deep now. I stay low, peering through the central gap in the desk, watching the door.

A moment later, a pair of orange-clad legs appear. I fire. There's a spray of blood and my attacker drops to the water with a scream of pain.

Our eyes meet through the gap. The guy has just enough time to form the word "no" before I shoot him in the head.

I wait a few moments, but no one else follows. I stand up warily, edge around the desk. I pull my attacker inside the room and push the door almost closed. Then I stand there and listen.

I can hear shouting and gunfire in the distance. Nothing close, though. Sounds like Preacher and his men have found someone else to chase down.

What the hell have I unleashed? Inmates trapped inside a prison, armed with rifles, shotguns, and handguns? And the armory still sits wide open, an invitation for anyone to go and arm themselves. It's going to be a bloodbath.

Hell, it already *is*.

Fourteen

2:50 a.m.

Two and a half hours to go.

Two and a half hours before the eye of the hurricane hits the prison. Two and a half hours to find our way through the prison units, somehow getting past inmates, gangs, rapists, murderers, and psychos.

I'm doing my best to avoid any contact. I have a goal now. Stay alive long enough to get to the Glasshouse. After that? Fuck it. I don't really want to be responsible for killing inmates who are scared, paranoid, or just plain crazy. Add to that the fact that I'm carrying a bag full of guns on my back, which makes me as much a target for attention as a young boy on his knees praying does to a Catholic priest. Best for everyone if I stay out of sight.

So I hop between offices and bathrooms, storage closets and prayer rooms, temporary sleeping quarters for the COs and shower rooms for when they work double shifts. Pausing to let inmates move past my hiding spots and running when I think I have a clear stretch.

I fail twice. Both times turning a corner to find myself face-to-face with groups of inmates. First time it's three guys, the second time a group of six.

But they don't attack. They just eye me warily as we move past each other on opposite sides of the corridor. That's when I realize the mood in the prison has shifted. It's gone from "every man for himself and let's settle old scores and kill anyone we feel like" to "shit, this is bad, maybe we should be focusing on surviving." Fat lot of good it will do them.

I make it back to the gym without shooting anyone else, something I take as a personal victory. I'm already responsible for too much of the mayhem going on around here. Preacher's guys now have total access to the armory. They'll *definitely* kill other inmates. Preacher and his crazy-ass brimstone-and-hellfire judgments. Plus, it's guaranteed they're going to lose some of the weapons. So guns will fall into other prisoners' hands, which means all-out war is going to kick off, even if some of the inmates *would* rather focus on finding shelter. It's inevitable.

I shift the heavy weight of the bag on my back. My muscles ache from carrying it all this way. The water is now up to my knees and still rising. I'm not sure if it means the flooding outside is the same level as in here, or if the water is higher outside and is just taking a while to find its way inside. Either option is terrifying. The walls and windows of the prison—safety glass or not—will only withstand so much pressure. I don't know what's worse. The walls holding and the prison slowly filling up with water, or the walls coming down and everyone being crushed or ripped apart by the hurricane.

I can't really think about that right now. I have more immediate problems. I can't give Castillo the guns. That was never my intention. It's just...wrong. Insane. Plus, there's absolutely no guarantee he won't just shoot us straight away. Fact is, I bet that's *exactly* what he plans to do.

I have to think smart here. I have to plan ahead.

I retreat up the corridor and take refuge in a closet that holds towels and antibacterial spray.

I dump the bag on a shelf, unzip it, and eject all the magazines out of the M9s. I then take out all the bullets, laying them out in piles. It takes me about ten minutes; then I move on to the shotguns. Once I'm done, I have huge piles of 9mm bullets and shotgun cartridges, and lots of guns with no ammunition in them.

I place Sawyer's keys on a high shelf. Castillo's bound to ask for them back. This way he can search me all he wants, but I'll just say that Preacher's men got them.

I pack the guns back in the bag. I make sure the Beretta stuck in the elastic of my underwear is secure at my back, then head to the gym.

I'm halfway there when I hear sounds behind me. The close echo of splashing water, raised voices. I pause, head tilted, but the sounds fade away. Whoever made them is going in another direction. I wonder if it's Preacher and his men. Did they follow me? Or Kincaid, even?

What difference does it make? Everyone's an enemy in here. I start walking again and arrive at the door leading into the gym. I try to push it open, but it's blocked from the other side. I kick it a couple of times and wait.

The door opens a crack. Silas peers out, gives me a cold look. He leans forward, checking both ways along the corridor, then frowns at me. I know what he's thinking. Ramirez.

I show him the canvas bag. "You gonna let me in, or am I dropping these in the water?"

He pulls the door open against the floodwater and steps aside. I enter the gym. There's no sign of Felix or Sawyer. About half the Kings are standing around, leaning against the gym machines or lounging up against the walls.

I dump the bag on top of a treadmill as Castillo strolls out of the changing rooms. He glances around.

"Where's Ramirez?"

"He didn't make it."

A heavy silence fills the room. Castillo moves toward me. The others straighten up, readying themselves, watching for his reaction.

"The hell you mean, he didn't make it?"

"We ran into Preacher and his men. You know how crazy that guy is. They chased us. He got hit."

"And you didn't?"

"What can I say? I'm a lucky guy."

Castillo stares at me. I can hear the rest of the Kings muttering.

"It's not like I just ran away and ditched him. I took a few of them down. And no offense, but Ramirez was a stupid fuck who thought he lived in a movie. He probably thought bullets would bounce off him or something. They got the keys too. Made it into the armory."

Castillo continues to stare at me for a long time, clenching and unclenching his jaw. Then he gestures at one of his guys. "Search him."

One of the Kings gives me a pat-down. He shakes his head once he's done. "Nothing."

Castillo scowls and finally turns his attention to the bag. "Is that all you got?"

"You want to try carrying that thing on your back while getting chased down by psycho Bible-bashers? You're lucky I brought anything."

"No. *You're* lucky you brought anything. And I'd seriously reconsider the tone of voice you're using with me."

"Where are Sawyer and Felix?" I ask.

"In the changing rooms."

I nod and start walking.

"Where the hell are you going?"

"I did my part. We're leaving now."

I can see Castillo trying to figure out his next move, can almost hear the thought process in the guy's head, trying to decide if it's easier just to kill me now and get it over with. I can already feel the pressure building up inside me. There's no time for this. I want to be long gone before they check the magazines.

I leave him to it and head into the changing room. Sawyer is pacing back and forth, rubbing her hands nervously together. Felix lies on one of the benches, arm over his eyes to block out the light.

"Enjoying your nap?"

Sawyer smiles in relief when she sees me. "Wasn't sure you'd make it back."

"I'm Connor MacLeod of the Clan MacLeod."

Her smile fades into confusion.

"I'm immortal?"

Nope. Nothing.

"Never mind. Let's go."

Sawyer joins me at the door, still looking at me sidelong. I realize I'm probably acting oddly. I feel different. Free. *Buoyant*. The realization you're going to die and the acceptance of that really does change your perspective. She's wondering why the hell I seem to be in such a good mood. I don't think I could explain it to her if I wanted to.

Felix hasn't budged since I entered the room. "Felix? You coming or you staying here to sleep?"

He sighs and sits up. "Just conserving my energy."

"Is he really letting us go?" asks Sawyer.

"I got him his guns."

Sawyer's face clouds over. She's not happy about it.

"What did you want me to do?" I ask. "Let you both die?"

She doesn't answer.

"Look—it doesn't matter. Just trust me, okay? But we have to get out of here. Right now."

Felix frowns. "Want to tell us why?"

"Just follow me and don't look back."

We head into the gym. Felix and his guys are standing around the treadmill, taking out the shotguns and M9s. My stomach clenches up. I hope my face doesn't look as panicked as I'm feeling.

Just play it cool. You're smarter than these guys. They're not gonna check the magazines.

I stare at the door. It's only about ten paces away. I pick up the pace. Silas is still standing there, watching us approach. I slow down, letting Sawyer and Felix pull ahead.

"Boss?" calls out Silas.

I look over at Castillo. He has a Beretta in his hand. Jesus. Surely he can feel how light it is?

He just nods and turns back to the guns. Silas braces himself, starts to pull the door open against the water.

Then I hear it. The ratcheting click of a magazine being ejected.

I lunge forward through the water, grab the door and try to heave it open.

"Go!" I shout.

Sawyer and Felix give me confused looks, but they dart forward, trying to squeeze through.

"Stop them!" shouts Castillo.

I punch Silas in the throat. I may as well have punched a wall of sand for all the good it does. The guy shrugs it off and grabs Felix by the collar, yanking him back. Felix flies backward and lands on his ass in the water.

I try to push Sawyer through the door, but Silas elbows me in the head. I stumble back, stars exploding across my vision. Silas shoves his back up against the door, pushing it closed with his weight.

Castillo comes for me, empty magazine in one hand, Beretta in the other. I glance around the gym, doing a quick count. There are about twenty other guys in here. All of them ready to fight. If I take my own gun out, I might fire off a few rounds before I'm overpowered. But it would be a waste of a gun, and a waste of all our lives. Better to keep it for when I really need—

Castillo hits me in the face with the Beretta. My cheek smashes up against my teeth and I taste the metallic tang of blood in my mouth. I stagger back, shake my head to clear it.

"You think you can mess with me? Seriously?"

I spit the blood into the water, probe the inside of my mouth with my tongue. Tooth's still there. That's something at least.

"Where are the bullets, Constantine?"

Sawyer is busy helping Felix to his feet. She looks sharply at me.

Castillo hits me in the head with the butt of the gun. I drop to my knees.

"Where are the bullets?" he shouts.

I don't know what to do. There's no way I'm going to get away with *not* handing the bullets over. Can I lie? Say I didn't bring them? No. Castillo won't believe me.

He looks over at Silas. "Grab one of them," he says, indicating Felix and Sawyer.

Sawyer is closer to him. Silas's hand closes around her arm. "What you want me to do?"

"That depends on Constantine."

Castillo pulls me to my feet and shoves me toward Sawyer. Her eyes are wide, but she's trying not to show fear.

Castillo takes a knife out of his pocket. Silas yanks Sawyer's hair, pulling her head back so her neck is stretched tight. Felix takes a step forward, but Castillo waves the knife at him.

"Just...don't. Okay? Or I'll kill you both."

Felix freezes. Castillo turns to me, waiting. He doesn't say anything this time.

I sigh. "The closet. About four doors down."

Castillo nods at a few of his guys and they hurry out of the gym. While they're gone, Silas pushes the three of us up against the wall close to the door. Sawyer is on one side of me, and Felix on the other.

"Do we have a game plan here?" asks Felix. "Because I'm pretty sure these guys are gonna shoot us in the head soon."

He's right. I realize I'm going to have to risk the gun. Best to do it now, when the Kings are five men down.

I wait until no one is looking, then quickly reach into my prison scrubs and pull the gun out, hiding it behind my back.

"Did I just see you pull a gun out of your ass?" asks Felix.

"It was in my boxers."

"Same thing."

"It's nowhere near the same thing. Resting a gun in your waistband and shoving it up your ass are so far beyond the same thing it's not even worth talking about."

"Whatever, man. I'm not touchin' it."

"I'm not asking you to touch it. *I'll* touch it. You don't have to touch anything."

"Will you two shut the fuck up!" snaps Sawyer. "Do we have a plan or not?"

"I was thinking I'd start shooting and we make a run for it."

"Good call," says Felix. "Now is—"

The door surges open against the water, forming a wave that carries across the gym. The Kings who went to fetch the bullets burst through, panicked looks on their faces. They're carrying some of the bullets in their scrubs and T-shirts, using them as makeshift sacks to transport the ammo. They look freaked out.

"Preacher!" one of them shouts.

Castillo frowns. "What?"

The inmates rush forward and dump the ammo into the gun bag. Silas closes the door, a worried look on his face, while they start loading up magazines as fast as they can, ramming shells into shotguns.

"Preacher. He's here. He's coming—"

There's a concussive blast and a massive hole appears in the door. Silas, who had been standing right in front of it, screams and goes down, his back shredded to pieces by wood, metal, and what I'm assuming are shotgun pellets.

The door slowly moves inward to reveal Preacher standing there, holding a shotgun.

I shove Sawyer to the right. Felix follows and we duck down behind a shoulder press machine.

"God has judged you all for trespassing!" shouts Preacher as he moves farther into the room. "You have come into the promised land as invaders. For did not the enemy say, 'I will pursue, I will overtake, I will divide the spoil; my lust shall be satisfied upon them; I will draw my sword, and my hand shall destroy them!'"

His followers step inside the gym behind him. They're all armed with handguns, rifles, and shotguns. I count seven of them.

"'And I will bring a sword upon you, that shall avenge the quarrel of my covenant: and when ye are gathered together within your cities, I will send the pestilence among you; and ye shall be delivered into the hand of the enemy.'"

There's a moment of silence. The figure next to Preacher leans into him and whispers something. Preacher frowns as he listens, then pulls back to give the guy a look.

"Man, do you not read the Bible? It's a prerequisite for being in my blessed army. What I'm saying is kill these motherfuckers. They're trespassing in my Canaan."

The guy hesitates again. Preacher sighs and pumps his shotgun. "Just shoot."

Preacher's men open fire, muzzle flare lighting up their faces. Some of the Kings scramble for cover behind the weight equipment. Others rush toward the changing rooms and are cut down in midstride, blood spraying into the air.

Preacher has his arms outspread, face raised to the roof. "For you know I am the *Lord*," he shouts, "when motherfuckers spray bullets in my name— *Oh shit!*"

His last words come in response to Castillo and some of his men grabbing the half-loaded guns and returning fire.

The noise of shotguns and semiautomatic weapons blasts through the confined space. Felix lunges out from behind the cover of the weight machine, grabs a Beretta from the guy standing on the end of the line, and shoots him in the head.

He then ducks down and darts through the gap that opens up, running straight through the door. Sawyer and I follow him. We sprint along the corridor as fast as we can, the sounds of gunfire echoing behind us as we go. I pause once to duck into the storeroom and grab the key ring, then we put as much distance between us and the gym as we can.

Fifteen

3:20 a.m.

Sawyer feels like she's losing control of everything.

Wait—who the hell is she kidding? She never *had* control. From the moment she arrived this morning, events have just snowballed, and she's been caught up in them, thrown about like a leaf in a...well, like a leaf in a goddam hurricane.

Right now she's utterly exhausted, freaked out, pissed off, fed up, terrified, and a lot of other things she's too stressed to even attempt to label.

"Man, I've *never* experienced shit like that," says Felix excitedly.

The three of them have ducked into what turns out to be a mail room. There are piles of letters everywhere, some bound by elastic bands, others piled up in wall nooks. Opened letters are spread across multiple desks. Magnifiers with lights attached and portable drug-testing kits stand ready to examine them for contraband. Some relatives spike the paper with LSD. Others spray Spice—synthetic cannabis—onto the pages; the drug soaks in and the inmates then smoke them.

They came in here to hide in case Preacher came after them. *And* to discuss their next move. Which to Sawyer is totally pointless, because if their next move isn't making their way through the prison units as fast as fucking possible, then they're all going to die anyway.

Constantine is sitting next to her on a desk chair while Felix has his face pressed against a crack in the door, watching the corridor.

"How long are we going to be here?"

"We'll give it five minutes," says Constantine.

Sawyer sighs and leans against the desk. She stares at Constantine for a long moment, a thoughtful look on her face. "Tell me about Amy," she says after a while.

He looks at her in surprise. "Why?"

She shrugs. "We've got five minutes to kill."

He hesitates for a moment, his eyes distant. "She was... amazing. And a pain in the ass. Stubborn. But not arrogant. She could change her mind, you know? She didn't think she was always right. If you could lay out your argument, and she saw sense in it, she would shift her viewpoint. I liked that about her. Most people just double down when they realize they're wrong. They get defensive, argumentative. But Amy never saw the point in that."

"How did you meet?"

"She stalked me."

Sawyer looks at him in shock. "She *didn't*."

He smiles. "No. Well... kinda. I was coming back from my veterans' support group meeting. I was on the train, just sort of... zoned out. You know how it gets when you have to deal with emotional shit. You're just mentally exhausted. So there I was, sitting there, minding my own business, staring at my hands, and I get this feeling someone is watching me. I look around, but I don't see anything suspicious. No one really paying me attention. Just normal people doing normal things. I look down again, but I can't shake the feeling. So I whip my head up and I catch her."

"Amy?"

He nods. "Staring right at me, but, like... *intensely.* Like she was concentrating on some math problem or something. I wasn't even sure she was looking at me. I thought she was just distracted—you know when you stare at nothing?"

Sawyer nods.

"But then she got up and came to sit next to me."

She laughs. "Just like that?"

"Just like that."

"What did she say?"

"Hi."

"What did *you* say?"

"Nothing."

"Nothing?"

"I may have grunted or something. See, back then I wasn't the suave ladies' man you see before you now. I was pretty screwed up. I was in the middle of realizing that I hadn't actually come back from my tour without any issues. Not like I first thought. I wasn't in the best of spaces."

"What did she do? When she sat next to you?"

"She stared at me."

Sawyer laughs again. "You're kidding. Like, from right next to you?"

Constantine nods. "Like she was trying to memorize my face. I could *feel* her looking. Then I start to go red. I can feel the color creeping up my neck."

"And she still kept staring?"

"Still kept staring. I finally turn to look at her. I can't take the social embarrassment anymore. And she breaks into this smile..." He trails off, remembering. "Her face just transformed. She has—had—these laugh lines around her eyes. They made her look like she was about to break into laughter even when she wasn't. But when she did...man, those eyes just lit up the room."

"What did she say?"

"She said, and I quote, 'You look like a puppy that's been yanked from a kid's warm bed and kicked out into the rain.'"

"What did you say?"

"Nothing. Then she asked if I wanted to go get a drink."

"Did you go?"

"Honestly, I don't think she'd have let me say no. So yeah, we went to a dive bar, played pool, talked about life. It was the first time I'd smiled since I came back from Afghanistan.

Looking back on it now, I think it was the best night of my life."

Sawyer is about to respond when Felix closes the door and turns to face them, interrupting their conversation.

"Coast is clear. I guess they're all still busy killing each other." He shakes his head in amazement. "Man, did you see that guy? I heard stories about Preacher, but that shit was crazy." He holds his arms up in the air. "And you know I am the Lord when motherfuckers spray bullets in my name."

Sawyer glances at Constantine. He shrugs and smiles. So much for conversation.

Felix turns his attention to her. "What's the word, little lady? You doing okay after all that?"

"I'm fine."

"Good to hear. You're tough, yeah? Or are you like my ex-wife? Hides all her emotions till they explode out and she comes at me with a knife." Sawyer doesn't even get a chance to answer before he turns to Constantine. Jesus. It's like he's on speed or something. "So what's the next move?"

Constantine suddenly holds a finger to his lips. They all fall silent as the sound of people wading through the water passes outside the door. He waits a couple of moments, then gets up, opens the door, and ducks his head briefly outside. He closes it softly. "Preacher and his men."

"They heading the direction we want to go in?" asks Felix.

"Looks like it." Constantine glances at Felix and then breaks into an unexpected grin. "I'd heard stories too, but, man... none of them do him justice. That guy is intense."

There's something off about Constantine, thinks Sawyer. He seems different since he came back from the armory. Somehow...lighter? She's not sure if that's right. But there's a barely suppressed energy about him that seems like it's about to burst out at the slightest chance.

"You sure the inmate corridor is out of commission?" he asks Felix.

"Saw it myself. Highway to the danger zone."

Constantine sighs and looks over at Sawyer. "What do you think? Stick to the plan? Go through the prison units."

"What about the staff corridor?" asks Felix.

Constantine shakes his head. "We can't."

"Why?"

"Kincaid was there. He chased us out."

"Constantine," says Felix patiently, like he's talking to a kid. "What do you think is the most immediate danger to us? Trying to get through seven prison units with one gun, or spooky Kincaid, who I'm telling you right now is *not* sitting in that corridor like a creepy doll in a horror movie just waiting for you to walk by?"

Constantine still looks unsure.

"Come on, man. No harm in trying. We have guns now."

"Yeah," says Sawyer. "But it seems everyone else does too." She looks at Constantine. "What's with that?"

He shrugs. "We were attacked. Preacher's guys got the keys, opened up the armory. I'm assuming it's been emptied by now."

"And Ramirez?"

"I killed him."

"*You* killed him?" asks Felix. "Why?"

"He shot up a lot of unarmed people. Then he killed Henry. Right in front of me."

"Henry's dead?" says Felix. "Fuck, man."

"Who's Henry?" asks Sawyer.

"The guy I worked with in the maintenance shed," says Constantine. "Old guy. But he was one of the good ones."

"Oh...I'm sorry."

He shrugs. "We've all got to go sometime. I guess tonight's as good a night as any."

She thinks this is an odd thing to say, but before she can question it, Constantine glances up at the old analog clock on the wall. "Five minutes are up. Let's go. We've got two hours till the eye of the hurricane hits." He hesitates, looking like he's going to say something more. But he doesn't. Instead, he opens the door and checks the hallway before stepping outside.

They leave the mail room. Sawyer can hear gunshots echoing around the prison, but they're not just coming from back in the direction of the gym. They're coming from up ahead too, from far in the distance. From everywhere.

The mail room is near the first door leading into the prison units. As they make their way through the corridors, Sawyer can't help noticing that the building is not coping well under the constant barrage of the hurricane. Lights dim and flicker. The floodwater actually moves, small waves rolling into the walls as the building sways and shudders. And the sounds of tormented metal, creaking wood, and rending concrete are constant. She's not sure the place is going to last two hours.

So where does that leave them? What the hell are they going to do?

She takes a shaky, worried breath. They keep going. They keep trying. That's something her mother taught her. You walk the highway and you keep going till it runs out. Then you drag yourself over the dirt until you can't carry on.

They move past the Unit 1 door and turn into the passage that eventually leads to the staff corridor. A hallway opens up to the left, and as they pass by, a quiet sound freezes them in their tracks.

They turn to find a group of seven inmates standing in the semidarkness. None of the lights are working in the side corridor. They're pressed up against the walls, tensely watching them.

The two groups stare at each other for a long moment. Finally Constantine steps forward.

"You guys looking for problems or just trying to survive?"

"Just trying to survive," says a voice out of the darkness.

Constantine nods. "We're gonna keep walking, then, okay?"

"Knock yourself out."

He turns and gestures at Sawyer and Felix. After a moment's

hesitation, Felix starts walking. Sawyer follows, jogging to keep up with the two of them.

"Good luck," calls out the voice.

Sawyer pauses and looks back in shock. The inmates exit the corridor and head in the opposite direction. Sawyer watches them disappear around the corner, then hurries after Constantine and Felix.

After another minute or so, they arrive at the door to the staff corridor.

"Okay," says Constantine. "We open the door, do a quick check and see if the coast is clear. Agreed?"

"So you the boss man now?" says Felix.

"Nobody's the boss, Felix. I just know Kincaid. He covers his back. I know he's going to have someone watching the corridor."

"And I will shoot whichever unlucky bastard got stuck with the job," says Felix.

He grabs the door handle and pulls.

The door doesn't budge.

"The hell?" he says.

"Is it locked?" asks Sawyer.

"Nah, man. I can feel it moving. It's like…someone's holding it."

Constantine and Sawyer both grab hold of the handle. They give it a tug. Felix is right. It's not locked, but something is stopping it. Maybe Kincaid has blocked it off.

Sawyer frowns, straining her ears. The hurricane itself overlays everything: the constant wind, the battering against the roof, the creaking of the entire building as it strains to resist.

But…somehow it sounds louder here.

Felix pushes down on the handle and tries to pull the door open again.

Sawyer suddenly realizes what's happened. She opens her mouth to warn him, but it's too late.

The sound of the wind drops slightly, and the door flies

open, accompanied by the howl and wail of the hurricane. Sawyer and Constantine slam back against the wall, and almost immediately Felix is yanked away, sliding toward the corridor. His gun flies out of his hand as he grabs hold of the door frame, screaming.

The wind shrieks and the rain pummels through ragged holes in the walls of the staff corridor. The outside walls are breached. The wind is trying to pull everything into the hurricane outside.

Sawyer and Constantine grab hold of Felix, bracing themselves against the door frame. The rain slams into Sawyer, into all of them. She can see Felix's grip slipping.

She lets go and scrambles behind the door, trying to push it closed. It bumps against Constantine's shoulder.

"What are you doing?" he screams over the noise.

"Just get ready!" she screams back. She can see the door is now pushing hard into his shoulder. The wind is trying to pull it closed again.

"Don't let me go!" shouts Felix.

Sawyer grips the edge of the door with both hands. The wind lessens slightly, just like it did before.

"Now!" she screams. "Pull him in!"

Constantine yanks Felix hard. Felix uses his own strength to help, clawing his way back against the door frame. Eventually Constantine manages to pull him around the side of the door and they both fall back into the corridor while Sawyer shoves the door shut. The wind sucks it out of her hand and it slams back into place with a loud crack.

The sound of the storm drops slightly. Sawyer stumbles away from the door and stares down at Felix and Constantine lying in the water.

"You two okay?"

Constantine rolls over and glares at a shell-shocked Felix. "What was it you said about the staff corridor? *No harm in trying?*"

Felix pushes himself to his feet. "Fuck off, Constantine. I'm not in the mood."

Sawyer holds her hand out to Constantine. He grabs it and she helps him up.

"No, I'm serious," he says, turning to Felix. "No harm in trying. That was what you said, right? Oh, hey, at least we've got guns now, in case anyone is in the corridor waiting for us. Oh, wait! You don't, do you? Because the fucking hurricane just took it."

"Constantine." Felix's voice is low. "I'm serious. I'm about to blow, man. I'm not in a good mood right now."

"Will you two please just shut up," snaps Sawyer. They both turn to look at her. "We have to go through the units now. It's the only way."

Felix and Constantine exchange uneasy looks, but they shut up long enough for them to retrace their steps back to the door leading into Unit 1.

It's unlocked. Sawyer pushes it open to reveal a passage running to either side of them. To the right is the door leading into the staff corridor, and to the left the door to the inmate corridor.

Constantine heads left and cups his hands against the glass, peering into the inmate corridor. His shoulders slump and he returns to the others.

"Didn't believe me?" asks Felix.

"Just needed to check."

"And what did you see, my white friend?"

"Broken walls. Lightning. Clouds."

Felix points his two index fingers at Constantine. "Exactly. Trust me when I speak, my young Padawan. Felix doesn't lie."

"No, but he makes stupid fucking decisions," mutters Constantine.

An open door leads into the sally port, basically just a long corridor that ends at a second door leading into Unit 1 of General Population. About a quarter of the way along the corridor is the security room that Sawyer used earlier that night.

Constantine tests the door that leads into the unit. It's unlocked, but he doesn't open it. Instead, he inserts key after key from Montoya's key ring until he finds the one that works. He then takes the key off the ring and slips it into his pocket.

"What are you doing?"

"I don't want to be fumbling around looking for the key if things get hot." He looks at them both. "Ready?"

Sawyer and Felix nod. Constantine takes a deep breath, and then pulls the door open.

The entrance into Unit 1 is totally sealed off. Tables, broken desks, smashed-up chairs, all the pieces jammed together like a puzzle blocking the doorway. Sawyer can't see a single gap through the barrier.

Constantine kicks at it, but it holds firm. Felix joins him, but their kicks do nothing at all.

"What the hell have they shored this up with?" growls Felix. "Okay, step aside."

Sawyer and Constantine move up against the wall as Felix takes a running start and hits the barrier with his shoulder. He bounces off and dances around in agony. "Motherfucker!" he shouts. "Christ, that hurt."

Constantine tries to pull something out of the blockage. Sawyer thinks he's hoping it's like Jenga; that if he yanks something free, the whole structure might weaken. As he's pulling on a table leg, a wooden pole emerges from somewhere and thuds into his chest.

"The hell?" He moves back a step, but the pole has vanished back inside the unit. He reaches out again. As he does so, the pole slowly emerges, like a turtle peering from its shell. Constantine stops moving. So does the pole. He takes a step forward. The pole inches farther out.

"Touch me with that again and I'll break your jaw!" shouts Constantine.

"Fuck off and leave us alone." The voice from the other side of the barrier sounds scared. And old.

"Don't tell me to fuck off," snaps Constantine. "Let us in. We need to get through the unit."

"Son, there's more chance of whoever that woman is getting on her knees and sucking my shriveled cock than there is of me letting you in here."

Sawyer's eyes widen in embarrassment. Felix chuckles, but quickly stops when she throws a glare in his direction.

"You're starting to piss me off," says Constantine.

"Ooh, look...I'm trembling. I've made the man angry. You think I give a shit? Just leave us alone. We don't want any part of whatever's going on out there. We've already had to let Preacher and his men through. No one else."

"You let Preacher through? When?"

"About ten minutes ago."

"Why?"

"*Why?* I'm not arguing with him. He's a goddam psycho. Easier to just let him through. Now fuck off!"

Constantine growls and kicks out. Felix joins him, and the two stand together, lunging in and hitting the barrier while trying to avoid the pole jabbing at their faces.

This goes on for about thirty seconds before Sawyer sighs and steps forward, putting a hand on Constantine's arm. He looks at her in surprise, and she gently shakes her head, then steps closer to the barricade.

"What's your name?"

"Carl."

"Carl. I'm Sawyer. What are you actually doing in there?"

"Hiding."

Sawyer glances back at Felix and Constantine. They both look surprised.

"Hiding from what?"

"The hell you think? You actually seen what's going on in this place? We let anyone get in here, we're all dead."

"You let Preacher in," she points out.

"Yeah, but he swore on the Bible he'd leave us alone."

"Who are you? Are you a gang?"

"Yeah. The over-seventy gang." The voice chuckles. Sawyer thinks she can hear appreciative laughter from inside the unit.

"So . . . what are you saying?"

"I'm saying me and everyone else who is too old to fight the psychos have all taken shelter in here, and we're not gonna let anyone in."

"But what about the hurricane?"

"What about it?"

"Well . . . this place is falling apart. It's not going to last."

"And what do you suggest as an alternative?"

Sawyer glances at Constantine. He shakes his head and mouths, "Don't you dare."

"We're going to make our way to the Glasshouse. It will hold—"

She's cut off by the voice bursting into laughter. "The Glasshouse? Jesus, woman. I've been there. If this place goes down, there's not a chance in hell the Glasshouse will stay standing. At least in here we're dry."

"Can you just let us through, then?" asks Sawyer. "We're not going to do anything. We just need to get to Northside."

"Through the prison units?"

"It's the only way."

"Then I'm saving your life by saying no. You try to go through the units, you're all dead."

"We're dead if we don't," says Felix. "Just let us through."

"Piss off."

Sawyer thinks about it. This isn't getting them anywhere.

"What about a trade?"

"What kind of trade?"

"You let us through, and we give you something to defend yourself with."

"What kind of something?"

"A gun."

"Sawyer—" Constantine's voice is urgent. She holds her hand up to stop him.

There's a long moment of silence from the other side of the barricade. Then, "Let me see it."

Sawyer turns to Constantine.

"I'm not giving up my gun," he says. "It's the only one we have now."

"We have no choice. If it gets us through the unit, it's worth the loss."

Sawyer can see Constantine doesn't want to do this, but he reluctantly pulls the gun out of his waistband and hands it to her.

"Hold it up," commands the voice.

Sawyer does as she's told. There's a noise from the other side of the barrier, and after a few moments, a larger hole opens up.

"Pass it through."

"No way," snaps Constantine. "Open up first."

"No. Hand it over first."

Sawyer ejects the magazine, handing it over to Constantine. She passes the gun through the hole and sees a liver-spotted hand pull it out of sight. "You get the magazine when you let us through."

"Give me a minute."

Sawyer hears whispered voices. Then silence.

A few moments later, she hears the sounds of the barricade being taken down.

"Go, Sawyer," mutters Felix.

Constantine doesn't say anything. Sawyer glances at him, but he's not looking happy.

After a few minutes, the gap is wide enough for them all to squeeze through.

Once inside, Sawyer straightens up and looks around the unit. It's like all the others she's been in. Two floors, with cells looking out over the rec area. The only thing that's different here is that the unit is filled with geriatrics. It's like pensioners' day at the local mall, except instead of coupons they're all holding weapons.

One of the inmates, an old man around five-five in height, orders the others to fix the barrier again. This must be Carl. He has wispy gray hair and a beaklike nose that juts out from a hollowed-out face. He glares at them suspiciously.

He finally turns his attention to the gun he's holding. He racks the chamber and peers inside.

"Ah, will you look at that? You left me with a bullet in the chamber."

He levels it at them. "A deal's a deal, but if any of you make a move I even *think* is suspicious, the bullet goes in one of your heads." He gestures toward the opposite end of the unit. "Move on. You're so eager to go to your deaths, who am I to stop you?"

Sawyer, Constantine, and Felix walk between the lines of inmates. There are already three of them dismantling a small section of the barricade at the exit, pulling out what look like sheets of corrugated metal from the roof, desk chairs, metal poles, and parts of bookcases that have been broken down and slotted into place like a jigsaw.

"What's going on in the next unit?" asks Constantine.

"Gang war," says Carl.

"What gangs?" Felix asks.

"First off, we thought it was East Bloods and West Bloods. You know, doing what they normally do."

"But it's not?"

"Nah. It's the Bloods against the Woods. As far as I can tell, they're fighting over control of units 2 and 3."

Sawyer thinks back to the intelligence pack she received when she got the job at Ravenhill. The Woods are white supremacists. The name is an acronym for Whites Only One Day. And if the Bloods have squashed their own intra-gang beefs to take the Woods on, it isn't going to be pretty.

The inmates quickly open up a three-foot hole through the barricade.

"How am I supposed to get through that?" asks Felix.

"Crawl," says Carl. "And while you're down there, you might as well start praying too. You're going to need all the help you can get." He holds out his hand. "Magazine."

Sawyer is about to hand it over when Felix makes a sudden lunge and snatches the gun right out of Carl's hand. He points it at the old guy. To give him credit, Carl doesn't panic. He just takes a step back.

"We had a deal."

"I'm aware of that," says Felix. "I'm also aware that we might need the gun more than you guys."

"I couldn't give a shit. You gave your word."

"Felix, back off," says Sawyer.

"Me?" says Felix in surprise. "The fuck you talking about? We need the gun."

"Like the man says, we made a deal."

"And that matters how?"

"It just does. Don't be an asshole. Constantine? Tell him."

Constantine sighs. He tosses the magazine to Carl, who catches it in one hand.

"Are you insane?" shouts Felix.

"No. Just being practical. We don't have time to screw around here. And Sawyer's right. We made a deal. Give it to him."

Constantine turns and gets down onto his hands and knees. The water touches his chin as he pulls himself through the small opening they've cleared in the barricade. Sawyer waits for Felix. He hesitates, then grudgingly hands the gun over to Carl.

"After you," says Sawyer.

Felix glares at her. "You're a pain in the ass, you know that?"

Sawyer shrugs. "So my ex-husband says."

He shakes his head and pulls himself through the gap.

Sawyer gets down into the water and is about to follow when she feels a touch on her shoulder. She looks up to find Carl holding the gun out to her.

"They're right. You will need it. But I think you should be the one to keep it. Don't let them know. In case you need to use it against one of them."

Sawyer hesitates, then takes the gun. "Thank you."

Carl nods amiably. "Now fuck off so I can close up."

She turns back to the hole and starts crawling. She's barely through before she hears Carl ordering the others to plug the opening up again.

Sixteen

3:45 a.m.

I crawl through the hole in the makeshift barricade, my mouth dipping into the warm water. I straighten up in a corridor identical to the one outside Unit 1. It travels about fifty feet to both left and right, ending at the doors leading into what were once the staff and inmate corridors. There are doors to offices and rooms along the wall in front of me, as well as the reinforced door that leads into the Unit 2 sally port. Lots of doors. Lots of corridors. I'm sick of them.

I can hear screaming and shouting coming from Unit 2. Felix straightens up beside me and gives me an "I told you so" look when he hears the sounds of fighting.

"Don't blame me," I say. "You think I wanted to give up the gun?"

"It was the only way," snaps Sawyer, pulling herself out of the hole.

"Not true," says Felix. "There was the option of violence. Violence solves many, many problems."

"And causes even more."

"How? Those guys were nearly eighty years old. I could have whistled in Carl's direction and shattered his bones." He turns his glare to me. "Why did we listen to her? Is she suddenly the boss now?"

"Why are you so obsessed about who's the boss?" asks Sawyer. "No one's the boss. I saw a quick way out of the situation and I took it. Time is ticking, in case you hadn't noticed. Now stop being a little bitch. You're so tough, you don't need a gun. I'm sure you can handle anything that comes at us."

Felix looks at her in shock. I kind of want to laugh, but on the other hand, I agree with Felix. I feel naked again without a weapon, and it sounds like we're about to walk into a war zone.

We approach the door to the sally port. I pull it open against the rising water, then pause, surprised when the screams and shouts don't grow much louder. I exchange a puzzled look with the others and pull the door all the way open, revealing the corridor and, at the opposite end, the open door leading into Unit 2.

From what I can see, the entire unit looks deserted.

We move cautiously along the passage and peer inside. Unit 2 is indeed deserted.

But it's not untouched.

There are bodies everywhere. Floating in the water, draped over the hexagonal tables, even hanging over the second-floor railings.

"Jesus," mutters Felix.

Most of the bodies seem to be white guys. There are a few darker skins among the dead, but I'd say seventy percent are white. Which means the Woods lost big time.

I step nervously into the rec room and pause, waiting to see if anything happens.

Nothing.

One thing becomes clear, though. The noises we're hearing are actually coming from Unit 3. And they don't sound like screams of pain. More like the shouting you'd hear at a sports event.

We wade through the water, skirting around the bodies. I check them out as we pass. Puncture wounds, bruises, slit throats...Some of their faces are so messed up they don't even look human anymore.

Felix reaches the door ahead of me and opens it a crack. He peers through, then pulls it open all the way. It's the same as the last two units. An empty corridor with the door into the Unit 3 sally port about ten feet in front of us.

The screaming and shouting is much louder out here. I can hear specific words now, chanted over and over. "Bloods, Bloods, Bloods!"

Same drill. Along the sally port passage and pause outside the door. Felix cracks it slightly. The roars explode into the passage. It reminds me of a boxing match.

He peers through, then moves aside to let me and Sawyer look.

All I can see are the backs of inmates as they jostle and shove each other, trying to catch a glimpse of something happening in the middle of the rec room floor. They're jeering and shouting, hands raised in the air. There are more inmates leaning on the railings. They're all staring down, cheering and laughing.

The crowd is so thick that I think we might actually have a chance. If we can circle around the outside of the spectators, maybe we can get to the door on the other side while everyone's attention is focused on whatever's going on.

"Are we really going to just walk through that?" whispers Sawyer. She doesn't even attempt to hide the fear in her voice.

"I'm open to alternatives."

"There aren't any," says Felix. "Okay, here's what I suggest. I go through first. No offense, but you two kind of stick out. If I'm caught, I'll holler something so you know not to come. If I don't, you follow on."

"What are you going to shout?" I ask.

"I don't know. Depends on the situation. Maybe something like 'Why did you stab me, you asshole?'"

He slips through the door and makes his way left around the ring of inmates, disappearing from sight. Sawyer and I wait, straining our ears for his shout.

"You think we're going to make it?" I ask.

"Do you?"

"If the storm was, like, an hour behind where it is now, maybe. But honestly, I think this building is going to come down before the eye of the hurricane hits."

"If you think that, why are you still trying?"

"What else am I gonna do? We all need goals, right? Some people want to make CEO by the time they're thirty. Some people want three kids and a picket fence. I want to kill Wright and Tully with my own hands."

"That's it? That's really what's keeping you going?"

"That's it," I say cheerfully.

"Constantine... are you all right? You've been acting weird since you came back from the armory."

"Weird how?"

"I don't know. Happy, I suppose. Buzzed."

"Call it a Zen-like acceptance of what is."

"What the hell does that mean?"

I shrug. "Just what I said."

I think Felix must have made it to the other side by now. There's been no shout of warning, so I think we're all clear.

"Same rule as Felix," I say. "I'll go first. There's more chance I'll be seen. Listen out for my shout."

I head into the rec room. The screams and cheers surge in volume. There's an animalistic sound to them. A bloodthirstiness that makes them seem barely human.

I keep low as I move around the outskirts of the crowd, keeping close to the wall and trying to stay out of view of those on the second floor of the pod.

There's no sign of Felix anywhere ahead of me. Which is good news. Well, for him. He blends in.

I wonder what he'll do if I'm caught. I wouldn't blame him if he hung back. No point in him being taken down with me. Still, I'd kind of like to know where he stands. Call it curiosity.

The crowd gets denser the farther into the room I go. The press of bodies forces me right up against the wall. I'm jostled and elbowed, but nobody actually turns around to see what they're hitting and bumping into.

I'm about twenty feet from the door when a huge cheer

explodes in the pod and the inmates all start jumping around as if celebrating. I'm shoved up against the wall. An elbow smashes into my head. I instinctively shove back, harder than I mean to. The person I push stumbles forward, then whirls around to fight back.

Shit.

He stares at me in surprise as I slowly straighten up.

"Hey!" he shouts. "Look what I found. A little white boy trying to sneak past."

People turn to see what's going on. It's only a matter of seconds before hands grab hold and drag me through the crowd toward the center of the room.

I'm shoved forward. I stumble out of the crowd and steady myself against one of the tables. I finally see what all the cheering is about. The inmates surround an open area in the rec room where two prisoners were in the middle of a fight.

Everyone is looking at me. Even the fighters.

Jesus. I peer closer at them. It's Travis and Deacon. Both of them are Woods. I haven't seen them since cleaning out the Glasshouse earlier in the day. They both look exhausted. Deep cuts and gouges cover their faces, dripping blood into the water.

"Mr. Constantine," calls a voice.

I look up. Leaning over the second-floor railing is an inmate called Dexter. He's a Blood, though I don't think he was ever the leader. More a lieutenant who did what he was told. But judging by the way everyone turns their attention to him, he's the boss in here.

"Welcome to our courtroom," he says.

I look around. There are bodies lying off to one side. All of them Woods. "Seems more like an execution chamber."

Dexter shrugs. "You say potato, I say righting a thousand years of wrongs done to the black man."

"Right..."

"Don't stress, though. You'll get your turn to sacrifice yourself to the cause."

"I'm not big on charity work."

"That's okay. You can just stand there and get killed. All the same to me."

Dexter turns his attention back to Travis and Deacon. Travis realizes the fight is about to kick off again and doesn't wait around. He rushes forward, leaping over one of the tables and launching himself straight at Deacon.

Cheers and screams erupt once again. Deacon turns in surprise. Throws his arms up to catch Travis in midair. They collide. Travis's arm is already moving. A blur. In and out, in and out. I can see something plastic in his hand. A toothbrush, by the look of it. Deacon uses the weight of Travis landing on him to flip him over and body-slam him onto a table. He brings his forearm down, trying to hit Travis in the throat. Travis rolls off the table. He lands in the water and surges to his feet. He's a wiry guy, fast.

The shouting and cheering is deafening now. Deacon is faltering. The adrenaline stopped him from maybe feeling the stab wounds, but now he looks down at his side. There are about ten small puncture marks there, all of them streaming blood.

Travis grins and goes for him again. He leaps in the air, kicking Deacon full in the chest. They both land in the water. Travis scrambles to his hands and knees, grabbing hold of a struggling Deacon and jamming the toothbrush into his throat.

Jesus. I wince as the volume of the crowd goes even higher. Inmates screaming in joy, others swearing and cursing over Deacon's body. Small bits of paper change hands. These guys are betting on the fights. God knows what they're using for currency.

Dexter raises his hands in the air and the Bloods gradually fall silent.

"We have a new contender!" he shouts. "Jack Constantine. Ex-cop, ex-army, ex-husband..." I tense up as this raises a few laughs. "An intense guy, I think we can all agree. Someone who likes to act as if he's pretty cool. Am I right?"

More cheers. The Bloods closest to me give me mocking shoves, and I stagger forward a few steps into the cleared circle.

"Now we'll see what all that experience has done for him. Never let it be said I'm an unfair man. Seeing as our friend here has had training, I think we need to even the odds a little."

He raises two fingers at someone in the crowd. The Bloods clear a path and two men are shoved forward into the circle.

I've seen them around. Sanchez and Jensen. They're not Woods, though. I think they're Ñetas. They're both armed. Sanchez has a bread knife, while Jensen is holding what looks like part of an office chair, a long piece of metal with the coaster still attached. Not sharp, but it's enough to brain me if it connects with my head.

The two of them share a look, then split up, coming at me from either side. I look desperately around. Most of the inmates surrounding us are armed. I try to grab a metal pole from one of them, but he holds on tight. Those standing next to him punch and shove at me until I'm forced to let go.

I turn back just as Sanchez comes for me, swiping the knife back and forth through the air like he's a ninja or something. He looks ridiculous. I wait for him to get within reach, throw a dummy punch that he jerks his head back to avoid, then lash out with my foot, kicking him in the nuts. He folds over and I follow through with a fast jab to his face. His head snaps to the side, but instead of going down, he lashes out blindly with the knife.

I jerk back out of reach. This is bullshit. I need a weapon. I lunge at the closest inmate and punch the guy in his throat. He's holding a smaller version of the cleaver that Ramirez carried around. I grab it from his hand, whirl around, and am barely in time to block a slash from Sanchez's knife.

I shove him away and bring the cleaver down on his forearm. I grabbed the cleaver the wrong way round, and it's the blunt edge that connects. I hear the crack of breaking bone. Sanchez cries out and drops the knife, falling to his knees.

Jensen has disappeared. Only one place he can be. I swing the cleaver around behind me and slam the same blunt edge into his windpipe. He drops, gagging, choking for breath.

There's a change in the noise coming from the crowd, a sudden drawing-in of breath. I whirl around and drop into a crouch. Sanchez's knife stabs into the air where I've just been standing.

Sanchez kicks me, sending me sprawling. The cleaver falls from my hand. He tries to kick me in the face. I grab his foot and twist, then shove him as hard as I can. He falls back on his ass and I scrabble around in the water in search of the cleaver. I hear him coming back, splashing noisily. My fingers curl around the handle and I roll onto my back, taking a chance and launching the weapon through the air.

It hits Sanchez right in the forehead, bringing him to a sudden halt. The shouting and cheering stop. Everyone stares at Sanchez as he just...stands there. Then a trickle of blood slides right down the center of his face and over his nose. He tips forward, falling into the water.

The crowd screams, laughing and howling. I push myself wearily to my feet—

—and something slams into my back. I grunt in pain and stumble forward, half turning just in time to stop Jensen's chair leg hitting me again.

I throw myself toward Sanchez and yank the cleaver free, then surge to my feet, and slam it hard into Jensen's ribs as he runs at me. He screams and drops to his knees. Blood bubbles from the huge gash in his side, pooling out between shattered ribs.

The crowd is chanting, "Finish him, finish him."

I hesitate, trying to catch my breath. I glance up at Dexter. He's waiting to see what I do.

Three gunshots ring out. Panicked shouting erupts as everyone tries to scatter, unsure where the danger is coming from.

Then something flies into the center of the room, spraying

clouds of white powder everywhere. The inmates push and shove each other to get away. The object rebounds off a wall and shoots past Dexter, clipping him on the side of the head as it does so. He goes down.

I scramble into the crowd, staying low. Everything is chaos as the white powder sprays over the rec room. I head for the door leading out of the unit, shoving inmates out of my way. I see Sawyer to my left, sprinting around the side of the wall as she runs through the pod.

The missile drops into the water, spinning around and around, still spraying spirals of white powder. I suddenly realize it's a fire extinguisher that's been punctured. Simple as that.

I hold the door as Sawyer bursts past me, then pull the key out of my pocket and shove the door closed. Some of the prisoners try to get out, but Felix is there waiting, and he holds the handle up while I ram the key home and lock the door.

I let out a shaky breath and sink down into the water, my back resting against the door.

"You okay?" asks Felix.

"What do you think?"

"I think you're damn lucky to be alive."

"Yeah. I could've done with some help in there."

"You had it covered. I was watchin'."

I turn my attention to Sawyer. "Thanks. Quick thinking."

"No problem." She holds up the gun. "Actually, slight problem. There were only three bullets in the magazine. I used them all."

Felix snatches the weapon from her. "Where the hell did you get that?"

"Carl gave it back to me. Guess he liked me."

"And you used all the bullets?" He ejects the magazine and stares at it in dismay.

"I didn't know there were only three left."

"Neither did we," I say wearily. "Doesn't matter now."

Felix angrily rams the magazine home and throws the gun

along the corridor. It spins through the air and lands with a splash.

"What the hell, man? We might be able to find bullets for it." I push myself to my feet and wade through the water, heading toward the door leading to the inmate passage.

"Just leave it," calls out Felix. "We're not gonna find any bullets."

I ignore him, feeling around with my feet as I get close to the door. My foot bangs into something heavy and I bend down to grope for it. As I do so, something catches my eye. The water seems to be pulling away from me, currents streaming toward the door. I move closer and see that the door has been pushed inward. There's a gap between it and the frame.

I frown and straighten up. I put my hand in front of the gap. There's wind, but not much. I crack the door slightly. It opens at my touch, moving inward.

The sounds of the storm grow louder. I can feel gusts of wind, but nothing like what I would be feeling if the whole corridor outside had been destroyed. I open the door wider. Still, nothing. No wind sucking me out to my death. No lashings of rain.

Now I'm confused, because Felix said this corridor had been destroyed. I pull the door wider. The area outside seems to be intact. Dark, but dry.

I hear Sawyer calling out. I can't hear what she's saying, but she's probably telling me not to do anything stupid. I ignore her and step out into the passage. Wind hits me from the left, shoving me forward. I steady myself, turning to face it. The wall to my right—the outside wall of the prison—is still holding together here. The whole thing has collapsed, leaning in against the wall to my left to form a sort of triangular passage.

I duck down and take a few steps, peering into the darkness. There is a blockage up ahead. I crouch down, my hand touching the leaning wall just above my head. Felix was right. The corridor *has* been totaled, twisted wreckage and bricks lying everywhere, broken stone piled up and blocking the way. Wind buffets through unseen gaps, blowing against my face. I gently prod the rubble, but it doesn't shift.

I turn around, facing back toward the right. I can't see from here, but if the corridor is still in one piece going north, we can use it to slip around Kincaid's unit. We won't even have to go through Unit 4.

I retrace my steps through the water, moving at a crouch as my head skims against the tilted wall. I move past the door leading back into the passage and keep going, blindly feeling my way. I count about twenty paces before I trip over something beneath the water, almost falling flat on my face. I throw my hands out to steady myself and hit up against another blockage in the tunnel.

Shit.

I stretch up, feeling along the fallen rubble. It goes right up to the ceiling, but there's a breeze coming from somewhere. More than a breeze. It's a steady wind.

I follow the flow of air to a gap in the rubble, then get down on my knees and peer through. There's light coming from somewhere on the other side. I reach through with my arm, trying to test the thickness. I can feel a breeze on my fingers. I reach up, then down, but all I can feel is cold metal and more bricks.

Shit.

I briefly consider pulling on the rubble, seeing if I can bring the blockage down, but I manage to stop myself. That's the kind of thinking that gets you killed. Best to just head back to Felix and Sawyer.

I start to pull my arm out. The bricks shift suddenly, the grating sound of concrete echoing around me.

I freeze.

The sound stops. I slowly move my arm again, pulling it back toward me.

Then the whole pile shifts and a heavy weight slams down

on my arm. I try to yank it out, but I already know it's too late. The shattered concrete and debris only digs deeper.

Jesus Christ. Please do not tell me this has just happened. I tug gently, but I can feel the edge of the concrete digging into my skin.

"Hey!" I shout. "Guys!"

Nothing. Where the hell are they?

Seventeen

4:10 a.m.

Sawyer watches Constantine disappear through the door into the inmate corridor. She throws a shocked look at Felix. "Uh…?"

"Don't look at me like that! I checked the corridor from Admin. There was no way in."

"Looks like there is now."

Felix brightens up. "Well…that's good for us. It means we don't have to go through there." He gestures to their right, then suddenly freezes. "For fuck sake."

Sawyer follows his gaze to find two men standing by the door into Unit 4.

Two men holding M9s.

"Felix," one of them says, nodding as though greeting an old friend.

Felix sighs. "Cassidy. You still alive, huh?"

"Still alive." Cassidy waves the gun in a "come here" motion. "Why don't the two of you just step into Kincaid's office? I'm sure the big man will want a chat."

Sawyer glances at Felix. He nods subtly but urgently in the direction of Unit 4. She gets the hint. They need to get out of the corridor in case Constantine comes back. At least if he's free, he might be able to do something to help.

Cassidy nods amiably at her as she approaches. "We haven't had the chance to properly introduce ourselves yet. I'm Cassidy. This is Veitch."

The other guy lifts the barrel of his gun to his forehead, like he's touching the brim of a hat.

"If you'll be so kind as to step this way." They move aside to let Felix and Sawyer go ahead of them into the sally port. The door at the other end stands open.

"All the way through," says Cassidy.

Sawyer and Felix step through the door into Unit 4. There are two men sitting opposite each other at a table in the exact center of the rec room, easy for everyone to see.

Kincaid lounges on a chair close to them. He looks... *bored*. His eyes briefly come alive when he sees the newcomers, but the spark quickly fades when they're followed into the unit by Cassidy and Veitch.

"Where's Constantine?"

"He wasn't with them," says Veitch.

"He's already dead," says Felix. "One of Castillo's guys—Ramirez—took him down."

Kincaid stares at Felix, trying to figure out if he's telling the truth. Sawyer quickly scans the rec room. It's mostly empty, except for the two seated men and a bunch of terrified inmates crammed inside one of the lower-level cells. They don't seem to have anything in common apart from the look of fear on their faces. They're from all races. Some have gang signs, some don't. Some are in their sixties, while a couple look barely out of their teens. None of them try to step out of the cell, despite the fact that the door stands wide open.

Her heart starts to beat faster as she focuses on the two men. An old-fashioned revolver lies between them. There's blood all over the table, some of it sticky and old, some fresh and dripping over the edge into the water.

Kincaid turns his attention to her. "I wasn't sure if my eyes were playing tricks on me. You know how it is. Age. Creeps up on us all. I thought, that can't be a woman running around with Constantine. And yet here you are." He chuckles. "Bet you've had a helluva night." He stands up and approaches. Sawyer tenses as he walks behind her, leans close to take in her scent. "How do you still smell so nice after everything that's happened?"

One of the men at the table tries to speak. "Kincaid—"

Kincaid turns to him. "You want to say something?"

The man nods gratefully. Kincaid steps away from Sawyer, approaches the table. When he gets there, he casually picks up the revolver and shoots the man in the head. His head jerks sharply to the left as the gunshot echoes around the confined space.

Sawyer screams in shock as the body slumps sideways into the water.

Kincaid bursts out laughing. "Jesus Christ, that is one unlucky guy."

He holds the gun out. Veitch takes it and slips a single bullet inside the chamber.

"Where did you get that?" asks Felix.

"Sheriff's office. You never see him carrying this thing around in his holster? Guy was stuck in the past. Thought he was in the Wild West or something."

Veitch hands the gun back to Kincaid. He spins the chamber and snaps the gun closed. "Bring another one."

Cassidy and Veitch hurry over to the cell. There's jostling and fighting inside as everyone tries to move out of reach. A skinny guy is shoved forward. He looks like he's in his early twenties, sobbing and begging them to pick someone else. The two men ignore him and drag him to the table. Cassidy shoves him down onto the bench, while Veitch grabs the body in the water and starts dragging it toward the stairs leading up to the second level.

Sawyer watches him shove it behind the stairs. Her eyes widen. There's already a pile of bodies dumped there. There must be about twenty of them.

Kincaid passes the gun to the skinny inmate. "I think you've got the idea by now."

The young man takes the gun in trembling hands. He looks at the guy sitting opposite him. He's older, Mexican. His eyes don't hold the same fear as the other man's. He just looks angry.

"Let's go," says Kincaid. He's still standing by the table. "We don't have all day. Do it or I do it for you."

The young man slowly lifts the gun toward his temple. His hands are shaking so hard Sawyer is surprised he doesn't drop it. Kincaid watches from about two feet away, positioned directly between the two men.

Then the young man turns suddenly and points the gun at Kincaid, pulling the trigger.

The gun clicks.

Kincaid doesn't even flinch as Cassidy lunges forward and grabs the inmate's arm. He turns to Veitch with a grin. "How many is that now?"

"Four."

"Four out of...what? Twenty?"

"Nineteen."

"Nineteen? Shit. Guess I'm just a lucky guy."

Cassidy tightly grips the man's hand, lifting the gun up to his temple.

"You are going to feel *so* stupid if the bullet is in that chamber now," says Kincaid.

Sawyer doesn't want to watch. She turns back to Kincaid, grimly fascinated by what she's just witnessed. She's sure she saw a look of disappointment on his face when there was no bullet in the chamber.

The young man is sobbing and begging, pleading with Kincaid to pick someone else.

"Either you pull the trigger or I shoot you in the stomach and let you bleed out," says Kincaid. "You've got three seconds to choose. One..."

The young man squeezes his eyes shut.

"Two..."

His finger curls around the trigger.

"Three."

The gunshot echoes throughout the rec room. The inmate's head jerks to the right, blood and skull fragments exploding outward.

He falls into the water. Kincaid turns his attention to the

Mexican guy sitting on the other side of the table. "You sure you're Mexican? You not messing with us? Because you've got the luck of the Irish, my friend. Get up."

The guy looks at him in confusion.

"Get up. Go back to the cell. The fuck you staring at me like that for? Go!"

The guy stands up hurriedly, tripping over his own feet and sprawling into the water in his haste. He pushes himself up and scurries back to the cell, trying to burrow as deep into the press of bodies as he can.

Kincaid turns his attention to Sawyer and Felix. "Your turn."

Veitch shoves Sawyer forward. She stumbles and catches herself on the table. Cassidy tries to do the same to Felix, but the big man doesn't budge.

Kincaid sighs. "Jesus, must everything be difficult? Sit or I just shoot the woman in the face."

Veitch grabs Sawyer's arm. She tries to fight him off, but he punches her in the side of her head, hard enough for stars to erupt across her vision. He pushes painfully on her shoulder and she falls onto the bench.

Felix reluctantly sits down opposite her. Kincaid hands him the gun.

"You first."

Felix takes the revolver. He glances at Veitch and Cassidy, then over at Kincaid.

"I'd think about that *very* carefully," says Kincaid.

Sawyer shakes her head in an attempt to clear it. She glances around unsteadily. At Felix. At Cassidy, at Veitch. At Kincaid. She feels a moment of utter depersonalization. What the hell is happening? Why is she here? Everything feels so surreal. She can feel her breath coming in short gasps. Panic wells up inside, rising from the depths of her soul into her tightening chest. Tears sting her eyes, blurring the image of Felix sitting before her. This isn't fair. None of this is fair.

A loud bang echoes from somewhere overhead, a heavy

thump, then the sound of rolling and crashing. Sawyer jumps, whimpering in fear, but is unable to look away from Felix. His eyes stay locked on hers, but everyone else glances upward, making sure the roof isn't about to come down on them.

Sawyer takes strength from Felix's implacable gaze. She quickly wipes her eyes. *Pull yourself together. Don't you fucking dare let them see you weak. You can get through this.*

She almost bursts into hysterical laughter. How? They're not getting out of here. Constantine was right. She was a naïve idiot for ever hoping they could. They're all going to die tonight. The only thing she can control is how much dignity she has when the time comes.

She straightens up in her chair, staring at Felix. The banging sound shifts from the roof and seems to drop down to echo from somewhere over in the staff corridor. More walls being torn down by the hurricane, probably. She wonders which would be worse. The gun or the hurricane. Probably the hurricane. At least the gun is fast.

Kincaid claps his hands together once. "Let's go. If this place is going to come down around our heads, I want to see one of you shoot yourself first."

Felix doesn't hesitate. He moves so fast Sawyer barely has time to register it, raising the gun to his temple and pulling the trigger. He doesn't even blink.

No gunshot. Just the click of the hammer striking the empty chamber.

"Jesus, Felix," says Kincaid as Felix slams the gun down on the table. "What's the rush? Give it some buildup. Some drama." He shifts his gaze to Sawyer. "Your turn."

Sawyer hesitantly reaches out for the gun. As her fingers curl around the grip, Felix lunges for Kincaid.

Kincaid is expecting it. He slams a fist into Felix's face, then launches an uppercut as Felix falls. Cassidy and Veitch grab him and yank him back into the chair.

Kincaid has a glint in his eye as he bobs around like a boxer, striking the air with his fists. "Still got it. That's the problem with you big guys. You don't *think*. You think your weight is all you need. See how wrong you are? That's a lesson for you. Free of charge. You've got about three minutes to ponder it."

He stops bouncing around and squats down, leaning his elbows on the table as he turns his attention back to Sawyer.

She slowly lifts the gun, tilting it forward to locate the bullet in the chamber.

"Uh-uh," says Kincaid, pushing the gun sideways. "No peeking."

She takes a deep breath and slowly raises the gun to her head. The tears start flowing again. This time she can't stop them.

"Look at me," says Felix. "Sawyer. Look at me. Keep your eyes on me, okay?"

She nods and takes a shuddering breath. She focuses on his eyes. They're actually quite kind. She's never noticed before.

He nods gently.

Sawyer pulls the trigger.

The click is so loud in her head she thinks for a moment it really is a gunshot. But then she hears Kincaid laughing and she realizes she's still staring into Felix's eyes.

He looks briefly relieved. But the look quickly fades as he stares at the gun, knowing it's his turn next.

There's a screech of rending metal coming from somewhere in the staff corridor. The whole unit shakes. It feels like an earthquake, the water surging and slapping up against the walls.

Kincaid waits until the rumbling dies down, then smiles expectantly at Felix.

Sawyer can see that Felix fully expects the bullet to be in the chamber this time around.

He curls his fingers around the grip and slowly raises the gun to his head, his eyes never leaving hers.

Eighteen

4:20 a.m.

It's been five minutes since I acted like a four-year-old kid sticking his head through the railings at a shopping mall and got my arm trapped. Five minutes. And no one has come to look for me. Which means Sawyer and Felix are in trouble.

I've managed to pull the sleeve of my prison suit up over my elbow, but it hasn't done anything to help. The rubble itself is weighed down and off balance. No matter how I move my arm, the concrete and metal shifts and settles again.

The outside wall of the corridor, the part that has fallen diagonally over the passage to my left, is making ominous grinding and crumbling noises. Every thirty seconds or so, I hear concrete splashing into the water and the wind in the corridor increases in strength.

This is probably the stupidest thing I've ever done. And I once tried to leap over a pickup truck coming at me at 40 mph after drinking half a bottle of Jack. But I was hoping there would be a way through. If I'd just been able to get past the debris, we could have avoided Kincaid altogether. There might even have been a clear path along the inmate corridor all the way to Northside. I could have made it easier for everyone.

Could've, would've.

Moron.

I need some kind of lubrication. Water sure isn't doing it, but blood might. I steel myself, take a deep breath, then start pushing and pulling my arm against the jagged concrete. I wince at the pain. My arm isn't actually moving; just the skin, shifting and scraping and tearing. I grit my teeth as the concrete digs in. I can already feel blood, warm against my arm. I keep sawing it back and forth. I don't want to go too deep, just enough to see if it works.

After a minute or so, my forearm is slick with blood. I brace my shoulder against the rubble, pushing up in an attempt to lift it slightly, and pull. Pain explodes through me, slicing up my arm as the broken concrete digs in. But I can feel my arm moving slightly.

I can also hear the rubble shifting. Stones tumble from somewhere deep inside the huge pile. A few small rocks fall and hit me on the head.

Shit. No choice now. I pull as hard as I can, screaming against the pain. My arm starts to slide free, slowly, too slowly. Rocks tumble down, splashing into the water beside me. I pull harder, feeling my skin tearing away. I grit my teeth as more concrete falls. A huge triangular slab of roofing dislodges from the top of the pile, tumbling end over end to slam into the water about two feet from my legs. I pull harder. I can feel the whole pile shifting ominously. I yank my arm free and throw myself backward, scrambling through the water as the roof and walls of the inmate corridor slide and fall, the entire section of corridor tumbling down. The wind and rain roars inside, the destroyed corridor now completely exposed to the elements. I push myself to my feet and sprint back for the door, making it through just as the outside wall collapses inward. I get a brief glimpse of lightning and solid sheets of rain before I slam the door closed, holding it in place until I find the correct key to lock it again.

The wind buffets and shoves against the door, rattling it in its frame. I take a shaky breath and examine my arm. The skin has been ripped away, exposing patches of fat. The whole of my forearm is dripping with blood. I rip the right sleeve off my prison scrubs, wrapping it around my arm and tying a knot using my left hand and my teeth. Fuck, but it's painful.

The passage is empty. I glance through the doors opening

off the corridor. No sign of Sawyer or Felix. I check the door into Unit 3. There are three members of the Bloods smashing something into the glass, trying to force their way out. The door is still locked. Which means Felix and Sawyer can only be in one place.

I move along the sally port leading into Unit 4. I can hear talking as I approach. Low voices. I press myself up against the wall and peer through the door.

Sawyer and Felix are seated opposite each other at one of the tables. Kincaid watches them with an eager look on his face. Cassidy and Veitch stand to one side. They're both holding guns.

And then Sawyer lifts a gun to her head and pulls the trigger.

My heart almost stops, but the gun doesn't go off. There's no bullet in the chamber.

She drops the gun onto the table. Kincaid turns to Felix, and Felix reluctantly picks it up.

There's no time for thinking things through. I sprint back to Unit 3, give the guys smashing the glass the finger, then use the key to unlock the door.

I run as the door slams open behind me. I hear excited shouting as the Bloods realize they're free and spill out into the prison.

I burst into Kincaid's unit. He turns, a surprised look on his face. Felix still has the gun against his head. He sees me coming. His eyes widen in surprise and he lurches to his feet.

"Move!" I shout.

I keep running. Felix turns the gun on Kincaid and pulls the trigger. Nothing happens. He tries again, but Kincaid is already moving, rushing toward Veitch and Cassidy. Felix keeps firing. The gun eventually goes off, but the bullet misses Kincaid and slams into the wall.

Felix throws the gun away and sprints after me. Sawyer is already moving. I hit the door and shove it open, glancing over my shoulder to see the Bloods streaming into the unit. Veitch and Cassidy start shooting.

Felix makes it through the door. Sawyer is still about ten feet away, some of the Bloods close on her heels. She rushes past me. I follow, trying to push the door closed behind me. Too late. The Bloods are already here. They slam into the door, sending me stumbling back into the corridor. Felix hits the closest guy in the face and shoves him into the others, then grabs me and pushes me ahead of him.

"Go!"

We sprint into the sally port and then straight through the door into the Transitional Care Unit.

It's not like the others. The door doesn't lead straight into the rec room, but rather into a corridor that splits left and right. We head right, the sounds of chaos and shouting close behind.

The health and security units are much bigger than the previous blocks we traveled through. They're entirely self-contained, like mini versions of the admin building. They have office wings, their own infirmaries, cafeterias, changing rooms, the works.

Hopefully that's enough to lose ourselves in. We turn left into the next passage, then take another random turn and just keep going until the sounds of pursuit finally die away.

We slow down, listening intently.

"I think we lost them," says Felix.

We keep walking, trying to find our bearings. The unit is dimly lit. The lights pulse and fade, the generator struggling to do its job. I'm not sure of the exact layout in here, but I know we have to head north to the door that leads out of TCU and into the Mental Health Unit.

I glance at Sawyer as we move. She looks like she's taking strain.

"Are you okay?" I eventually ask.

She shakes her head, but doesn't say anything. Her face is

tight, cold. Her eyes glisten. She's trying to stay in control. Trying to keep it together. She needs a breather. A couple of minutes to take stock. I think we all do.

I check the closest door, but it leads into a storeroom. The next one is the bathroom, then a few offices.

"The hell are you looking for?" asks Felix.

I don't answer. A couple of doors later, I find what I'm after. A staff break room.

"In here."

I usher the others in and take a quick look around the room. I sigh with a small amount of happiness when I see a coffee pod machine.

"Constantine? What are we doing?" asks Felix.

"Taking a break."

I cross the room and put a pod in the machine, then grab a mug and place it beneath the nozzle. Sawyer slumps into one of the chairs around the small table.

Felix looks at me like I've just stripped naked. "Seriously? We're running for our lives and you want to stop for a break?"

"Don't you feel like a cup of coffee?" I hold up one of the pods. "*Real* coffee?"

He hesitates. He's been in here a lot longer than I have. I know he's craving something better than the shit we get from the commissary.

"I don't know, man. We should keep moving."

I nod subtly at Sawyer. He glances over at her and his face clears. He mouths, *Oh . . .* and winks at me. Good old Felix. As discreet as a brick to the face.

"I know what you're doing," says Sawyer without looking up. "And I'd like you to stop it. I'm not a child."

I hear the coffee trickling into the cup behind me. "No idea what you're talking about. Milk?" I turn around and grab a milk pod.

Sawyer doesn't answer for a moment. "And two sugars. Actually, make it three."

"Coming up." I swap the full mug for an empty and insert a new capsule, then pour in the milk and sugar. I pass the mug to Sawyer and wait for the next one to fill. Felix stands at the door. No one speaks.

I put two more mugs down on the table and sit opposite Sawyer. Felix joins us and we all stare contemplatively into our mugs.

"Well…" says Felix. "Isn't this nice?"

I nod. "We should do it more often. We never get a chance to just sit down at the end of the day and check in with each other, you know?"

Felix nods seriously. "I do, I do. So how *was* your day?"

I breathe out noisily and take a sip of my coffee. I pause to let the flavor hit. Christ, this is good. "Well…you know Sinclair? Over in accounting?"

Felix looks like he's thinking. "Tall guy? Skinny? Made a move on you at the Christmas party."

"That's the one. Threw himself out the top-floor window today."

"Is that right?"

"It is." I take another sip and smack my lips appreciatively. "Said he couldn't live without me. That if he couldn't have me, there was no point in going on."

"Poor guy. If only he knew the real you. Fucker dodged a bullet."

Sawyer stiffens at his words. I glare at Felix and mouth, *What the fuck?* He just shrugs helplessly.

Sawyer sighs and looks up. "You can stop now. Actually, I'm begging you. *Please* stop now. I'm fine."

"You sure?" Felix reaches out and puts a hand over hers. "Because if you're not," he says gently, "you can talk to Constantine." He takes his hand back and wraps it around his coffee mug. "I'm no good at all that feelings shit."

Sawyer laughs softly. "I'm okay." She pauses for a moment. "I mean, we're alive, right? What more can we ask for?"

I think about it. "Shelter that's not going to fall on our heads?"

Felix nods. "Guns?"

"Scuba gear?"

"A submarine would be nice," says Felix.

"I'm talking figuratively," says Sawyer.

"Well, shit," says Felix. "Why didn't you say? I mean, the woman is talking *figuratively*."

"Shut up, Felix," she says.

"Shutting up."

She bows her head and sips her coffee. Felix and I are watching her carefully. She eventually snaps her head up and glares at us both. "Will you two stop looking at me like I'm a baby bird that fell out of its nest or something. I said I'm fine. Yes, I was just forced to play a game of Russian roulette. But so was he"—she nods at Felix—"and so were about twenty other poor bastards who didn't survive. You want to feel bad for someone, feel bad for them."

"Okay," I say, "she's fine. Break's over. Let's go."

Felix looks at his coffee in dismay. "I want to savor it."

"Tough shit. You were right. No time for a break. Hustle up."

He sighs and gulps down his coffee, then glares at me. "That is *not* how coffee should be enjoyed."

As we make our way through the unit, I'm getting more and more worried about the prison's ability to hold up. The hurricane lashes us with a ferocity that builds with every minute. Every creak, every distant rumble is making me more and more jumpy. I just don't think this place is going to last till the eye of the hurricane arrives.

But what the hell else are we supposed to do? Stop? Hide under a desk somewhere? No. We have to keep moving forward. Because anything else is admitting defeat.

We carry on, wading through water that is almost up to my waist. The building creaks and groans like a pirate ship. The wind sounds like the ferocious howling of animals. It rises and falls. Grows louder, then fades. It feels like the hurricane is a predator circling a campfire, waiting to strike.

A lot of the corridors we try have already collapsed, forcing us to retrace our steps and find alternative routes. But going by the evacuation plans stuck on the wall, we're getting close.

We turn into a corridor and pull up short. About halfway along, a bent-over figure is trying to drag what looks like a huge slab of concrete through a doorway. He's not making much progress. The slab looks way too heavy.

"That's Leo," says Felix softly.

Which explains *why* he's not making much progress. The guy is about eighty years old.

"Who's Leo?" whispers Sawyer.

"Old guy," says Felix. "Always talking about escaping. He's been here since he was twenty or something."

"What did he do?"

"No one knows. There are rumors. That he went a bit crazy in the army. Killed some of his own squad."

"Leo?" I call.

Leo glances over at us, barely registering our presence before resuming his task.

"What you doing there?" asks Felix as we approach.

"Pole dancing," he says. He straightens up and arches his back with a wince. "The hell do you want?"

"Just passing through," I say. "Heading for the Northside staff room."

He snorts. "Not this way you're not."

"Why?"

"You can't get through. The Mental Health Unit is still locked down."

"We have a key."

He shrugs. "Whoop-de-fucking-do. Even if you get in there, you're going to have to fight off the retards and rapists. They've all been let out of their cells. Then you have to get into ACU. Last I heard—and this was before the staff corridor went down, mind—Preacher's followers had turned that place into some sort of crazy-ass church, waiting on him to return like he's the Second Coming or something."

Shit.

"We still have to try," says Sawyer.

I look at her. "We don't have any weapons."

"So we sneak."

"Why you got such a hard-on for the staff room?" asks Leo.

"I have a keycard to get out," says Sawyer. "When the eye of the hurricane passes over, we're going to the Glasshouse."

Leo still looks confused. "Why?"

"To ride out the storm."

He bursts into laughter. "Seriously? In the Glasshouse? You'll be lucky if that place is even still standing."

"But...they were shipping in prisoners from all over the place," says Sawyer. "They said it would be safe."

Leo shrugs. "They lied. Or they're lying to themselves. Trust me, I've been inside the Glasshouse. The foundations in that place are crumbling. The mortar holding the bricks together is like sand. Not a chance it's going to survive."

I can see the dawning realization settling on Sawyer's face. Her shoulders slump and she turns away from us, walking off a few steps as she tries to think her way out of this. I glance at Felix, but he just shrugs.

Sawyer finally turns back. She looks at me numbly. "So that's it? We're dead?"

"Not if you help me here," says Leo.

"Why?" I ask. "What are you doing?"

"Trying to get to the tunnels."

Jesus. This again. "There *are* no tunnels, Leo. You've gone on about them for as long as I've been here—"

"Longer," says Felix.

"Longer. Exactly."

"So?"

"So they're not real."

He laughs. "Oh, so you know so much about this place? How long you been here exactly?"

"Three years."

He turns to Felix. "You?"

"Eight."

"Want to know how long I've been here? About sixty years. Sixty fucking years. You don't think that gives me some special insight?"

Felix shrugs. "Don't really care, Leo. You're starting to bore me."

"Oh, I'm boring you, am I? Tell me—you guys know about the history of this place, right? The Cross-Florida Barge Canal project?"

"Sure," I say.

"Right. And do you know about the floodwater system below the prison? It's like the G-Cans in Tokyo."

"What the hell are the G-Cans?"

"It's this huge storm sewer that's supposed to protect Tokyo from floods. An underground tunnel system, about four miles long. The tunnels connect up to these silos that drain into this massive room they call the Temple. The place is like…a *cavern*. Two hundred and fifty feet deep and nearly five hundred feet long. The floodwater from the city's drainage heads through the tunnels and ends up in the Temple. Then it's pumped out into the river."

I can see Felix is starting to get annoyed. He's looking around, deciding which way we should go.

"What does that have to do with this place?" I ask.

"We started building a smaller version of the G-Cans here in the sixties, when construction started up again on the canal project. So there are all these tunnels underneath us. The first set joins up with the Glasshouse, then to the flood system below us. But they were never used. When the project was canned, we didn't bother connecting the tunnels and silos up."

"Wait. Back up." I stare hard at Leo. "These tunnels. You say they connect to the Glasshouse?"

"Yeah. The basement tunnels in here join up with the basement tunnels in the Glasshouse; then they lead down to the flood system."

I try to fight down the excitement building inside me. "So... we can gain access to the Glasshouse through these tunnels?"

"I suppose."

"That means we can get inmates from here *and* the Glasshouse to safety," says Sawyer excitedly.

Everyone looks at her.

"What?"

"I don't get it," says Felix, ignoring her and turning back to Leo. "Won't we just drown in the tunnels?"

"Are you stupid?" snaps the old man. "If the tunnels are going to carry floodwater, they have to be waterproof. Which means water can't get out and water can't get in."

I nod to the corridor Leo was trying to clear. "This leads to the basement tunnels?"

"Yeah. These buildings are all part of the original build. Admin too. From when this place still belonged to the Engineer Corps."

We're all thinking about what he's saying. If it's true, it means we don't have to even head outside. We don't have to wait for the eye of the storm to arrive. We don't have to hope and pray the building holds.

"Are you sure you're not crazy?" asks Felix.

Sawyer shakes her head. "Martinez told me the same thing this morning, when she was giving me the tour. She mentioned the storm tunnels."

Leo looks smug. "See?"

"But we can't just hide underground without telling anyone on the outside," says Sawyer. "We have to get word out."

"Why?" asks Felix.

"What if Ravenhill comes down on top of everyone? We'd all be trapped in the tunnels. No one would know we're down there."

"Wait," says Leo. "What exactly do you mean by *everyone*?"

"Everyone who's sheltering down there. The inmates—"

He shakes his head firmly. "Not gonna happen. Who *are* you anyway? Why is there a woman wandering around...No, doesn't matter. I don't care. This is *my* escape route. I've been planning it my whole life."

"You can't just keep it to yourself," says Sawyer sharply. "You have a chance to save hundreds of lives."

Leo shrugs. "Fuck 'em."

I burst out laughing at her look of shock. Even Felix has a grin on his face. Not because Sawyer doesn't have a point, but because Leo does as well. Not one inmate has done anything to help us during the night. They've been trying to kill us, torture us, or let us drown. But that still doesn't stop her wanting to save them. Castillo nearly killed all of us, but I guarantee she doesn't regret rescuing him from the flooding room.

"I wouldn't even bother arguing, Leo."

"Why would anyone argue?" she asks earnestly. "What's the choice here? Letting hundreds of people die, or saving their lives?"

I leave Leo to deal with Sawyer's sense of moral outrage and peer into the passage he's been trying to clear. It's about fifteen feet long, but the roof and the left wall have caved in, leaving huge slabs of concrete completely blocking the way.

"Leo," I say, "if you won't do it for altruism, you need to do it for survival. Because there's no way we can clear this rubble. Not before the building comes down. We need *way* more hands."

Leo gestures hopefully at Felix. "Not even with this guy?"

Felix checks out the corridor and shakes his head. "I know I have the physique of a Nubian god, but even I can't move this much without help. We need some of the other inmates in here."

"*And* get word to the outside," says Sawyer.

"How do you suggest we do that?" asks Leo.

"What about the radios in the security room? I was talking to the COs on the bus when they crashed."

I shake my head. "Not powerful enough."

But Sawyer has given me an idea. A couple of years ago, when the inmate corridor was on lockdown, the COs brought me through this unit to get to my job at the maintenance shed. They took me other ways as well. Through the yard outside—though I don't think that's going to work right now—and once into the staff corridor and through Northside itself.

The point is, the shed isn't separate from the rest of the prison. It's part of the same building. I can get to it from here—and that's where Henry had been building a ham radio for the past couple of years. It was a secret project, right under the COs' noses. There were no nefarious reasons for it, as far as I could figure out. He just wanted to chat with people outside the prison. But he never completed it. He wanted my help to run the antenna up into the ceiling space so the radio would get a signal. We just never figured out a good time to do it. The shed was always under observation.

I tell the others. Sawyer breaks into a smile, then hesitates. "Where's the shed? Can we get there?"

"Yeah. I think so."

"Okay," she says. "Let's go."

"You don't need to come. You can stay here with Felix. Help clear this rubble away."

"Take her," says Felix. "You might need someone to steady the ladder."

"What ladder?"

"I don't fucking know. I'm assuming. I've never been in the shed."

I shrug. "Fine. Come if you want. Felix..." Felix glances over from where he's studying the collapsed passage. "Do what you can here. We'll be back in ten minutes."

He nods. "On it."

Nineteen
4:50 a.m.

We don't get back to Felix and Leo in ten minutes. It takes us that long just to reach the maintenance shed, moving through semi-collapsed corridors, backtracking to find a different path when the way forward is blocked, taking cover every time it sounds like the ceiling is about to come down on top of us.

And with every passing minute, the storm grows stronger. There's no difference in the volume of the wind, no increase in the shrieking, the howling. How can there be? It can't get any louder than it already is. No, I can *sense* it. Feel it weighing down on me. It's a rising pressure, a steady mounting of tension that has nowhere to go. It fills me with a sense of urgency that has no outlet. It just keeps building and building. Like I've put my hand on a hot plate and now I'm waiting for the pain to hit, for the stench of burning flesh to fill my nostrils.

Add to that, I'm sure we're being followed. I can't confirm it, and I don't have time to wait around to find out. I hope it's just coincidence. Inmates moving around the unit, exploring, looking for a way out, for weapons. If it's not?

Shit, I don't know. Deal with it the same way we've dealt with everything else tonight. Wing it and hope for the best.

After those ten minutes, we finally reach our destination. The maintenance shed is more like a miniature airplane hangar than anything else. Over to the left sits a tractor with its mower detached. The tractor is blue, but the paint is chipped away, revealing the original green underneath. The six-foot blade attachment sits on a workbench against the left wall. Henry and I took it off yesterday. It looks like Henry had already been sharpening it. The metal gleams in the light.

In the floor toward the middle of the shed is an inspection pit with chains hanging from the ceiling, just in case any engine work has to be done on the prison vehicles. Henry said it was left over from the time this place was the base for the army engineers, when they were still trying to get that canal project off the ground.

I never really understood how the shed was allowed to exist. It's still part of the prison complex, with the same thick brick walls and locked exterior doors to keep everyone inside— although the doors are wide enough to drive a bus through if needed. But there are so many dangerous objects here that I was constantly amazed Henry and I were even allowed to enter.

I suppose it's like the prison barbershop. Only the most trusted inmates are allowed to work there. I only got in because I kept mostly to myself the first year of my sentence. I didn't talk to many people until Henry struck up a conversation with me one time in the cafeteria. Henry was another ex-cop, except he was inside for going on a vigilante spree when he busted down the door of a pedo ring. He got me the job as his assistant.

I look around uneasily, realizing with an abrupt skip in my heart that I'll never see Henry again. This was the old guy's home. Everything in this place reflected who he was.

And now he's dead. Just like that. Because of a split-second decision made by fucking Ramirez. It feels like I'm intruding. I've never been here alone. Never been here without Henry prattling on about circuit boards or soldering technique.

Sawyer looks over at me. "You okay?"

I nod, turning my attention to Henry's office. It stands against the shed wall, a small roofed-over cabin about the same size as an RV. We wade through the water and climb the steps. A wooden bench runs around three walls of the office, the surface covered with loose wiring, toolboxes that have already been ransacked, old radios, an ancient lamp, and a clear plastic television set. There's a *Playboy* calendar from 1983 on the wall. I once asked Henry why he didn't get a new one. He just shrugged and said it was a good year.

I take a moment to look around. The old guy's presence is everywhere. This was his space. He told me he didn't even mind that he was in prison. He said he'd spend his time the same if he was on the outside, and at least in here he got food and a roof over his head.

The workbench to the far right is where he was building his ham radio. It's not much to look at. It's made up of a base transceiver Henry had pulled out of one of the old prison buses, to which he'd jury-rigged a handheld microphone using cables and wiring from old radios.

There's a kid's toy sitting on top of the radio, a little Winnie-the-Pooh figure.

I've never seen it before. I reach out to touch it, but pull my fingers back before I do.

"What's wrong?"

"Henry must have hidden this whenever I came in," I say softly.

Sawyer frowns. "A kid's toy?"

My eyes are fixed on the figure. "I . . . told him a story once. About how Amy and I were going to decorate the baby's room with all this stuff. The Hundred Acre Wood. All the characters, you know? They were my favorite stories as a kid."

I slump onto a stool, still staring at the toy. I feel tears in my eyes, a sharp pain in my chest. The memories rush back. Buying the little hardcover books in preparation. Way too early, but we couldn't wait. Little onesies with Tigger and Piglet on them. Looking for wallpaper, blankets.

"We'd been trying for a while," I say. My voice sounds distant, far away. "For a baby. Then one morning I wake up to find her staring at me. It was four in the morning."

"Again with the staring? She liked to look at you, huh?"

"Yeah, she did. I never understood why. Never got used to it, either." I smile sadly. "So I wake up to her staring at me, this huge grin on her face. And then she flicks the pregnancy test at me. I swear to God, I think I got some of her pee on my face."

"Gross."

"Yeah. Anyway, she throws it at me and starts bouncing around on the bed, screaming. Neighbors called the cops. They sent a car around. I had to smooth that over, and all the while I'm sort of just... stunned. Me, a dad."

"But you were happy, right?"

"I was... in shock. You always hear people say how their lives change when they find out, or when the baby actually comes. A whole new life opens up for you, one you've never really trained for. It's like those old choose-your-own-adventure books."

"Huh?"

"If you want to remain happy, solvent, and child-free, use a condom and turn to page thirty-four. If you want to be broke, worry all the time, and have your sex life reduced to quickies in a locked bathroom, do not use a condom and turn to page one hundred."

"Come on. You didn't *really* think that, did you?"

I smile. "Not really, no. But when you find out, your whole world changes. Just like that. Expands into all these new possibilities. Babies, diapers, schools, college... It takes you on a different path."

"A good path."

"Sure. A good path. But... different."

"You... don't sound sure you wanted a baby."

"I definitely did. But listen, I won't lie. It scared the shit out of me. When I found out, it made me realize just what a total fuckup I was."

"You're not a fuckup. You served. You were a cop."

"Doesn't matter. I think it's what every dad feels. You wonder if you're going to repeat the same mistakes your parents made, the ones that messed you up as a kid. You wonder if you're going to be good enough to look up to. Everything you've done in your life up to that point becomes meaningless, because suddenly you've created this innocent soul who's coming into this absolutely fucked-up piece-of-shit world and you realize it's on you to protect them. Suddenly there's this terrifying need...this *awareness*...that you have to step up. You have to become the man you always see in crappy movies or read about in books."

"No one's like that. No one's perfect. You shouldn't put that much pressure on yourself."

I'm silent for a moment; then I shrug. "Didn't matter in the end, did it? Novak, Wright, and Tully saw to that."

There's a sudden booming from somewhere outside. We both freeze, listening as something slams onto the roof. Metal scrapes on metal, rising above the noise of the rain and wind, sounding like fingernails on a blackboard.

Enough with the wallowing. I grab the Winnie-the-Pooh figure and stick it in a drawer, then turn my attention to the makeshift radio, fiddling with switches and turning dials.

"It doesn't look like much," says Sawyer doubtfully.

"Henry said it's as good as the ones you buy in the shops. He said you can bounce the signal off the rain, weather systems, that kind of thing."

"What's its range?"

"Hundreds of miles. At least."

"Bullshit."

"That's what he told me."

"You know how to use it?" Sawyer asks.

"Not really."

"You ever see *him* use it?"

"He *hadn't* used it yet. Don't think it's much different to a police radio, though."

I push the power button.

Nothing happens.

"Is it plugged in?"

I lean over the back of the desk. There's a trail of red and black wires sprouting from the back of the radio. Most loop around and plug straight back into another part of the transceiver, but there are two insulated cables that don't. One slips down behind the workbench, while another has been nailed up the wall in a neat straight line, disappearing through the roof.

I push back the chair and get down on my knees. The wire that goes behind the workbench disappears into a junction box. The junction box itself has a thick wire that snakes out through a hole in the wooden wall of the cabin.

I straighten up, try the desk lamp. It doesn't turn on. Neither does the desk fan when I try it.

"And now?"

"I'm working on it."

I exit the cabin and move around the side of it, where the cable exits through the wall. It's attached to a small generator raised on a metal trolley. Trust Henry to fix his own power source. I remember him requesting the generator when we had all those blackouts last year.

I yank on the rip cord. It grumbles and dies, like a geriatric lawn mower. I pull it a few more times until the generator finally kicks in, spluttering and chugging, the loud noise echoing in the large space.

I return to the cabin. The lights on the front of the radio are on. A hissing sound can be heard coming from the speaker. Sawyer already has the transmitter in hand. She pushes on the button.

"Anyone there?"

She releases the button. Static. I skip to the next saved frequency. Again, nothing but static. Same for every other frequency Henry has taken the time to store in the radio.

"Shit. Guess it really does need the antenna."

I exit the cabin again and peer into the small gap between

the makeshift office and the shed wall. There, spooled neatly and resting on a hook on the side of the cabin, is what looks like about fifty yards of insulated copper wire.

I squint up at the ceiling. There's a small trapdoor directly above the cabin that leads into the hidden roof space. That's where Henry wanted me to attach the wire that would act as an antenna. I sigh. Nothing else to do. I grab the spool of wire and toss it up onto the cabin roof.

There's an old extendable ladder leaning against the wall behind the tractor. I carry it over, lean it up against the cabin, then climb onto the roof. I pull the ladder up, then place it against the wall of the shed, bracing the base against the lip of the cabin roof. It isn't much to anchor it, but it's all I have. I loop the wire over my shoulder, then grab hold of the ladder and give it a shake.

"What the hell are you doing?" shouts Sawyer.

"Trying to get the radio to work! Just hold tight!"

I climb up slowly, tensing with every shift in weight and creak of metal. The ladder itself is one of those that bends in the middle to fold into a manageable size. But the joints have long ago rusted, meaning it's extended all the time. That isn't to say the rusted hinges will hold my weight. It could collapse beneath me at any moment.

I think I hear a noise from somewhere down below. I pause, stare over my shoulder to the door leading into the shed. I can't see anything. I wait another few seconds, then carry on climbing until I reach the trapdoor in the ceiling.

I push it open, peering up into the darkness, then pull myself up into the roof space and straighten up, careful to stand on the struts. I reach up and feel for the metal framework of the roof, just like above the gym. The frame isn't there to hold the roof up, but rather to stop anyone trying to escape. If I want an antenna, I'm not going to get anything much better than this. A metal framework that travels the length and breadth of the entire shed.

The heavy chains that are used to support the weight of engines in the inspection pit travel up into the ceiling space, bolted directly to the support framework. I bite the insulation off the end of the copper wire, stripping it down and peeling away about two feet. Then I move slowly over to the chain and wind the copper up through the links as far as I can reach.

I head back to the trapdoor and kneel down. I'm about to call out to Sawyer to ask if it's working when I see two figures moving through the repair shed.

It's Veitch and Cassidy. The last of Kincaid's men.

Note to self: listen to your gut next time.

I need to do something. Fast. They're going to investigate the cabin. Either that or Sawyer is going to come out to see what I'm doing. Veitch and Cassidy are both holding metal piping they've ripped from somewhere. No guns, though, which is good. I wonder what happened to them. Did the Bloods steal them when they stormed Unit 4? If so, I offer up a silent thank-you to Dexter and his crazy-ass followers.

I lower myself gingerly onto the ladder, carefully placing my weight on the first rung, wincing at the creaking sound it makes. I glance over my shoulder. Veitch and Cassidy are looking through a toolbox on the other side of the shed. I start to climb down, willing myself to be as light as possible.

I feel the ladder shift slightly on the roof of the cabin.

I freeze and look around again. One leg of the ladder has slipped over the lip of the roof.

Veitch is still nosing around in the toolbox. He takes out a heavy wrench that has been missed by the other looters and hefts the weight in his hand. Cassidy, however, is wading toward the cabin, a frown on his face.

I lick my lips nervously. Don't look up. Whatever you do, don't look up.

Then two things happen at once. Sawyer shouts from inside the cabin: "Constantine. I think it's working!"

And the ladder slides over the cabin roof.

I drop straight down with the ladder, hitting the roof hard and rolling to the side. I wince and push myself painfully to my feet.

And lock eyes with Cassidy.

Then I hear the clump of footsteps from below as Sawyer approaches the door.

Fuck it.

I leap from the top of the cabin, aiming directly for Cassidy. To his credit, he actually manages to stay upright when I hit him. He staggers back slightly as I collide with him, but it's me who ends up flat on my ass in the water.

I scramble to my feet and lash out, hitting Cassidy in the chin with my good arm. He stumbles back, falling against the tractor. I follow up with a kick to his stomach. His breath explodes from his lungs and he drops to his knees, wheezing erratically.

I throw a look over my shoulder to see Sawyer standing in the doorway, taking a hesitant step toward us.

"Go!" I shout. "Use the radio."

"*Watch out!*" she screams.

I whirl around to find Veitch swinging the heavy wrench at me. I duck away, tripping over Cassidy's sprawled legs. Veitch keeps coming. He brings the wrench down. I roll away just in time and he smashes it into Cassidy's shins instead.

Cassidy screams. I scramble to my feet, splashing through the water, and dart behind the tractor. Veitch comes after me. I look around desperately for something to use as a weapon. There's nothing close. My foot slams up against something beneath the water. I trip, manage to right myself against the tractor, and turn just as Veitch is aiming the wrench for my head. I grab his hand. I'm face-to-face with the guy. My gritted teeth are only inches away from his face. We stagger backward, locked together, Veitch trying to pull away, me trying my hardest to hold on.

We bump up against one of the workbenches. I have my

back against it, Veitch using my weight to try to force me off balance.

I crane my head around and see it's the bench where Henry had been sharpening the mower blades from the tractor. The long, curved blade just sits there, the newly sharpened edges winking in the light.

Veitch's face is right in front of me. I can smell the guy's bad breath. See the black staining between his teeth from too much smoking.

I push back, forcing him to strain even harder against my weight.

Then I spin aside and shove him as hard as I can, slamming his head downward.

He hits the mower blade face-first. Blood sprays upward in a wet spurt and his whole body stiffens. Then he sags against the workbench, blood pooling into the grooves of the blade.

I turn. Cassidy is on his feet, moving toward me as fast as his injured leg will allow.

My face hardens. I'm sick of this shit now. Sick of all of it.

I run at him.

His eyes widen in surprise as he sees me coming, but neither of us slows as we head toward each other.

Cassidy arrives next to one of the pulley chains used to lift the engine blocks. I grab one side of the chain, leap in the air and swing around him, then drop down to the ground and whip the chain around his neck, looping it twice. Then I grab the other side of the chain and haul hard on it, yanking it down and lifting him into the air.

He drops his metal pipe, fingers scrabbling at the chain around his neck. I keep pulling until he is halfway to the ceiling, his stupid thick face turning blue, eyes bulging in their sockets.

His legs spasm. His body rocks and arches wildly, swinging from side to side. He pisses his pants as his struggles become weaker and weaker before finally stopping.

I leave him dangling there and wearily climb the three steps into the office. Sawyer throws a terrified look in my direction, but she relaxes when she sees it's me and turns back to the radio.

"Please pass it on," she says. "I bet there are over a hundred of us here. Maybe a lot more."

She releases the mic and a burst of static comes from the speaker, followed a moment later by a male voice. "Roger that. We'll make sure someone gets to you as soon as the hurricane passes."

"Thank you..." Her voice almost cracks as she says it. She drops the mic on the workbench and sits back in the chair, glancing up at me as she does so.

"I talked to four different people. They said they'd pass on word."

Before I can answer, the sound of a throat being cleared issues from the internal PA system of the prison.

"Hello? This thing on?"

It's Felix's voice.

"Yeah, so...we kinda got a sort of tunnel system going on beneath this dump that might actually be waterproof. No promises, 'cause it's Leo who says it's there and you all know what he's like..."

There's the sound of scuffling; then another voice speaks. Leo.

"There are tunnels leading into a floodwater drainage system beneath the prison. My advice is to make your way to the office corridor in the Transitional Care Unit."

More scuffling sounds. Then Felix speaks again.

"We're not hanging around for any of you, though. Just get your fucking asses to the basement door. If you're not there, we're not waiting. I'm serious. We're going down to the tunnels and sealing them off, because as soon as the eye of the hurricane passes, this prison is going down."

Even as he says this, the lights flicker and dim. In the

distance the sound of a terrific rumbling crash sets the ground vibrating beneath my feet.

"You see?" says Felix over the intercom. "You feel that? Now get your ass to Mars—or in our case to the basement. Probably the same thing in the end. No air, dying slowly from asphyxi- ation, but you know how it is. A snowball's chance in hell is still a chance."

There's a click and then silence.

Sawyer and I exchange weary glances; then Sawyer heaves herself up off the seat.

"Let's go," she says.

Twenty

5:20 a.m.

Sawyer and I eventually arrive back at the basement to find a long line of inmates helping Felix and Leo clear the rubble from the corridor leading to the basement.

Felix grins when he sees us approaching through the flickering lights.

"Hey, man, you're still not dead."

"Nope. Sorry." I squint along the dim corridor. "Looks like you got some help."

"Yeah. Who'd've thought? The specter of approaching death is actually enough to get people to put aside their grudges and work together."

He's right about putting aside grudges. I see Bloods, Crips, Woods, Ñetas... All the gangs who were trying, often successfully, to kill each other only a couple of hours ago are now working together in an assembly line to shift the fallen rubble from the basement passage. It's not a total surprise. Inmates were already giving up fighting to look for shelter or protection after we left the gym. By now *everyone* must be realizing that things aren't looking too promising for the Ravenhill Correctional Facility.

Sawyer peers through the doorway. "How's it going?"

"Nearly through," says Leo, wiping sweat from his brow. "Looks like the whole roof caved in. Pipes and shit came down too."

"And a geyser," says Felix. "Thing was still full of water. Had to borrow a gun from one of our fellow inmates to shoot it a couple times, let the water out."

"Because what we need right now is more water around our feet," I say.

"You want to try moving a fifty-five-gallon geyser filled with water, be my guest."

I turn to Leo. "I hope you're right about these tunnels. You're going to have a lot of pissed-off convicts if it's all just your imagination."

"If it's just my imagination, pissed-off convicts will be the least of our worries. And relax, I'm old, not senile."

"But you always just sat in the cafeteria on your own, muttering about getting out of here," says Felix. "Everyone thought you were a bit...out of it."

"Because I didn't want to talk to you idiots? I think that makes me intelligent, not senile."

More inmates are arriving in the corridor, nervous, wary, in response to Felix's call. Their arrival is making me worried. I keep peering at faces—most of them frightened and freaked out because of the damage the hurricane is doing—to see if any of them has an agenda. Preacher and Kincaid are still MIA, and I'm uncomfortable not knowing where they are.

The building rumbles again. Dust sifts down from above, settling in a fine film across the water. And even though there's a steady flow rushing through the door and down the steps into the basement, it doesn't seem to be lowering the water level at all.

A commotion from the far end of the corridor distracts me. Felix and I wade forward to see what's going on. In the low light I can see four men approaching. One is holding a shotgun, one an M9, and two have Ruger rifles. They've obviously been to the armory. Felix takes out a Beretta he'd tucked into his boxers.

"Where'd you get that?"

"It was a donation. From one of our new arrivals."

"You got another one?"

"Sorry, man. Was hard enough to get this one."

I stop in front of the four men. "Hold up."

They stop walking. I squint in the dim light. I think these guys are Preacher's men. Yeah, they've got the cross tattoos on their necks.

"We don't want trouble," says one of them. "We just want to get to the tunnels."

"Not with those guns you're not," says Felix. "No offense, but I don't trust you freaks with guns of any kind. Anyone who follows Preacher is crazier than a fifth-generation inbred from Alabama."

The four men glance at each other uncertainly. One of them steps forward, slightly raising his shotgun. It's still pointed away from us, but he's brought it up to hip height. "We're not giving up our weapons."

"Then you're not coming with us," I say. "Nobody knows how long we're going to be stuck in those tunnels. We don't want anyone getting funny ideas. Maybe deciding to settle a few grudges to pass the time."

"We're not with Preacher anymore."

"I couldn't give a shit. You *were* with him. So that means I don't trust you."

"Maybe we'll just use the tunnels ourselves," growls the man. "Leave you all here to swim."

"You can tr—"

A gunshot explodes right by my ear. The guy who was speaking stumbles back into his friend's arms, blood pulsing from a bullet wound in his neck.

I turn to find Felix standing there with his gun still leveled. "Dude, what the fuck?"

"Anyone else want to argue?" he says, ignoring me. "I got more bullets."

"That was *right* by my ear."

Some of the prisoners who were helping shift the fallen ceiling move closer, eager to see where things are going. I can see this turning into another bloodbath if we're not careful.

I step forward. "Look, you say you're not with Preacher

anymore. Prove it. Otherwise you're not coming down there with us. End of story."

The three men glance uneasily at the other inmates. They're trying to see if I have them on my side, if I speak for everyone. No one argues, something I'm actually pretty surprised about. It looks like they've got my back.

"I won't ask again," says Felix. "I'm serious as fuck. I will shoot all three of you where you stand."

The guy in the middle sighs and holds out his Beretta, grip toward me. I wade forward and take it, then feel around beneath the water for the shotgun the dead guy dropped. I find it, straighten up and look at the others. They reluctantly hand over their Rugers. I sling one over my back and hand the Beretta to Sawyer, who has crept up to watch with the others.

"You know how to use it?" I ask.

"Don't be even more of an asshole than you already are. You think we're not given training before we turn up here?"

"All right. Jesus. Calm yourself."

We wade back to the door to find Leo watching us nervously. "Hey...you sure about all this?" He indicates the inmates with a tilt of his head.

I know what he's thinking. Are these guys really going to be able to forget their tattoos and gang signs, the man-made loyalties forged over the years and decades?

But I'm not feeling any fear on that front. I don't see murderers or robbers or drug dealers right now. I see people who want to survive. I feel a strange moment of...pride? Is that right? Maybe not pride. But a connection. A connection with a group of people I have nothing in common with besides the fact we're all human. Half of them would have killed me as quick as look at me an hour or so ago, but right now, all we want to do is get out of this alive. Our real enemy is the hurricane, and it's not going to have any mercy. It doesn't care what colors you wear, what leader you swear loyalty to.

Jesus Christ. What's happened to me? I've become a pussy.

Or…maybe not that bad. I was a cop once. Maybe I'm just remembering what that felt like. Maybe Sawyer was right when she said there was still some part of me that cared.

And then a sudden silence falls across the prison. The roaring of the wind stops, the constant hammering against the walls of the prison fades away.

We all look at each other in shock. The silence echoes in our ears.

The eye of the storm has arrived.

It takes us another ten minutes to clear a path. Leo already has the basement door open, and is holding on to the frame as water surges past his legs, almost pushing him off his feet. I join him as he peers down into the darkness.

"No lights?" I ask.

"I think they're downstairs."

"You think?"

He shrugs. "As far as I can remember. Last time I was down there was a good fifty years ago."

I try to see down the stairs. It's pitch-black. All I can hear is the water coursing down the steps like a waterfall.

"How many you think are back there?" asks Leo.

"More than a hundred."

"Christ. This place housed eight hundred people."

I shrug. "We made the announcement. Maybe more will come."

"Felix was right, though. We can't hold the doors open for them. Once we're down in the tunnels, we have to close everything off. End of story."

"Fair enough." I nod at the stairs leading down into the darkness. "You okay with this? You need a hand?"

"I'm nearly eighty years old. The fuck do you think?"

I smile. "I'll go first. If you fall, grab onto me. Don't suppose you have a flashlight?"

"Sure. Right here on my utility belt. Next to my cell phone and batarang."

"Right."

I move through the door, feeling for the first step. The water surges past my ankles, almost yanking me off my feet. I grope around on the wall until I find the rail.

"Guardrail," I say over my shoulder.

"Yeah, I'm old, not blind and stupid."

"Jesus, Leo. Why did you even say you needed a hand? You want to lead?"

"Nah, you're good."

"Shut the fuck up, then."

I slowly descend the stairs. I can hear the others following. Voices calling out—loud, raised, trying to hide fear behind bravado and forced jokes.

"Yo, man. Who's got my cane?"

"Where the fuck's my Seeing Eye dog?"

"This place is darker than your mama's soul."

"Nah, brother. It's blacker than the line outside KFC when they giving out free chicken wings."

"Who the fuck said that? You can't say that, man."

"I'm black!"

"I don't give a fuck. So am I. You don't say that shit."

I count twenty steps before I arrive at the bottom. The water comes up to my thighs.

"Keep moving forward," says Leo. "Should be a door ahead. You got those keys?"

"Yeah."

I wade through the water, hand outstretched, until I hit up against a thick metal door. I run my fingers over the handle and keyhole, trying to get a feel for the type of lock it is. I think it's the same as all the others. I breathe out softly, a sigh of relief. I was worried that the lock would be old, that maybe no one came down here, so the locks wouldn't be updated.

I try the key I used for the unit doors first. It doesn't fit. I take out the key ring and try the rest of the keys, one after another. It takes a while, but the lock finally clicks and turns. I drop the keys back into my pocket and test the door. It opens toward me.

"Need a few people to give me a hand here," I call out.

I wait for the inmates at the front of the line to edge forward. I can hear worried breathing, nervous whispering. We're all operating blind.

I push down the handle, feel other hands grab it, and we all brace our feet as best we can and pull against the floodwater.

It takes a few tries before we can even budge the door enough for the water to start pouring through the gap. We heave slowly, pulling it gradually open, the water streaming, then gushing past our legs and into whatever lies beyond. The water level drops lower and lower until it's just a calf-deep stream cascading from the prison above us and down the stairs.

"Should be a light switch to your right," says Leo.

I move through the door, bumping up against inmates who either twitch and pull away or stand their ground as I try to pass.

"Get the fuck outta my way. Let me find the switch."

I finally make it past the inmates and feel around on the wall. I find the switch, an old-fashioned one that sticks out from a round panel. I flick it up, and strip lights surge to life above me, humming and flickering as they switch on, illuminating everything in a sickly yellow tinge.

Another passageway reveals itself. I can't see the floor, but the walls are covered in old white tiles. Most of them are cracked. When I put my hand out to touch them, I can feel water trickling through the cracks. A worrying sign.

A few of the tiles have fallen off the walls completely, but I'm not sure if that's just because they're old or because of the hurricane. Closed doors line the passage. I try one and it opens to reveal a storeroom, mildew-covered boxes piled up against the far wall, the cardboard soaking up the water that now pours into the room.

"Just old storerooms," says Leo. "Keep moving. End of the corridor."

I throw a quick look back toward the stairs. Sawyer is right behind Leo, with Felix following her, then the line of inmates packed into the stairs and up into the prison.

I move through the flickering light to the end of the corridor. The door at the end is locked too. I use the keys to reveal another dark space beyond. I flick the switch and more strip lights flutter weakly to life. These ones are a lot older, covered in dust. Some aren't working at all, while some give off a muted green-tinged glow that illuminates a large room that looks like an old bomb shelter. Heavy-duty metal shelving holds crates with the U.S. Army insignia stamped on them in faded paint.

There are desks around the remaining two walls. They're covered with yellowing paper, in-boxes coated in dust, desk lamps with green shades, and metal filing cabinets. There's a huge map on the wall showing the path of the Cross-Florida Barge Canal project.

"This is the old bridging room between the bosses upstairs and the workers downstairs," says Leo. He nods to a door on the far wall. It looks normal. Metal, but not like the prison doors upstairs.

The room is rapidly filling up with inmates, pushing and jostling each other. Those still in the corridor beyond are shouting out, asking why no one is moving.

The door is unlocked. Leo opens it. I lean in and turn on the lights. They're not strip lights this time. They're big, old-fashioned globes hanging from cloth-covered wire insulation, metal lampshades casting wide shadows up to the ceiling. The room is filled with metal bunk beds, all of them without mattresses or pillows.

"Is this place really an army barracks?" asks Felix, moving past us to sit on one of the beds. The springs squeal in protest and he quickly stands up again.

"Yeah. Engineers, grunts for the manual labor. Officers. Eventually military prisoners who were put to work digging the tunnels for the storm drains. That's how I got involved. We didn't all sleep in here, though. We were kept above ground in Admin. Although it wasn't Admin back then."

We move through the room into another tunnel. This one is about ten feet wide and slopes downward at a steep angle. The same hanging globes light the way, but only about a third of them work. Even that surprises me. You'd think that after so long, none of them would light up. But I guess they built things to last longer back in the day.

The water is still pouring down behind us from the prison. Some of the inmates are pushed off their feet by the force of it, sliding down the decline, only to be caught by other prisoners and helped back up again. The sounds of the rushing water echo loudly in the confined space.

The tunnel levels off after we've descended—by my estimate—around thirty feet or so. It takes a sharp right and disappears into the distance.

"This is the last tunnel," says Leo. "It opens into a room that the Glasshouse tunnels connect to as well. From there it's down fifty feet into the flood drainage system."

"That's pretty deep," says Felix. He looks around uneasily. "Am I the only one here feeling a bit...claustrophobic? If anything happens down here, we're never getting out."

"Relax. I know what I'm talking about. We just need to get out of these tunnels. Everything beyond that room is sealed off. Watertight."

"And if the drainage system is actually open? Won't it be flooded by now?"

"It was never finished. We didn't even link up the flood tanks to the surface. Nothing's getting in. Trust me."

"So what's your *actual* escape plan?" I ask. "You've been muttering about tunnels for as long as anyone can remember. How did you plan on getting out?"

"I was going to use the aqueducts that drain the water out into the ocean. Just walk my way to the sea."

"That's it?"

"That's it. Nice and simple. Why complicate it?"

We keep walking through the tunnel. Sawyer catches up with me and touches my arm.

"You see this?" She gestures over her shoulder.

I follow her gaze and am shocked to see that the number of inmates has grown by a *lot*. There must be at least two hundred now. Sawyer the Samaritan looks happy. I suppose she has a right to. If we pull this off, it will be something to be proud of. That isn't a feeling I've had in a long time. But doing this feels right. It feels *good*.

"You see Kincaid anywhere?" asks Felix.

I shake my head.

"You not worried about that?"

"About him not being here? No. I'm pretty fucking ecstatic, actually."

"Yeah, but... it's *Kincaid*. He's not just gonna sit this out, is he? He's not just gonna hang around up there till the roof falls in on him."

"We've got guns."

"So does he."

"There's nothing we can do about it." I walk on, then glance back. "But just keep your eyes open, yeah? Tell me if you see him."

"Nah. I was thinking of keeping that to myself."

After about five hundred and fifty yards or so, the end of the tunnel appears, a solid brick wall with a thick rust-colored metal door blocking the way. It looks like it's about ten feet high by ten feet wide. I knock on it. It gives off a dull metallic thud. No echo at all.

"That's a pretty solid door right there," says Felix, knocking on it hard with his own knuckles. "I've seen thinner doors in bank vaults."

A silence has fallen behind us. I glance back and can almost feel the whispered murmurings passing back through the inmates. This is it. Salvation. I'm sure they think it means freedom too.

I think most of them believe they'll be able to run once the hurricane has passed. So did I a couple of hours ago. Although how we all plan on moving around in a flooded county with FEMA and cops and firefighters conducting salvage operations is another matter entirely.

I turn back, push down on the heavy handle, and give the door a shove.

It doesn't budge.

I push harder, then try pulling, even bracing my foot against the wall, but the door is closed tight.

"It's locked." I look at Leo. "Leo. It's fucking locked."

Leo's face shows confusion. "But...it can't be. It wasn't locked before..."

"Fifty years ago maybe! But it sure as shit is locked now!"

Leo gestures helplessly. "There's not even a lock on it, though."

I look. He's right. No keyhole. Nothing.

"It must be locked from the other side," he says.

I try my best to restrain my anger, but it's sure as hell getting hard. "There's no *keyhole*, Leo."

"Maybe there's a bar across it or something? I don't know!"

Jesus suffering fuck! Why did I believe a word this senile old goat said?

I fight down the rising panic. There's still time. I still have time. I turn around and set off back the way we came, wading through the water, pushing past the huddled mass of inmates.

"Where are you going?" shouts Sawyer.

"I can get to the Glasshouse. I'll open the door from the other side."

"Are you insane?" shouts Felix. "The prison is falling apart. The hurricane..."

"...hasn't come back yet. The eye is still right above us. It will last about three quarters of an hour."

"It's already been over twenty minutes," says Sawyer.

"So stop talking and let me go!"

"You can't, man," says Felix. "You heard Leo. The Mental Health Unit is locked down. So is the ACU. It's suicide."

"And waiting down here isn't? Once the eye passes over us, this place is going to flood. We'll all drown. Every single one of us."

"There has to be another way."

"There isn't." I turn to Sawyer. "Time to put your money where your mouth is. Give me the keycard."

Sawyer hesitates.

"Come on, Sawyer. The clock's ticking."

"I'll hang on to it."

"Sawyer, there's no time—"

"I'm coming with you."

"Me too," says Felix.

"Don't be stupid. I'll do this on my own."

"Look. I don't think you're a bad guy," says Sawyer, "but forgive me if I don't quite trust you."

"Trust me to do what?"

"What's to stop you just going off on your own to get those two guys who killed your wife?"

"You think I'd let everyone here die? I said I'd open the door, and that's what I'll do."

"Maybe you will. But I'd like it opened *before* you head off on your suicide mission, and I get the feeling you might not agree with that."

We stare each other down. I can see there's no way I'm going to convince her to stay.

And why bother anyway?

If she and Felix come with me, *they* can open the door to let the inmates through, and I can go for Wright and Tully.

It's win–win.

Twenty-One

5:50 a.m.

It seems to take so much longer to retrace our steps back up to the prison than it did to get down. We wade along the tunnels, then up the slope, pushing through the water that surges against our legs and knees and makes every step harder than the last.

I try to count heads as we move. I figure that our first guess was pretty close. Nearly two hundred inmates have responded to Felix's call, most of them shouting questions at us as we try to get past, questions I don't want to answer in case I set off a riot.

Sawyer, of course, doesn't think like that and eventually decides to try to calm the inmates down by doing something no one should ever do.

She tells them the truth.

Not the best move, all things considered. They don't take it well, hurling abuse at her as if she personally locked the door and put their lives in danger.

Things aren't totally out of control. She's handling the insults and the questions pretty well. Until someone—I see it's Dexter, the guy who organized his own personal fight club— mentions rape.

That's when Sawyer steps back, takes out the Beretta I gave her, and points it at his face.

"Say that again."

Dexter stares at the barrel of the gun. He licks his lips, frowning. His eyes flicker right and left, taking in the other inmates watching this go down. I can see exactly what will happen. He won't want to lose face in front of the other prisoners, especially not to a woman. He's not going to back down.

I rest my hand on the Ruger, making sure he notices. "Don't be a moron, Dexter."

"Jack," says Sawyer kindly, her arm not wavering, her voice as steady as before, her eyes on Dexter. "If you don't back off right now, I will shoot you both."

I look at her in surprise.

"I'm serious. I can fight my own battles."

I shrug, swing the gun onto my back, and move a few steps away to join Felix. We watch as Sawyer and Dexter stare at each other for a full twenty seconds before he laughs, nervous but trying to hide it behind volume.

"Just messing with you, sister. We all good."

"You sure?" asks Sawyer.

"Yeah. You're cool. We cool."

"Everyone's cool, huh?" says Felix, amused.

We set off again and finally arrive in the large room that holds the army beds. I shut the door behind us.

Sawyer frowns. "What are you doing? You can't lock them in."

"I'm not *locking* it. But a closed door will stop more water than an open one."

She nods. "Fair enough."

We move through the rooms and back to the basement stairs. They're hidden behind a literal waterfall that is so strong we have to pull ourselves up by the handrail. It's way worse than before. The roar of water echoes in the small space, cutting off any chance of communication. The spray gets in our eyes, up our noses, in our mouths. I think the whole of Ravenhill has started to breach. Whether the floodwater is pouring in through the walls or the windows, I'm not sure. But if it *is* the windows, then that means the water has risen high enough that the entire prison will soon be submerged, tunnels and all.

We arrive at the top of the stairs and make our way past the remnants of broken rubble and into the corridor beyond. The water is up to our stomachs now. We push on, heading in the direction we were going before we bumped into Leo. We should have just fucking left him and carried on with our own plan. I should have known Leo's plan wouldn't be as easy as that.

The lights are failing all over the building. I can feel water sluicing down the walls every time I touch them, an invisible curtain that pours into the prison.

There are other noises too. Louder now that the hurricane has died down. Creaking, rending sounds. Crashing. Metal under pressure, bending, making loud wailing noises as roof supports sag and buckle.

We pass more inmates on the way. Most of them are already heading for the corridor in response to Felix's announcement. But there are some who aren't, some who still seem ready to fight when they see us. They look like trapped animals, eyes wide with fear and panic. We explain to them about the tunnel—in case they missed the announcement—and without fail they head off without giving us any more trouble. I mean, that *could* be because of the guns rather than our skills of persuasion, but either way, I'm not complaining.

And after what seems like way too long, we finally arrive at our destination.

The Mental Health Unit.

I unlock the door using Sheriff Montoya's magic keys and push it open.

The first thing we hear is the screaming. A constant shrill shriek that goes on and on, pausing only for whoever is responsible to draw breath.

Most of the lights are down. Only a few remain, casting cold cones of harsh white over a deserted nurse's station. We move slowly past the desk and enter a long corridor with cells to either side. Felix is in the lead. I can see he's nervous. He has the second Ruger we took from Preacher's guys raised in the firing position, swinging it left and right at the slightest sound.

The cells all have windows in the doors. Dim light filters

out. I glance into a couple as we pass. They all have padded walls and a single bed with leather restraints attached to top and bottom.

Felix is getting more and more agitated. He's gripping the gun tightly, his knuckles white.

"I don't like this, man. I can't take crazies."

"They're not crazies," says Sawyer. "They're sick. They need help."

"Not sure they really deserve our sympathy," I say. "The people in here are rapists, mass murderers, torturers...the worst of the worst. They're all here because the judges ruled them insane. Either that or they were mentally unfit to even stand trial for what they did."

"So don't try any kind of Mother Teresa act on them," warns Felix. "They come at you, you do not talk. You shoot."

Sawyer throws me a worried look but doesn't reply.

We move slowly along the corridor, guns held at the ready. After a while, I notice a sound coming from one of the cells up ahead. Felix stops walking, levels his weapon.

Sawyer pushes the barrel down. "What are you doing?"

"There's something in there."

"Some*one*, you moron."

He frowns at her and backs up. I move slowly to the door and peer inside.

There's a man sitting on the bed. He's not moving. He's just sitting there, staring into the corner of the cell.

Felix reluctantly joins me and peers over my shoulder. "What's he doing?"

The man hears him and slowly turns his head to look at us. "Can you see her?" he says.

Felix doesn't answer.

"Can you see her?" His voice is more urgent.

Felix shakes his head.

The man points into the corner. "She's standing right there. The woman in black." He smiles at Felix. "She's watching you."

Felix turns and starts walking away. "Uh–uh. I'm out. That's a big nope from me."

I shiver and follow him, Sawyer at my side.

"Can't that bastard stop screaming?" says Felix, now even more on edge. "Shut the fuck up!" he shouts.

"What the hell are you doing?" I snap. "You've just announced our presence here."

"Good. Then I can shoot something."

"Jesus, Felix. Stop being an asshole. You could have stayed in the tunnel. We don't need anyone panicking."

"I'm not panicking. Don't tell me I'm panicking."

I can hear the brittle edge to his voice. I try a different tack. "Listen, I get you don't like it in here."

"Do you now? Do you really?"

"Yeah. I don't like it, either. But can we *please* just try and keep quiet? The quieter we are, the faster we can move."

"I see your point," he says grudgingly, "but I'm not promising anything."

He walks on. The passage we're in leads to a security door that opens into the staff section of the unit. The screaming is getting louder. We move at a faster pace. There are inmates in some of the staff rooms. Most of them are busy in their own worlds and don't even look up when we pass. One of them stands on a desk, arms spread wide, talking in Spanish about angels and God. Another lies in the floodwater, his head the only part of his body above the surface. He smiles as we glance into the office. "Don't tell anyone," he says. "I'm at the beach."

We leave him to his vacation and enter an open ward with about fifteen beds around the walls.

We all stop walking. Even Sawyer brings her Beretta up into firing position as she looks nervously around.

The beds are empty, but every one of them is stained with blood. We move slowly through the ward. There are cards propped up at the bottom of each bed. I grab the closest.

Touched children. He has been judged and sent to hell.

I stare at the bloodstains, then glance at the other cards. All bear mention of crimes and punishments.

And all the cards are signed by Preacher.

Sawyer looks around nervously. "Do you think he came back here after moving through Carl's unit?"

I really hope not. I'd thought maybe a few of his followers would be trapped in the Administrative Control Unit. That we'd be able to sneak through. But if he's there, that's a different story. His congregation of psychos would have followed him. They'll be everywhere, and I don't think we'll have enough bullets for them all.

We move through the ward and out into the corridor beyond. The screaming is still going on. We're all on edge. Tense. But we finally make it to the door leading out of the unit.

It's unlocked.

That's a bad sign. We step through into the passage beyond. The door at the far end of the sally port stands wide open.

We slowly enter the corridor. The security control room to our left has been destroyed, wires hanging everywhere. There's writing on the wall. In blood, by the looks of it. One message reads, *He shall also make restitution for what he has done amiss.* Another says, *Depart from me, you cursed, into the eternal fire prepared for the devil and his angels.*

"I think I had that on my doormat," says Felix.

Sawyer glances nervously between us. "So are we thinking Preacher is in there or not?"

I really hope not. Because we now only have minutes left before the eye of the storm passes over.

Twenty-Two
6:10 a.m.

The entrance to ACU leads into a rounded corridor that curves away to the left and right. There's an open door directly opposite us that leads us into a large octagonal room.

The room is lit by red emergency lights mounted in the ceiling. The octagon has doors on each wall—the entrances to the cells. There are four levels in the room, making thirty-two cells in total. The doors are all closed, but I don't know if they've stayed locked the whole night or if someone has closed them again.

I turn in a slow circle, checking out the higher levels to make sure no one is up there watching us.

The place seems deserted.

"How big is this unit?" I whisper to Felix.

"No idea."

"You've never been in here? No violent outbursts?"

"Shit, yeah. Lots of outbursts. Solitary confinement, though. I was never brought in here."

The room is about fifty feet wide. There's an open door opposite us leading into a dim corridor.

Curiosity overcomes me. I move to the closest cell and peer through the safety glass. It leads into a small sally port about the size of an elevator. I test the door. It opens. I enter the confined space beyond and peer through the window into the cell.

There's blood everywhere. On the floor, smeared over the wall. There are even spatters on the ceiling. The cell is illuminated by a harsh white light recessed into the ceiling. It makes the blood look black.

There's a man sitting on the bed staring intently at something in his cupped hands. He senses my presence, or maybe I make a noise or something, because he suddenly looks up.

His eyes are empty holes. Black, gaping wounds with tears of blood caking his face. He holds his hands up as if in offering. His eyes nestle together in his palms. I look away, feeling sick, and my gaze falls on the writing on the wall. It's scrawled in blood.

And if your eye causes you to sin, tear it out and throw it away.

Sawyer and Felix have joined me in the cramped sally port and we stare at the tableau for a long moment.

I've seen a lot of shit in my time. A lot of it objectively worse than this. But there's something intensely disturbing about the scene in the cell. There's no logic behind it. Not that there's any logic in war, but this...this is sick. Demented. It's almost like I'm staring at a piece of modern art.

We back out into the octagonal room. Nobody says a word. I move to the next cell, enter the sally port and look through the window.

Someone has been burned alive. A charred body lies curled up on the floor, black scorch marks haloing around him like wings. The ceiling is dark from the smoke, the recessed lighting dimmed with soot. I can just make out writing on the wall to the left.

Depart from me, you cursed, into the eternal fire prepared for the devil and his angels.

Preacher needs to get more material. He's starting to repeat himself.

I rejoin the others. "Why wasn't Preacher in the Mental Health Unit?" I ask. "He wasn't, right? He was here? In ACU?"

"He was in Mental Health a while back," says Felix. "But he did something like this before. They had to move him here. They figured the best way to deal with him was to lock him down twenty-three hours a day."

"Looks like he's making up for lost time."

Felix nods. "He's probably been taking notes on everyone in here. Now he's free, he's doing what he likes to do best."

"Well…they do say to find a job you love."

Sawyer throws me a disgusted look.

"Relax. It's just a joke."

"Not a good one. Are we going to stand around and stare at the dead people, or do you think we should actually get moving before the hurricane comes back?"

"The second one."

"You sure? I mean, don't let me stop you. If it's your thing…"

I sigh and head toward the door. We move faster, driven by Sawyer's words. She's right. We have to get out of here.

The corridor beyond leads to another octagonal unit. We don't pause in this one, heading straight through and into a staff reception area with a long counter along the far wall holding monitors and tower cases. Behind the counter is a staff bulletin board, flyers for various events happening in town, a few personal ads from COs looking for roommates or selling items.

The door behind the counter leads deeper into the wing, heading in the direction we need to go. We wade through the water and into the passage. It stretches ahead to a T-junction. Empty. Silent.

Maybe Preacher didn't come back here after all. All the crap we've seen could have been done earlier in the day, when the cells were first opened.

We reach the T-junction. I'm trying to imagine the layout of the prison in my head, wondering which way gets us closer to Northside. I'm thinking right. Left will just take us toward the inmate corridor, and that's all blocked off.

We turn right, moving past closed doors. We keep going, heading closer and closer to the opposite end of the unit, closer and closer to getting out of here, to getting to the Glasshouse.

I feel my spirits rising. We might just make it in time. It's going to be tight, but—

We turn into the next passage and freeze. Up ahead is a

slow-moving line of inmates. They're walking away from us in single file, murmuring something as they go. They're all armed. Shotguns and rifles mostly, but a few have M9 Berettas.

They turn the corner to the left and vanish from sight. We move slowly through the water and pause at the turn. The inmates are heading away from us, so we leave them to do their thing. It just means we have to be more careful. Quieter.

We wait in the corridor for about thirty seconds, just to be sure. Then we turn right—

—and come face-to-face with ten of Preacher's followers, all of them armed, their weapons trained directly on us.

I turn around and see the same thing. The group we thought had disappeared along the corridor is standing there with their guns pointed at us.

I turn back, my stomach sinking. One of the inmates smiles at me, and his smile is tinged with madness. It's too wide, too gleeful, and it definitely doesn't reach his eyes. In fact, *all* their eyes have a blank, empty look to them. Almost as if they're not actually seeing us, but are focused on something else happening in the far distance.

The inmate giggles, then tries to stop himself. His mouth twitches as he speaks, the corners trying to stretch themselves into a Joker-like rictus. "If you would be so kind as to drop your weapons, we will escort you to your judgment. Preacher is going to be so happy with us. Amen and hallelujah. Praise be on me."

The inmates all respond simultaneously. "Amen and hallelujah."

We've got no choice except to go along with them. They lead us along the passage—heading in the direction we wanted to go—and through a set of double swing doors into what appears to be Preacher's church.

It definitely wasn't a church to start off with. It was a cafeteria. But Preacher has done his best to change that. All the tables have been ripped out and lined up along the walls. They hold wooden crucifixes they must have gathered from the prayer rooms throughout the prison. Crosses fashioned from twisted cutlery.

And one Bible.

Only one, though, because they've used the rest as decoration. The walls are covered with pages ripped from the holy book. Roof to floor—or at least roof to floodwater—and corner to corner. I'm not a hundred percent sure how Preacher got them to stick, but judging by the dark staining seeping through some of the pages, I'd say it was blood.

Preacher himself is at the far end of the cafeteria, standing behind a makeshift pulpit constructed from two of the tables piled one on top of the other. Hanging on the wall above and behind him is a cross made from two long pieces of wood. The vertical piece is at least ten feet long and the horizontal one about six feet.

I have no idea where he got the wood, but that's not important. What *is* important is the inmate who has been nailed to the cross. It looks like they used nine-inch nails, ten or so for each wrist and foot. The nail heads stick about five inches out of the poor bastard's skin like needles in a pincushion. A crown fashioned from barbed wire has been forced onto his head, the blood from the puncture wounds completely covering his features.

The rest of Preacher's disciples all sit on the cafeteria chairs, formed into lines like traditional church pews. He looks at us with a huge smile when we're led into the room. A few of the inmates keep us covered with their guns, prodding us so we move toward Preacher, while the rest fill up the seats at the back of the room. The followers don't even look at us. Their attention is focused wholly on Preacher, their faces rapt in worship.

"A full house!" says Preacher. "How fortunate I am to have such a loyal ministry."

The guy behind me tries to shove me to my knees in front

of Preacher's makeshift pulpit. I resist, but then something slams into the back of my legs and I drop into the water. Sawyer and Felix are forced down as well.

Preacher looks down on us. "I was thinking of delivering a sermon on family today. About the importance of faith in keeping those fucked-up children from straying. I mean, I did what I could, you understand? I tried to teach them the Way back in Mississippi. But the agents of evil put a stop to that. They prevented me from doing the work of God Almighty!"

The congregation, if you could call it that, all start shouting.

"Shame!"

"Agents of Satan!"

"Unbelievers!"

"Heathens!"

Preacher holds his hands out for silence. "But seeing as we have guests awaiting judgment, I will postpone the sermon." He stares down at us. "'Do not marvel at this; for an hour is coming, in which all who are in the tombs will hear His voice, and will come forth; those who did the good deeds to a resurrection of life, those who committed the evil deeds to a resurrection of judgment. I can do nothing on my own initiative; as I hear, I judge; and my judgment is just, because I do not seek my own will, but the will of Him who sent me.'"

"Amen! Hallelujah!" shout the inmates.

Preacher stares intently at each of us in turn. "This hurricane is sent to us by God to cleanse the world of wickedness. You understand that, yes? For does it not say in Psalm 135:7, 'He causes the vapors to ascend from the ends of the earth; He makes lightning for the rain; He brings the wind out of His treasuries.' This is God's judgment on the wicked, and I am His sword."

He straightens up, filled with self-importance. He opens his mouth to say something else, but before he can get another word out, Sawyer speaks.

"James 1:20: 'Human anger does not produce the righteousness that God desires.'"

Everyone looks at her in surprise. None more so than Preacher himself. He stares at her a long time, confusion, then irritation, then anger twisting his features. "Are you...are you actually *daring* to judge *me*?" he shouts.

"'Do not be quickly provoked in your spirit, for anger resides in the lap of fools.' Ecclesiastes 7:9," says Sawyer.

Preacher's eyes widen. He leans on the pulpit and screams, spittle flying from his mouth. "'But I will warn you whom to fear: fear the One who, after He has killed, has authority to cast into hell; yes, I tell you, fear Him!' You do not lecture me in verse, you arrogant bitch! How dare you?"

Sawyer just stares at him, a mild look on her face. "You're scared. I can see that."

"Scared? I hold no fear in my heart. Except for the souls of those I have yet to judge!"

She nods, as if this confirms her thoughts. "'There is no fear in love. But perfect love drives out fear, because fear has to do with punishment. The one who fears is not made perfect in love.' 1 John 4:18."

"I never *claimed* to be perfect," Preacher snaps. "I only claimed to do His bidding. 'All who sin apart from the law will also perish apart from the law.' Romans 2:12." He stares at Sawyer challengingly.

I throw a confused look at Felix, but he just shrugs. I don't know what the hell is going on here, and neither does he.

"Ezekiel 33:11," says Sawyer. "'Say to them, "As I live!" declares the Lord God, "I take no pleasure in the death of the wicked, but rather that the wicked turn from his way and live."'"

Preacher leans over the pulpit. His eyes are almost black as he glares down at her. "'Know then in your heart that as a man disciplines his son, so the Lord your God disciplines you.'"

Sawyer smiles. "'Whoever sheds the blood of man, by man shall his blood be shed, for God made man in his own image.'"

Jesus. Where is all this coming from? Are they reading these things from somewhere?

"'And that servant who knew his master's will, but did not get ready or act according to his will, will receive a severe beating!'" Preacher is screaming the words and he slams his hands down on the makeshift pulpit. It shakes and trembles, almost collapsing under the blow. He points a shaking finger at Sawyer. "If you say *one more* word, I'll cut your fucking throat myself. Understand?"

Sawyer sighs as if in disappointment. "'But now you must also rid yourselves of all such things as these: anger, rage, malice, slander, and filthy language from your lips.'"

Preacher's congregation is muttering to one another, exchanging uneasy glances. Preacher notices too, because he points at Sawyer again. "Shoot her. She's the devil in disguise. She's in league with Lucifer."

The inmate standing behind us raises his gun. I tense up, ready to throw myself at him. I know it will end up getting us all killed, but what difference does that make now? The eye of the hurricane will pass over in five, maybe ten minutes. We're already dead.

"Wait!" says Sawyer. "I'm just trying to prove myself to you."

Preacher holds up a hand and the guy lowers his rifle. "Explain."

"I understand what you're doing. Why you're doing it. I want to help. I want to stand by your side as we cleanse the world. I can preach to the guilty, try to get them to see the error of their ways. If they don't, then you will deliver them to judgment."

Preacher pauses. He narrows his eyes, leaning forward to get a better look at Sawyer. I have no idea what her plan is, but goddammit, she's got the psycho thinking.

She stands up slowly, hands raised outward to Preacher. "'And these will go away into eternal punishment, but the righteous into eternal life.'"

Preacher's tongue flicks out like a snake's and he moistens his lips. "Matthew 25:46." His voice is husky. I realize this is like foreplay to him. He's getting off on it.

Sawyer nods. "Exactly. I want to prove myself to you. Please. Let me stand by your side. We can judge these two together."

Preacher's eyes flicker toward us, then back to Sawyer. She's looking at him with such an innocent, guileless expression that *I* almost believe her.

Finally he nods. "Come, then, child. Stand by me as my wife. For God is a righteous judge, but He rewards those who are loyal."

Sawyer moves slowly around the pulpit. There's some kind of step that Preacher has raised himself on. He holds out a hand to her and she climbs up to stand by his side, looking down on the rest of us.

She reaches over to touch something on the pulpit. "May I?" she asks.

He nods. "You may."

She lifts up the Bible. It's a big hardcover version. Without even pausing, she twists to one side, away from Preacher, then swings herself back around with all the force she can gather and slams the edge of the book into his throat.

His eyes go wide and he staggers back. His throat is crushed. He can't draw breath. Cries of shock go up from behind us. I surge to my feet, headbutt the guy behind me in the nose, and yank his weapon away. I fire at the inmates sitting in the back, the ones who led us in here. They're already rising, their own guns coming up to point at us.

Gunshots explode to my right and the disciples go down before they can open fire. I glance over to see that Felix has grabbed a Beretta from someone and is shooting at anyone else holding a weapon.

I turn back to see what's happening with Preacher. Sawyer moves quickly to the side as he staggers back, gagging for breath. His face is ashen. He bumps into the huge crucifix and it shifts in its brackets. He grabs hold of it, trying to steady himself, but all he succeeds in doing is pulling it off the wall. It falls and hits him in the back.

He goes down and doesn't move. I throw a quick look at the

horrified congregants to make sure they're not doing anything stupid, then move around the pulpit to look.

I can see why he's not getting up. The five inches of nails that were sticking out of the guy's right wrist are now buried in the back of Preacher's skull.

I grab Sawyer and we move back around the pulpit, joining Felix, who's still covering the inmates. Most of them are crying, wailing at Preacher's death. We move along the aisle, Sawyer pausing to grab a Beretta from one of them, and duck through the door.

No way to lock it. We'll have to run.

We move as fast as we can through the floodwater. No one follows us. Guess they're too broken up about their holy prophet being killed by a crucifix.

We keep going for a couple more minutes, then turn a corner to find the exit to ACU right in front of us. I unlock the door. We slip through and I lock it behind us again.

We pause on the other side, staring at each other.

"Is this it?" asks Felix. "Northside?"

Sawyer nods. "This is it."

We did it. I can hardly believe it. We actually made it through the prison units in one piece.

"You know where we are?" I ask Sawyer.

She nods. "Follow me."

She leads the way through the corridors, Felix and I on either side.

"The hell was all that Bible stuff about?" I ask.

She glances at me. "I told you my mother was religious."

"Yeah, but how did you remember it all?"

"She was *really* religious. Believe me, if your mother reads you the Bible every night for a bedtime story, it tends to stick in your head."

"It was awesome," says Felix. "It was like watching a tennis match or something. You, him. You, him." He shakes his head. "Crazy."

We turn into a narrow passage with doors to either side. The first opens into a small staff room, the next a bathroom, and the next few lead into offices.

Sawyer glances over her shoulder, a smile on her face. "It's just around the—"

She's cut off by the sound of gunfire.

The wall next to my head explodes, sharp fragments cutting into my cheek.

Sawyer and Felix, about five steps ahead, make it around the corner to the next passage. I throw myself through the closest door into one of the offices, and swing the Ruger around from my back, holding it at the ready.

"Jack?" shouts Felix.

"Go!" I shout. "Just leave the door open."

"Hey, Jackie-boy!" It's Kincaid's voice. "What's the word?"

Jesus Christ. Why won't he just fuck off? "Nothing much!" I shout.

I wait.

"Jack?" Felix's voice again.

"Fuck sake, Felix. Go!"

"You sure?"

"Yeah, I'm sure. I'll take care of this asshole."

Kincaid laughs. "What a hero," he says. "How you gonna take care of me, boy?"

Another burst of gunfire erupts in the hallway. The water explodes into fountains just outside the door.

"You ever going to leave me alone?" I shout.

"Don't think so."

There's another burst of gunfire. I wait for it to stop, then duck my head quickly through the door and back in again. I see the barrel of a rifle one room down. In the staff kitchen.

I point my own rifle at the wall inside the office. I aim it toward where I think Kincaid is standing and open fire.

The bullets rip through the internal walls. I hear a heavy splash in the passage outside the room and instantly dive to the side. Bullets punch through the wall, shredding the shelves and books behind me.

I fire back, keeping my aim low.

I take my finger off the trigger. I hold my breath, listening.

Silence. Did I get him? I push myself to my feet, head for the door. I pause just inside the room. Listening.

Nothing.

I peer around the doorway and the butt of Kincaid's rifle hits me in the temple. I stumble back, falling into the water. Kincaid comes after me, rifle raised to strike again.

I kick out, sweeping his legs out from under him. I push myself to my feet, fighting off waves of dizziness. I realize I've lost my rifle. I look around. Where the hell did I drop it?

Kincaid launches himself at me, grabbing me around the stomach and sending us both flying backward. I hit the edge of the desk, pain exploding up and down my spine. He forces me back, hand pushing at my chin, then shifts his weight, both hands coming up around my neck. He digs his fingers in. I try to pull away, but he won't let go. I reach out to grab something from the desk, anything I can use as a weapon. My fingers curl around the desk lamp and I smash it against his head.

Kincaid grunts and loosens his grip. I bring my knees up and shove him back, then launch myself after him, splashing through the water. He is still on his feet. I lash out and hit him in the jaw. That's the only punch I land before he raises his fists to protect his face.

He jabs at me. I block, but he follows it with a lightning-fast uppercut I don't even see coming. It smashes into my chin. My mouth slams shut, pain and blood blossoming in my mouth as I bite my tongue. Rapid body punches connect with my ribs, my kidneys. I try to keep myself protected, but every time I shift my guard, Kincaid finds an opening and lands another punch.

I can't keep this up. I drop my guard and grab him around the body, pinning his arms to his side. I lash out with my head, slamming it into his face. Then I bring my knee up into his stomach. I feel the explosion of breath against my neck and shove him away. He stumbles into the wall, his face contorted in pain as he tries to catch a breath.

My arm is killing me. The makeshift bandage has come loose and the wounds are bleeding freely again.

The building suddenly starts to shake, the walls trembling. The remaining books fall off the shelf, splashing into the water. I stagger, steadying myself against the desk.

I glance out the window, and what I see makes my stomach lurch with fear. The eye has almost passed completely over us. The hurricane wall is only a few hundred feet away.

I dive toward where I think I dropped my Ruger. My fingers curl around it and I heft it up from the water, rolling over to fire at Kincaid. But he's already moving, disappearing through the door. I fire along the wall until the magazine is empty, then push myself up and stagger out into the passage.

Nothing. He's gone. I want to go after him, but I don't have time. The shaking is growing more violent. It feels like an earthquake. The gun is out of ammo. Useless now. I drop it into the water and wade back along the corridor, turning into the passage Sawyer and Felix took.

It leads into a staff changing room. All the lockers have been forced open, the contents floating around. Civilian clothes, textbooks, novels, plastic lunch containers.

The exit is on the opposite side of the room. Felix and Sawyer have left the door wedged slightly open.

I take a deep breath, yank on it, and step out into the open air.

Twenty-Three

6:30 a.m.

I feel the sweat prickling instantly on my skin. The humidity and heat out here is like nothing I've ever experienced, a suffocating, heavy dampness that crawls down my throat and makes it difficult to breathe.

The wall of the hurricane surrounds me. To my left, west, the wall looks to be about ten miles away. But I can see it easily, a solid wall of writhing gray-black clouds that climb into the sky. Lightning flashes within the wall, a constant flickering, pulsing glow that illuminates the coiling clouds from within.

I turn to my right with a sense of rising dread. The wall of the hurricane to the east is almost upon me, about four hundred yards away and crawling across the landscape. It's as if the clouds are alive, reaching out with writhing, probing tendrils, mini cyclones that dance and skitter across the water, pulling waterspouts back into the cloud wall.

I can already see loose debris being sucked up into the hurricane. Fencing, broken telegraph poles, metal signs, all pulled into the heaving mass. It's alive, a monster devouring and chewing up everything that comes into its path.

I look up. The sky directly above me is blue. To the right, streamers of sunlight burst up past the top of the hurricane wall, limning the topmost clouds with burnished gold. It's an oddly beautiful moment, serenity within the violence.

But when I drop my gaze, everything is destruction. The entire area is flooded, sitting under about four feet of water. And if the water is four feet deep up here at the top of the hill, that means Miami is completely underwater. There can't be anything left. Houses totally submerged. Hospitals, shops, every-thing, just...gone. There can't be anything left of Florida. It must *all* be underwater.

This is a disaster that will change maps, and we're not going to escape the devastation. The hurricane has already half destroyed the prison. I have no doubt it's going to complete the job.

I'd briefly entertained the idea of escaping after I killed Tully and Wright. But I can see now what a stupid, childish thought that was. Where would I go? As soon as the eye passes over us, the 200 mph winds will return. If I'm not in the tun-nel with everyone else, I'll be crushed, drowned, ripped apart, or any one of a hundred other grisly deaths.

I have to move. The wind is warm and clammy against my face, like sticky fingers stroking my skin. I wade forward through the water, pushing debris aside as I go. The wall of the hurricane is a solid mass a few hundred yards to my right, while the Glasshouse is a few hundred yards ahead. I can actually see the hurricane creeping forward, moving at a fast walking pace. I don't know if I can reach the prison before it does.

I can just make out Felix and Sawyer moving toward the Glasshouse building, wading as the crow flies, since the fences and walls have all been pulled down. I follow them as quickly as I can, but the depth of the water makes speed impossible. My feet keep getting tangled in debris. Wires, cables, cloth, tree branches and roots. And if I'm not getting tangled up, I'm smacking my feet into concrete, rubble, unseen detritus that has been plucked up in the hurricane and dropped in my way.

Felix and Sawyer disappear from view as they approach the front doors of the Glasshouse, but then reappear again as they make their way around the side of the building, heading toward the loading bay where the bus took us earlier. Before they van-ish from sight, I see them pause and look back. I wave my hands in the air to indicate I'm on my way. They wave back and then head for the relative safety of the building.

The wind picks up. I can hear it, a whistling, howling echo, close but somehow sounding like it's coming from far away. A waterspout leaps up directly in front of the Glasshouse doors. It hovers in the air, leaning in toward the hurricane. A cyclone branches out from the wall, stretching toward the waterspout. When the two touch, the spout explodes into movement, dancing and skittering across the water, throwing branches and debris into the air in a triumphant display before finally being sucked into the hurricane wall.

It's too close. I'm not going to make it.

I'm going to let Amy down again.

I push my aching, burning legs on, jumping and wading, doing anything I can to try to speed up my progress.

I make it to where the perimeter fence used to stand. The Glasshouse is directly in front of me now. A hundred feet away. But the storm is closing in fast from the right. I can feel the sheer power of the wind. The water surges all around, white-caps rising, waves blowing past me.

I'm being pushed off course. I have to angle into the wind to keep on track, but it's slowing me down. My hair whips around my head, wet prison fatigues billowing against my body. Debris flies through the air. Broken wood, stones, bricks even, thrown out of the hurricane wall like missiles.

The eerie silence that accompanied the eye of the storm is gone. The wind howls and shrieks, whistles in my ears and roars like a demon. The light drops suddenly, like someone has flicked a switch. I shield my eyes and look up. The blue sky has vanished, shifted way over to my left. Roiling gray clouds toss and writhe above me, the wall of the hurricane folding into them and starting to drop down toward me like a collapsing wave.

I try to move faster, but for every step I make, I'm pushed two steps to the left.

There's a huge downed tree about fifteen feet ahead. I remember that tree, an enormous sycamore that cast shade over the grass outside one of the rec yards. Now it lies half submerged in the water, pointing toward the Glasshouse.

I bend low and aim straight for it. The wind grows stronger, louder, screaming in my ears, slicing water into my face so hard it feels like glass shards.

The tree doesn't seem like it's drawing any closer. I keep my feet firmly on the ground as I try to reach it. The wind picks up even more. I'm shoved upright, almost thrown over onto my back. I drop into the water, knowing that if I'm tossed even a few feet back, I'll never make it to the Glasshouse.

I keep my whole body except my head submerged, pulling myself along the ground, clutching at rocks and grass, anything I can grab hold of.

The hurricane wall is about thirty feet away. The door into the Glasshouse is fifty feet to my left. I almost scream in frustration. There's just no way I can get ahead of the wall. Not at this pace.

My fingers curl around the roots of the tree. I grip them tight, yank myself forward, pulling myself arm over arm until I'm able to grab the trunk. I use it as a windbreak and keep moving, dragging myself up to the branches. By now I've covered ten feet. I glance at the hurricane wall. It's twenty-five feet away.

The water level drops as I climb the last bit of the hill toward the Glasshouse. I keep going until the water sits below my thighs, then my knees.

And that's when I can run.

I put everything I have into that final sprint. The wind tries to fight me, tries to shove me away. It's like a huge hand trying to throw me back into the water.

I see Felix and Sawyer waiting at the metal doors to the loading bay, watching with wide eyes as I draw closer. I also see the looks they throw over my shoulder and I know the hurricane wall is closing in. There's a terrific crashing sound, and a second later, a massive tree branch hits the water directly in front of me, almost crushing my head. I leap over it and keep going, putting everything I have, everything I've *ever* had, into that last burst of speed.

I make it with barely a second to spare.

I leap forward and splash to the ground. As Sawyer and Felix drag the shed doors closed, I roll onto my back, gasping for breath, staring up at the corrugated roof as it billows and rolls like waves on the ocean.

I feel hands dragging me up, hear Felix shouting at me. I struggle to my feet, following them through the door and finally—*finally*—into the Glasshouse itself.

I slam the door shut behind me and slump against it.

We made it.

We fucking made it.

"Jesus Christ!" shouts Felix. "I mean...did you see that? I absolutely cannot believe what we just did."

I feel a tremor of excitement rush through my body. It's tangible, contagious, like a jolt of adrenaline to the heart. This is it. This is the moment I've been waiting for. Ever since I walked down those stairs and found Amy lying in the living room.

I straighten up, pull out my gun, and eject the magazine. Five bullets left. Plenty. I ram it back in place, stick it in my waistband, and start walking.

"Constantine?" says Felix. "Where you going?"

I turn back. "Where do you think? To find Wright and Tully."

Sawyer looks at me with disappointment. I've just confirmed her fears.

"What about the door?" says Felix.

"You guys can do it. I'll find you later." I start walking again.

"Jack!" shouts Sawyer.

"I'm doing it, Sawyer. You always knew I would."

"I can't let you do that, Jack."

I can hear a shift in the tone of her voice. Something there I haven't heard before.

I turn around to find her pointing her gun at me.

"I need you alive, Jack. I can't let you out of my sight."

Twenty-Four

6:40 a.m.

I stare at Sawyer in confusion. "What are you talking about? Need me alive for what? What difference does it make? I'll take Wright and Tully out. I'll even open the cells for you. Help you be the Good Samaritan and get the inmates down to the tunnels."

"No. I need to keep my eyes on you."

Felix tenses as if getting ready to move for her gun, but I hold out a hand to stop him.

"Let her talk." I shift my attention back to Sawyer. "Why? Why do you need to keep your eyes on me?"

"Kincaid."

"What about him?"

"You framed him."

She knows about that? Did I tell her? I don't think so. Did *Felix* tell her? I glance over at him, but he gives a subtle shake of his head.

"He deserved it."

"I'm not saying he didn't." Sawyer takes a shaky breath. "My little brother was running in his gang at the time. He was just a kid. Twenty-two. Pulled in by Kincaid's lieutenants. I was trying to get him out. He was finally *talking* to me. He was ready to come live with me. Ready to get clean. Then *you* turned up. My brother got taken down with Kincaid. He's serving ten years because of you."

Felix whistles.

My memory drifts back to that night. The kid in the dining room. He looked a bit like Sawyer. He wanted to leave. Wanted out.

And I didn't let him.

"Sawyer...I'm sorry. I didn't know..."

"I don't want your apologies. I want you to help me fix it."

"How am I supposed to do that?"

"I want your confession. On record. That you framed Kincaid."

I look at her with dawning realization, then shake my head slowly. "Was this your plan all along? Is that why you came to work here? To get to me? Is that why you came in during a fucking hurricane?"

"I thought it might be my last chance."

"And how exactly do you want me to confess? Got something to record me? No? What about pen and paper?" I pat my prison scrubs. "I seem to have left my journal in my cell."

"Jack," says Felix softly. "Ease up, man."

"No. I want to know." I take a step toward Sawyer. "What the fuck is your plan, Sawyer?"

"I don't know!" she shouts. "Jesus! I've been planning this for a year now. Training, moving here, applying for a job. I thought it was all working out; then this fucking hurricane hit...I panicked, okay? I *had* to come in to work. It could have been my last chance. I didn't plan on hanging around here, believe me. I'm not insane. But when I was left behind, I thought...why not just go through with it? I saw you being taken to the infirmary this morning. I thought I'd...I don't know, get you out of here before the hurricane hit. Thought I'd get you before a judge or something, get him to hear your confession."

Felix shakes his head. "You know how crazy that sounds?"

"I know, Felix! Jesus Christ. What else was I supposed to do? Just sit around here and die?"

"And what made you think I'd even do what you wanted?" I ask.

Sawyer hesitates. Her hand drops slightly. "I...don't know. Like I said, I wasn't thinking straight..."

I wait for her to glance away, then grab the gun from her, turn it around and point it in her face. I step back, gun still leveled. "I'm sorry about your brother, okay? I really am. I didn't mean for that to happen."

"You think that makes me feel any better?"

"No. No, I don't think it does. All the same, I *am* sorry."

Her shoulders sag. "So you're going to go kill them now?"

"Always said I was."

Felix steps forward. "Jack. We need to open that door. Get everyone to the storm tunnels."

"The fuck you care, Felix? You hate everyone."

"It's...different now," he says, looking almost embarrassed.

"Why?"

"Because we're all just trying to survive. Look at what we've been through tonight. Doesn't that count for anything?"

I hesitate. Felix almost gets through to me, mainly because he's repeating the same thoughts I've been having over the past hour or two.

But then I get a flash of Amy lying on the living-room floor, her head smashed in, the two men responsible only a few hundred feet from where I'm standing.

I've been waiting too long for this. *Amy* has been waiting too long.

I tighten my grip on the gun. "I have to do it. I'm sorry. You two can open the door. You don't need me."

I turn and start walking, leaving them behind, heading deeper into the Glasshouse.

I follow the exact same route we took this morning. The rotting magazines that were piled up in the rooms now float across the surface of the floodwater. Old *TV Guides* from the eighties. A few *Playboys* from the seventies. *Omni* magazines. Gossip rags with stars of bygone years staring up at the ceiling with rotting faces and mold-smeared eyes.

At least the lights—those that were working this morning—are still on. Whatever generator powers this place is industrial in design.

I enter the laundry. The washing machines are now half submerged. The sheets, black with mold, float and bob across the room, looking like an oil slick coating the water. I exit into the corridor covered in old white tiles. I remember that the ones underfoot are orange-brown, like they were lifted from a Spanish villa.

The metal gate that Evans unlocked still stands open. I step through, following the winding corridors lit with hanging bulbs that cast a jaundiced glow over the water. It feels more like a morgue now than anything else. Which is kind of fitting, seeing as we're all probably going to die here.

Unless I just let the prisoners out and go back to help Sawyer and Felix with the door.

No. I can't. I have to do this. I didn't protect Amy. Didn't protect our child.

I owe them...

There's a high-pitched wailing coming from somewhere up ahead. It grows louder as I approach the reception area of the prison, the one that looks like it belongs in an old hotel.

The walls have been breached. The noise is the wind howling through holes in the bricks. Rain surges through the gaps like water from a hose, flicking into the room in windswept sheets.

The entire building shakes suddenly, almost throwing me off my feet. I start to run. This whole place is about to come down. If it does, fine, but I want Wright and Tully first. They have to die by *my* hand.

I sprint through the corridors, barely remembering where I'm going. I know I'm heading in the right direction, though, because I can hear the inmates shouting for help, a cacophony of voices raised in panic and fear.

I finally burst through the door and into the Rotunda.

I remember being impressed by it this morning, the colossal

circular tower containing tier after tier of cells. But now, as I wade through the floodwater, staring up at the ruptured roof a hundred feet above, rain pouring down into the cylindrical prison, I think it looks more like a zoo.

The inmates are all hanging on the cell doors, pulling, pushing, slamming themselves against the metal in an attempt to get free. When they see me, the shouts rise in volume until they're all screaming and begging to be let out.

The noise is overwhelming. I try to filter it out, scanning the cells, looking for Wright and Tully. But it's no use. I can't see clearly enough.

Then, as I'm standing there wondering what to do, a portion of the wall about sixty feet up suddenly collapses. Plaster, concrete, and metal supports plummet down the central shaft of the Rotunda.

I throw myself out of the way, landing with a splash as the huge chunks smash into the water, the falling debris just missing the COs' security tower.

I push myself shakily to my feet. I'm running out of time here. "Where's Wright and Tully?" I shout.

No one hears me. The inmates are busy panicking, shouting and swearing at me, begging with one breath and threatening with the next.

I cup my hands to my mouth. "Wright and Tully!" I shout.

Again no one hears. I pull out the Beretta I took from Sawyer and fire it into the air. The shot splinters through the inmates' shouts, echoing back and forth around the walls.

The Glasshouse falls silent, everyone's attention focused on me.

"Wright and Tully!" I shout. "I want them. Point them out, and I'll release you all. We've got a way to safety. Underground. You want to live, show them to me."

All the inmates start shouting over each other, pointing toward a pair of cells on the fourth level. I look up and see Wright and Tully holding on to the bars, staring down at me.

I feel a surge of excitement as I look at them.

Finally...

Another rumble sounds from deep within the building. The floor shakes. I steady myself and run through the water, heading toward the elevator. It isn't there. I peer up the shaft. It's stuck on the top floor. I take the metal stairs instead, sprinting up to the fourth level. My feet clang over the metal grating. Inmates shout as I pass, reaching out between the bars to try to grab me.

I ignore them all. My attention is focused on Wright and Tully. They watch me coming, fear in their eyes. As I get closer, I keep seeing the same image over and over in my head. The moment I entered the living room and found Amy lying on the floor, her blood soaking into the carpet. I'm so close. I can almost feel it. Justice. Revenge.

I'm about ten feet away when the wall to my right collapses.

One moment I'm running, the next a huge section of wall just sloughs away. Wind and rain explode inside. The walkway buckles, tossing me into the air. The gun flies from my grasp and I land heavily, the walkway tearing away from the bolts that hold it in place. I hang on for dear life as it swings outward, dangling thirty feet above the Rotunda floor.

The wind slams against me, tossing me back and forth. I blink through the pouring rain, my eyes darting back to Wright and Tully. Their cell is still in one piece. I can still get to them.

I hear the scream of tortured metal and peer over my shoulder. The remaining supports that hold the walkway in place are buckling. The grating shifts suddenly, then lurches to a stop, the bolts sliding partway out of the wall.

I wait, holding my breath.

Then one of the bolts drops out and tumbles into the water below. The walkway sags even more. I look down. I'm hanging directly above the fallen debris from the roof. Jagged rocks, metal struts, and poles...

I reach up and force my fingers into the square holes of the walkway, slowly dragging myself up. The grating drops slightly, then jerks to a stop. I'm about five feet from the still-intact section. I hesitate, then slowly reach up.

The walkway lurches again. I freeze.

"Jack!"

I look up to see Sawyer leaning over the edge, her hand stretched out toward me.

I reach up and grab it, but I'm way too heavy. She slides partway through the gap, just managing to stop herself from falling by hooking her other arm around the railing support. I swing for a brief, terrifying moment, then use the momentum to grab the lip of the walkway with my free hand. Sawyer takes as much of my weight as she can and I slowly rise up, hooking my elbows over the edge and pulling myself onto the metal grating.

I lurch quickly to my feet, turning to stare across the gap in the walkway. It's about twelve feet. I'm sure I can make it. I can still get to Wright and Tully.

I brace myself.

Sawyer grabs my arm. "Jack!" she shouts. "Don't be stupid."

I try to pull away, but she digs her fingers in.

"Let go!"

"No!" She's screaming to be heard above the wind. "You're going to get yourself killed!"

"I don't care! Let me do this!"

"I can't!"

"Sawyer, I have to do it! Don't you understand?"

She moves closer until her face is inches from my own. "No. I don't. Look, I get it. You think you failed your wife and kid. But you *didn't.* There's not a single husband in the world who wouldn't want revenge. But if you kill those two men, you cross a line you can't come back from."

I hesitate.

"What would Amy say to you right now? Would she want you to do this?"

What *would* Amy say?

I turn around, glance across at Wright and Tully. They're gripping hold of the bars, watching me.

I turn back. I can almost see Amy standing next to Sawyer. Staring at me. Frowning in the way only she could. I know exactly what she'd do. The same thing she'd have done if she found out I was planning on shooting myself with the fourth bullet I'd cast. She'd kick me in the nuts and call me an asshole.

"It's not worth it, Jack!" shouts Sawyer.

I stare at her. At this woman who has been by my side the whole night, helping me survive despite what I did to her brother.

She's right. It isn't worth it. It never was. I open my mouth to say something—

—and the walkway lurches beneath our feet.

I barely have time to shove Sawyer to safety before the structure gives way with a grinding shriek, and I fall.

There is a moment of emptiness, followed by the jarring thud as I hit the water. Stars erupt across my vision as my head hits submerged concrete. My eyes close and I feel myself sinking down into nothingness. Darkness enfolds me, embraces me. It's like a lover's caress. Comforting. Calming.

It would be so easy just to let go.

To drift away.

No.

My eyes snap open.

Blackness greets me. My chest is tight, my lungs empty. I open my mouth for air, swallow water instead. I surge upward in shock and fear, breaking the surface. I retch, vomiting water as I stagger to my feet.

The sounds of the hurricane burst against my ears, broken only by the shouts and screams of the inmates. I turn in a confused circle. I look up and see Sawyer moving toward the stairs, peering down at me with wide eyes. She gestures frantically toward the guard tower.

The cell doors.

I limp to the tower and climb painfully up the stairs that corkscrew round and round, emerging into the security room at the top. The windows have cracked and splintered, some of the frames now entirely empty. The wind and rain pummel me, a physical force trying to shove me back down the stairs.

I glance quickly around the room. There isn't much in here. Nothing electronic. It's all old-school. I see a series of heavy levers sticking out from a metal control panel. There are faded signs underneath them: *Level 1, Level 2...*

I yank the levers in turn, pulling them all the way down. I can't hear anything over the storm, but I see the cell doors slide open, one after the other, level by level, all the way up to the top of the Glasshouse.

The inmates explode outward, sprinting along the walkways, lowering themselves down over the broken sections, and dropping to the floors below. I retreat back down the stairs to find Sawyer waiting for me at the door to the tower.

The inmates are already milling around by the time I get there. I cup my hands around my mouth. "You want to live, follow this woman! We've got a place to hide out from the hurricane!"

Sawyer heads toward the exit, then pauses when she sees I'm not following. "You coming?"

"I'll bring up the rear. Make sure everyone gets out."

She hesitates.

"Go. I'm not going to do anything stupid."

She nods and disappears through the door, the inmates following. There's another crash, and more bricks fall from the wall, tumbling down into the water. I step back and wait while the inmates make their way into the corridor beyond.

I'm waiting for a reason.

Wright and Tully appear. They hesitate when they see me.

I stare at them, not moving. They glance at each other, then slowly move past me and through the door.

I wait until there's no one left; then I turn and follow them.

Twenty-Five

7:20 a.m.

As I make my way back through the Glasshouse, I feel shell-shocked. I can't believe I let them live. After all these years. After what they did...

Was Sawyer right? I try to imagine having a conversation with Amy, talking it through. I try to add my viewpoint, but every time I do, Amy shuts me down.

She wouldn't want me to ruin my life. Not any more than I already have. I'd convinced myself I was doing it for her. For our child. And in a way, that was true. But really it was for me. I'd hoped it would lessen the pain. Would give me...I don't know. A sense of peace? Closure? But that was just stupid. If I'd gone through with it, I would have been signing my soul away.

And Sawyer knew that. Just as Amy would have.

Nobody speaks as we hurry through the corridors. There's no point. The deafening sounds of the hurricane overwhelm everything. The threat of destruction, of death. So close to all of us, held at bay by a few bricks and tiles and ninety-year-old mortar.

We retrace the steps I took earlier, arriving back in the corridor where we first entered the Glasshouse and following Sawyer down into the depths of the old building.

There aren't many lights that work down here. We make our way through long patches of darkness, broken only by an occasional bulb hovering in the distance like a streetlamp in the night. The water is deeper here, past our waists, and the lower we go, the higher it rises.

Finally the line of inmates comes to a confused stop. I wait at the back. I can't find the energy to move forward, don't have the will to shove my way through the crowd to see if there's a problem.

We start moving again after a few minutes. I push myself off from the wall and wade through the water, eventually emerging into a wide room. There's a huge rusted door to the left that has been pulled open, and inmates from the Ravenhill side are now shuffling through. Some of them are holding flashlights. Someone must have had the bright idea of raiding a supply cupboard.

Felix and Sawyer stand by the door as Leo guides everyone through, pointing to an open door to our right.

"Through there. Keep going. Come on, people. Move it."

Felix sees me and approaches. "So? Did you get them?"

I shake my head. "Sawyer talked me out of it."

Felix glances over at her, surprised. "Okay..." he says. "Didn't see that coming. But...I'm glad."

"Yeah?"

"Yeah. The coldhearted-killer thing—it's not you. You need to leave that to those of us with the experience." He slaps me on the shoulder and heads back to the door.

I feel distant as I watch everyone move to safety. Over two hundred inmates. Say three hundred, counting those from the Glasshouse. That's all that's left from the eight hundred or so that were locked up here.

I should feel...something, surely? Relieved? Proud? But I don't. I feel nothing. Just...empty.

And then it's just me and Sawyer left. She stares at me slumped against the wall.

"You okay?"

"Not really."

She nods. "You waiting here to drown, or you coming?"

I don't answer. She waits, watching me.

Then holds out her hand.

I look at it, and the tears that have been threatening finally fall. Why does she care if I don't? Why does she give a shit after what I did to her brother?

I hesitantly reach out and she clasps my hand tightly. She smiles, and we move into the dark corridor. Once inside, I let go so we can pull the door closed. Water trickles through invisible gaps between the door and the frame. We're not safe yet. We still have to get to the actual storm drains.

Someone has given Sawyer a flashlight. She shines it around as we walk. The corridor is lined with avocado-green tiles. There's hardly any dirt on them. No one has been down here for half a century.

We reach a long flight of stairs. At the bottom of the steps is a tunnel that looks more like an aqueduct, an arched passage about ten feet wide with raised walkways to either side. We've caught up with the inmates now, and follow them until the tunnel finally opens into an old-fashioned control room. We push through the crowd to get inside. It looks like something out of a sixties science-fiction movie. Hulking machines and analog control panels.

There's no power down here. Inmates shine their flashlights around, beams of light picking out computers and file cabinets.

Leo stands in the center of the room, looking around with satisfaction. He sees me and nods toward a metal box mounted on the wall. "Jack? If you please."

I pull it open. There's a huge circuit-breaker switch inside. I push it up and a loud hum vibrates through the air.

Dim lights flicker to life, but not only in the control room. The walls are lined with viewing glass, and beyond it distant lights switch on, revealing what I can only describe as a cavern.

I peer through the window. The space below is utterly massive. Easily a hundred and fifty feet high and a hundred wide, an enormous concrete room that disappears into the distance, the arched ceiling supported by huge, hulking pillars.

"This is the final flood chamber," says Leo, appearing at my side.

"You weren't lying when you said it was big," I say softly.

"There are five more just like it heading north. All connected by about twenty miles of tunnels."

"Watertight?"

"Watertight."

We leave the room and descend the steps into the vast chamber. Leo leads the way, heading toward a service door about fifty feet ahead.

"That door connects to the storm tunnels," he says.

"Why don't we just wait in here?" asks Felix, his head arched back as he tries to make out the distant roof.

"This place wasn't finished," says Leo. "I don't think it's sealed properly. Look around. There's been deep water in here."

He's right. The walls are covered with tidemarks and old algae stains.

He kicks at the ankle-deep water covering the chamber floor. "See? Already filling. The storm drains are watertight, though. We can wait there till the floodwater recedes."

"How long will that take?" asks Sawyer.

Leo shrugs. "Your guess is as good as mine. Might be a couple of days. You got any better ideas, though?"

She doesn't, and so the inmates trudge wearily across the chamber floor, remove the heavy bar locking the door, and file into the storm tunnels beyond. Despite the uncertainty, there's a feeling of relief in the air. We all thought we were going to die tonight. This is a second chance.

The four of us hang back until the last of the inmates have gone through. Leo goes next, Sawyer close behind him. Felix glances over at me. He opens his mouth to say something—

—and the top of his head bursts into a fine red mist.

The crack of automatic gunfire erupts, the chamber amplifying the noise to ear-shattering levels. The echo makes it sound like a hundred rifles are going off at once.

I feel a massive punch to the back of my ribs. I stagger and look down, staring in amazement at the blood spreading across my prison scrubs.

Felix topples over. I drop to my knees, see Sawyer's shocked face as she watches from inside the storm tunnel.

The shooting stops. Sawyer hesitates, then steps forward as if to help. Gunfire erupts again, chips of concrete exploding around the door. She yelps and ducks back inside.

I turn painfully around.

Kincaid strides toward me, a Ruger rifle raised to his shoulder. He fires at the tunnel again. Sawyer has no choice but to yank the door closed.

I fall back against one of the massive pillars, slumping down into the water, my hand going to my ribs. I can feel my blood pulsing, pumping from the wound.

Kincaid keeps his gun trained on me as he approaches the door and slides the bar back in place.

"Better," he says. "We don't want any interruptions."

He backs up a step and leans against a pillar. I can't take my eyes off Felix. His face is turned away from me, the wound submerged in water. Maybe he'll get up. Maybe he's fine...

"We were interrupted earlier," says Kincaid casually. "Back when we were cleaning the cells. There was something I wanted to talk to you about. To tell you."

I wrench my attention away from Felix. Kincaid cocks his head to the side. "You took my wife from me."

"You...already told me that," I say, gritting my teeth against the pain.

"I know. But I didn't get to tell you everything. I wanted to savor it." He smiles briefly. "See, I couldn't let it pass. I had to return the favor."

I frown. "The hell you talking about?"

"You think Novak, Wright, and Tully just *happened* to be at your house that night?"

I stare at Kincaid, struggling to understand the words. He can't be saying...

"I see your mind working. Wondering. Let me clarify. That was me. You took my wife from me, so I took yours from you." He frowns. "I don't like that phrasing. Makes them sound like property. Something we own. But we both know that's not how it was." He watches me for a moment. "I get what you're feeling. It's like it's just happened, right? You're hurting all over again. But this time, you've got the guilt too. Because it's all your fault. Your wife's death. Your kid's death. It's all on you, Constantine."

I feel my body go cold. My whole world drops away from me, like I've fallen over the edge of a cliff. I shake my head, not wanting to believe it.

"See? That right there. That's the look I wanted to see," says Kincaid in satisfaction. "*That's* what I've been waiting for. Why I wanted us to be alone for this."

I let out a scream of fury and pain and launch myself at him.

He tries to swing the gun around, but I grab it, throw myself against him. I slam my forehead into his face, feel the crunch of breaking cartilage, then bring my knee up into his stomach. His breath explodes outward and I yank the Ruger from his grasp. I stumble back, swing it around so it's pointing at him.

Our eyes lock. Kincaid straightens up. There's something in his eyes. Resignation. Acceptance.

Hope?

"Do it, then," he says.

I hesitate, confused.

"Do it!" he shouts.

I pull the trigger.

The click echoes through the chamber.

A look of disappointment flashes across Kincaid's face. I

stare dumbly at the gun, then stagger back and slump against the pillar, sliding into the water again.

Kincaid sighs, then reaches into his pocket and pulls out a revolver. I'm assuming it's the same one he forced Sawyer and Felix to play Russian roulette with. He checks the chamber, turns it slowly, then carefully closes it again.

"When I found out my wife was gone..." He shakes his head. "No words can describe it. Everything you say is a cliché, right? *It doesn't feel real. It feels like a movie.* But it's true. I still thought she was going to walk through the door, come visiting day." He sighs. "But she never did. And when that finally sinks in, when all the denial is gone, when you're sitting there feeling like your insides have been scooped out, you realize what loneliness really is. That utter emptiness of the soul. You know what I'm saying? There was a part of me that was entwined with her. Our history, our memories. Our love. And she took it with her when she died. You become less of a person. A ghost."

Kincaid looks around the chamber, then smiles sadly at me. There are tears in his eyes as he holds the revolver up in the air. "One bullet left. I don't think I'll waste it on you, Jack. I think I'd like you to suffer a bit longer with what I've told you." He thumbs back the firing hammer. "But you know what? If tonight has taught me anything, it's that I just don't care anymore. About anything."

And with that, he puts the revolver under his chin and pulls the trigger.

I shout out in shock as the gunshot booms around the chamber and Kincaid falls back into the water.

I sit for what feels like forever, my eyes fixed on his body. After a while, I notice that the water is rising. It's up past my stomach now, pouring in through the roof. There's been no maintenance in these flood chambers. Leo said they weren't even completed. This place is going to fill up. Just like Ravenhill. Just like the Glasshouse.

I push myself painfully to my feet and turn to face the door that Sawyer and the other inmates went through. I take a step toward it, but then stop. Why go that way? Do I want to spend the rest of my life in prison?

Do I even want to live anymore? Maybe I should follow Kincaid's example. The only thing keeping him going was the thought of telling me what he'd done. He wanted me to hurt. Once he'd done that...

I pick up a flashlight someone dropped, limp over to Felix. I squat down, put a hand on his chest.

"See you 'round, buddy."

I straighten up and study the chamber. I find what I'm looking for and head toward the far side. There's a series of round tunnels cut into the wall. They must be how the water exits the flood chambers.

Which means they connect to the ocean.

I step into the closest one and shine the flashlight around. The tunnel is concrete, gray and rough, unfinished.

I start walking. I walk until the pain is too much. Then I rest against the curved wall until I find the energy to push on again. My clothes stick to the bullet wound, forming a make-shift bandage. I'm not sure how much blood I've lost. A lot. Enough that I don't think I'm going to make it.

I don't care anymore. I don't deserve to live. All this was my fault. Everything. *I* killed Amy. *I* killed our daughter. It's all on me. If I die, I die. If I don't...well, I have a lot to make up for, a lot of guilt to pay off.

I'm not sure how long I keep walking. How many minutes or hours pass as I stagger through the pain and the haze of delirium.

I finally reach a door in the tunnel. No, not a door. A round metal gate that sits flush with the tunnel walls. I can't see how to open it. I feel around for some kind of switch or lever before I finally stop.

What am I even doing? The hurricane is still raging. What's the point?

I chuckle to myself, slump down in the water. The tunnel is filling up. The water is up to my ribs.

Not much longer now.

I close my eyes.

Epilogue

Four months after the hurricane, Keira Sawyer sits at a table on Venice Beach, sipping a cold beer.

She stares out over the ocean, smells the salt in the air, watches the surfers and families playing in the sand. She shivers a little as the waves crash over the kids, listens to the laughter and screams of teenagers. She has to fight down a flash of fear at the sound. Has to remind herself that everything is fine. That no one is going to die.

Thirty hours they were trapped in those flood tunnels. Thirty hours. The weird thing was, she never once felt in fear of her life. Not from the inmates, at any rate. All that mattered was surviving. At that moment, they were just human beings trying to stay alive, nothing else, and they all looked out for each other.

It was a strangely uplifting thing to experience. The world might be a shit show, but there *is* some decency left. Humanity has a way of pulling together when the chips are down. It makes her feel optimistic about the future.

A shadow falls across her table.

"This seat taken?"

She takes off her sunglasses and glances up. Her eyes go wide as Constantine lowers himself gingerly into the seat opposite. He's holding a bottle of Bud that he sips from while she gets over her shock.

"Jack . . . I thought . . . we all thought . . ."

"That I was dead? Yeah. Me too. It hasn't been a pleasant few months, I can tell you."

"But . . . *how*?"

"I made it into the outflow tunnels. Couldn't get through the gate, though. Didn't realize it opens automatically when the water pressure gets high enough. The weight of the water just sort of pushes it open. I was thrown out into the ocean during the tail end of the hurricane."

"And you didn't drown?"

"Nearly did. Washed up on the beach. Just managed to strip my jumpsuit off before passing out. FEMA found me, took me to the hospital."

"How did you explain the bullet hole?"

"Looters. They didn't make a big deal of it. There was too much going on."

Sawyer nods. She stares hard at him, then takes a big swallow of her beer. "Why are you here?"

He places something on the table. She leans forward. It's a memory stick.

"What's that?"

"My confession. About how I framed Kincaid. How your brother shouldn't be in prison. It's all there. How I stole the drugs from dealers. Planted them at Kincaid's place. Set up the bust for when I knew he was at home."

She reaches out and takes the memory stick with a shaking hand.

"I'm sorry," he says. "Really." He finishes his beer and stands up.

"Wait." Sawyer looks up at him. "What are you going to do?"

"Not sure. I've got a few contacts. People who can make me a fake ID. Maybe I'll go up north. I'm sick of the heat. I'd like to see some snow." He gives her a small smile, and she can't help noticing the sadness behind it. "Or maybe I'll take up a hobby. Storm chasing sounds interesting."

She smiles. "Take care, Jack."

"You too, Sawyer."

She watches him disappear into the crowd. She clenches her hand around the memory stick and sits back with a contented sigh, watching the setting sun flash orange on the tips of the waves.

Acknowledgments

I would like to extend appreciation and thanks to my amazing agents, Sandra Sawicka and Leah Middleton, and to my editors, Toby Jones and Wes Miller. Your suggestions and comments without a doubt made the book much stronger and tighter.

Also, I would like to say a special thank-you for your empathy and concern during a very difficult time. It was (and is) greatly appreciated.

About the Author

Paul Herron is a Scotsman struggling (and failing) to survive the heat and humidity of South Africa. Although *Breakout* is Paul's debut thriller, he also writes computer games and comics, and has worked on over twenty-seven television shows, one of which was nominated for an International Emmy Award. One of his previous works of fiction is being developed by Jerry Bruckheimer Productions and CBS as a television series. Paul lives with his wife, Jo, on the east coast of South Africa. He has three children.